"Intense, chilling and fille
Aftermath is a book that wi
long into the night. I couldn
of *Between You And Me.*

"Dark and suspenseful. I loved it." – Tana Collins, author of the Inspector Jim Carruthers series.

"I was gripped from the first page to the last because nothing - and no one - is as it seems. **The Aftermath** *is mesmerising."* – Roger Corke, author of *Deadly Protocol.*

"Another triumph from Gitsham - dark, tense and compelling from the first page until the last chilling twist. I read it in one nailbiting sitting."' – Lucy Martin, author of *Last To Leave.*

"Nail-biting twists that will keep you guessing until the very end." – Antony Johnston, author of the Brigitte Sharp thrillers and The Dog Sitter Detective Series.

About The Author

Paul Gitsham started his career as a biologist, working in laboratories in Manchester and Toronto, before retraining as a secondary school science teacher.

He now tutors in science and writes crime fiction.

Paul always wanted to be a writer, and his final report on leaving primary school predicted he'd be the next Roald Dahl! For the sake of balance it should be pointed out that it also said "he'll never get anywhere in life if his handwriting doesn't improve".

Decades later and his handwriting is even worse, and unless Mr Dahl also wrote crime fiction under a pseudonym, he has failed on both counts!

Paul lives in the West Midlands with his wife, in a house with more books than shelf space.

Also by Paul Gitsham

DCI Warren Jones Series
The Last Straw
No Smoke Without Fire
Blood Is Thicker Than Water (Novella)
Silent As The Grave
A Case Gone Cold (Novella)
The Common Enemy
A Deadly Lesson (Novella)
Forgive Me Father
At First Glance (Novella)
A Price To Pay
Out Of Sight
Time To Kill
Web Of Lies

The Aftermath

Paul Gitsham

To Diane,

Hope you enjoy something a bit different.

[signature]

16/11/24

STRAW HAT CRIME

Not for distribution or resale without written permission from the author.

Copyright © Straw Hat Crime 2024

Copyright © Paul Gitsham 2024

Paul Gitsham asserts the moral right to be identified as the author of this work.

A catalogue record for this book is available from the British Library.

This novel is entirely a work of fiction. The names, characters and incidents portrayed in it are the work of the author's imagination. Any resemblance to actual persons, living or dead, events or localities is entirely coincidental.

No part of this text may be reproduced, transmitted, downloaded, decompiled, reverse engineered, or stored in or introduced into any information storage and retrieval system, in any form or by any means, whether electronic or mechanical, now known or hereinafter invented, without the express written permission of Paul Gitsham.

E-book Edition ISBN: 9781068730504

Paperback Edition ISBN: 9781068730511

Cover design: BespokeBookCovers.com

Typeset in EB Garamond 11pt

For my beloved Cheryl.
This book would not exist without you.

Then

Prologue

Primary Fire. Serious risk to life and property.

The shed was fully ablaze as Crew Manager Matt Brown burst through the kitchen doors and out into the garden. He caught the familiar odours as he pulled his breathing mask across his face. Wood smoke, burning roof felt, and something no firefighter ever wanted to smell.

To the left of the shed, a man in a shirt and trousers was on his hands and knees retching. Beside him a garden hose pumped water ineffectually onto the path. The water pressure this far from town was crap; they'd have to pull their hoses through the house and use the appliance's water pumps to douse the inferno.

"I can't get the door open," the man wheezed. "I can't get in." A series of coughs wracked his body, and he threw up on the lawn.

Behind him, Brown heard the thud of boots as his colleagues followed him.

Pausing to size up the challenge ahead, he hefted the crowbar in his hand, then approached the conflagration.

The wooden outbuilding was completely alight, flames licking its roof.

Deliberate, he thought. Treated wooden sheds didn't just spontaneously catch fire.

The shed door was reinforced with a high-security lock and two padlocks, one at the top and one at the bottom. They were both hanging from their hasps.

He reached for the handle with his insulated gloves and gave it a firm twist. Nothing, it was locked.

"I can't find the keys," the man gasped, before coughing again.

"Come with me mate, it's not safe." Brown heard his crewmate's soothing voice behind him. Even through his protective suit, the heat was fearsome.

He inserted the crowbar between the lock and the door jamb and levered it back. With a splintering crunch, the door opened.

Behind him he heard scuffling and a surprised grunt from his colleague. "Woah mate, stay with me."

Turning, Brown blocked the entrance to the burning shed and grabbed the flailing homeowner.

"No mate, no mate, you don't want to see in there," he said, struggling to stop the man from going any further.

One glance and years of experience had told him that once seen, the inside of the shed could never be unseen.

The man let out a shrieking scream. "Carole!"

Now

Three Years After The Fire

Chapter One

Dominic Monaghan tapped the side of his champagne flute with a fork and stood. Raising his voice above the howling wind and pounding rain outside, he lifted his glass.

"Ladies and gentlemen, a moment of your time, please."

"I thought the speeches were supposed to be at the end of the meal?" someone called out.

"And give you the opportunity to sneak out early to relieve the babysitter? I'm wise to that one, Pete."

Seamus Monaghan gave a mock groan and placed his head in his hands. Beside him his fiancée, Andrea, laughed and settled back in her seat. Dominic was an entertaining and witty public speaker; she looked forward to what he had to say. She looked forward even more to the small glass of champagne she was allowing herself. Seamus reached for his red wine and finished it in one gulp.

Andrea squeezed his hand in support. Where Dominic was loud and outgoing, happy to be the centre of attention, Seamus was more quiet; shy even.

Seamus reached for the bottle and refilled his glass. "I think I'm going to need this," he muttered. The dozen or so friends gathered around the table chuckled at his discomfort.

"Grin and bear it sweetheart," she whispered in his ear. "He's picking up the tab, remember."

Seamus took a large swallow of his wine.

"Today we are gathered to celebrate my little brother," said Dominic. "Thirty years old and he doesn't look a day over forty."

"Piss off," said Seamus, as he emptied his glass. "Unlike some people here, I don't dye my hair."

"I think the grey makes you look sexy, Dom," piped up Anton. "I've always had a thing for silver foxes."

"You have a thing for anything with a pulse," said Dominic.

Anton gave a good-natured shrug. "There is that."

Seamus reached for the wine bottle again, and Andrea buried a twinge of jealousy. It was his birthday; if not tonight, then when? For months, he had abstained from drinking in the house. Their fridge was filled with alcohol-free beers and the spirit collection had been banished to the garage. It was a silent sign of support that reminded her why she loved him so much.

"Anyway, as I was saying before I was so rudely interrupted," continued Dominic, "tonight, we are here to celebrate my little brother reaching another milestone," his voice took on a mock wistful air. "Why, it seems like only yesterday, I was teaching him how to shave and talk to girls,"

"Oh, so that's your fault?" called out Andrea. "You and I need a chat." She kissed Seamus on the cheek. "No offence, sweetie."

"The bathroom looked like a murder scene," said Seamus. His voice was slurred, but he wore a sloppy smile. "I must have ended up with half a loo roll stuck to my face."

"Manual dexterity never was your thing," said Dominic, over the laughter. He spoke in a mock stage whisper. "It's why he's never beaten me at FIFA."

There was a chorus of "ooh"s, from around the table.

"Oh, that's a low blow," Andrea said.

Dominic gave an exaggerated shrug. "All I'm saying is that you should leave it to Uncle Dom to teach the bump how to play video games, change a tyre, wire a plug ..."

Seamus' retort was drowned out by a deafening crack of thunder. A moment later, the restaurant was plunged into darkness.

There was a collective gasp from the assembled diners and a squeal of surprise from one of the servers. After a few seconds the emergency lights above the fire exit blinked on, the flickering tealights the only other source of illumination.

Dominic stepped over to the full-length windows and peered through the glass.

"Looks like that took out the whole hillside," he said.

A low hubbub started amongst the other guests. Eventually Francesco, the restaurant owner, emerged from the kitchen, a torch in his hand.

"Ladies and gentlemen, I am so sorry," he said loudly. "We have completely lost power, along with the rest of the area. I'm afraid we are going to have to close for the night."

"What about the rest of our meal?" demanded a middle-aged man in a suit and tie. "Don't you have a back-up generator?"

"I'm sorry, but it only powers the emergency lights and keeps the freezers running," Francesco said.

"Don't you cook on gas?" asked the man's wife.

"Yes, but it isn't safe for my staff to work without proper lighting," Francesco said.

As the harried restaurant owner tried to placate the irate customers and stave off the one-star reviews, Seamus stretched his back.

"Spared by a divine act," he said to his brother.

"Don't worry, I'll save it for team briefing," Dominic said, clapping him on the back as he headed for the young waitress who had been serving them.

"I take it the tills are down?" he said.

"Yes," she said. She nodded anxiously.

"Don't worry," Dominic said. "Frankie's a mate. I'll pop back later in the week and settle up for the wine we've drunk."

He opened his wallet and took out a twenty-pound note. "Stick this in the tip jar, it's not your fault the weather's so bad."

Back at the table, the rest of the party were getting their coats and saying their goodbyes. Andrea grabbed a couple of handfuls of bread from the baskets on the table; it was already an hour past the time she and Seamus usually ate, and she was ravenous.

She looked at her champagne flute, before deciding she'd earned it.

"You stay here," Dominic said, materialising at her side. "I'll bring the car around."

"No rush," she said patting her swollen belly. "Bump needs a wee."

***

Maurice Seacombe peered through the windscreen of his elderly Subaru, the headlights barely cutting through the pounding rain. Another flash of lightning left coloured spots dancing in his vision. Beside him, his wife shifted in her seat.

"Slow down, Maurice," she said. He ignored her, concentrating on the road ahead. His daughter had offered them her spare room for the night, but Winnie was hosting tomorrow's Macmillan coffee morning and she wanted to get up early to do some more baking. He should have put his foot down and insisted they stay. But after forty years of marriage, he'd learned to pick his battles.

"You're going too fast," she said, as if a lifetime of knitting in the passenger seat had somehow made her an authority.

"Do you want to drive?" he asked, glaring at her.

"Look out!"

Snapping his attention back to the road, he hit the brakes, feeling the wheels lock and the car start to slide.

He caught a brief glimpse of the woman's face as she tumbled down the embankment, and then she was gone.

Wrestling with the wheel, he felt the drumming through the brake pedal as the car's ABS fought for grip on the slick tarmac, before they finally came to a scraping, juddering halt, resting against the crash barrier.

He let out a deep breath.

"Are you OK?" he asked, turning to his wife.

She pointed at the huge crack in the windscreen, her voice a whisper. "I think you hit someone."

Chapter Two

WIND BUFFETED THE CAR as Dominic steered it carefully along the country lane, the rattle of the rain all but drowning out the faint whine of the Tesla's electric motor.

"Ah, shit," said Seamus as they pulled up to the electric gates at the end of the driveway. The house beyond was in total darkness; not even the security lights came on.

"You know I'm not one to say I told you so ..." Dominic said.

"It's pitch black," Seamus said. "Solar panels don't work at night. You'll be sitting in the dark, just like us."

"Are you sure you don't want to stay over?" asked Andrea. "The weather is appalling."

Dominic gestured towards the traffic update on the car's display. "The main road is still open," he said. "I'd rather get home before it floods." He turned to his brother. "And you're forgetting; I have battery back-up. Forty-eight hours of lovely lighting, TV, heating, cooking ... You know I might even turn the hot tub on ..."

"Anyone ever tell you, you're a knob?" Seamus asked.

"Only you," Dominic said. He turned to Andrea in the backseat. "You know what, Andy, why don't we leave Seamus to sit in the dark with a candle and eat cold baked beans, whilst we go back to mine, reheat last night's lasagne and chill in the hot tub?"

"That's sweet, Dom, but I really wasn't planning on a water birth with you as the midwife."

Dominic shrugged. "Your loss. If you change your mind, I've got loads of fresh towels, and I've watched videos on YouTube; it doesn't look that difficult."

Andrea leaned forward and kissed him on the cheek. "You're such a charmer."

Seamus reached across the centre console and gave his brother an awkward hug.

"Sorry about tonight," Dominic said. "I'll have the two of you over next week and I'll cook us something to celebrate properly."

"Looking forward to it," Seamus said before stepping out into the rain. Opening his umbrella, he sheltered Andrea as she heaved herself out of the car.

Dominic waited until he was sure the side gate had opened, before turning the car around. He quietly beeped the horn and glided away.

Sheltering under the porch as Seamus unlocked the door, Andrea watched as the Tesla's rear lights disappeared from view.

She shook her head. "What are we going to do about him?" she asked. Not for the first time. "What was the excuse this time? Too needy?"

"Something like that," Seamus said, as he let them into the house. "You know, when we were younger, he was the one who all the girls liked. He was handsome, funny and smart. He can cook, and he had his own company by the time he was twenty. I figured for sure he'd be married with kids by the time he was twenty-five. Meanwhile, I was short, spotty and shy."

"Yeah, it's weird how one of you got all the good genes," Andrea said. She kissed him. "No offence."

He swatted her backside. "It's my birthday, you're supposed to be nice to me. It's the law."

"You know, I've been wondering something for a while," Andrea said. "Dominic's always pulling lovely girls, but they never seem to last very long. I was just thinking ..."

"That he might be gay," Seamus finished.

"You've got to admit, it's a possibility," she said.

Seamus puffed out his lips. "It's crossed my mind," he admitted.

"Do you think we should say something?" Andrea asked as she groped around in the junk drawer for candles.

"By we, you mean me?"

"Well, he is your brother. But seriously, Seamus, if you would find it too awkward, I don't mind."

"I'll think about it," Seamus muttered.

"I'll tell you something, though," she said, moving the subject to safer ground. "He might be right about the solar panels and battery back-up. It'd be nice not to have to dig the candles out every time there's a storm."

"Yeah, I'll look into it," Seamus said. "To be honest, I've been thinking about it for a while. Our last electricity bill was horrific, and it's only going to get worse. It's just Dominic can be such a smug git when he's right."

***

Dominic drove through the pounding rain. The live traffic updates had shown the most direct route to be blocked, so he took the longer main road. Even so, he kept his speed low. The powerful headlights struggled to penetrate the blackened gloom and the wipers were swishing flat-out.

Eventually he turned off the wide A-road, and started down the narrow, single-lane track towards his house. The rain running off the embankment had turned the road into a muddy quagmire, and he was glad he'd not waited around any longer. Much more of this and it would be impassable.

Finally, his house came into view.

"Shit."

The house was pitch black. He thumped the steering wheel in frustration. The battery back-up had cost a small fortune; it was supposed to store unused electricity from the array of solar panels on the roof and mean he wasn't reliant on the National Grid at night, or in the event of a power failure. This was exactly what it was supposed to prevent.

Thank God Seamus wasn't with him; he'd never live it down.

Then

The Morning After The Fire

Chapter Three

Seamus Monaghan cradled the cup of coffee in his hands; a thin film had formed as it cooled. It was his third that morning. It too was destined for the sink.

The two detectives were sympathetic, expressing their condolences; he'd barely heard them. All he could see were the flames engulfing the body. And the smell ... oh the smell ... he knew he'd never forget it.

The younger of the two, a black woman with braided hair, sat awkwardly, clutching her own coffee whilst her partner, an older white man in his fifties with greying hair and a thin moustache, made notes in his pocketbook.

DS Freeland had asked most of the questions so far.

"Was your wife depressed or upset?" he asked.

Seamus shrugged. His brown eyes were bloodshot and puffy, his blonde hair tousled where he'd been running his hand through it. "Not really. We've had a tough couple of years, obviously, but I thought she was coping. She never said anything ..."

"What about recently? Was there any change in her mood? Anything worrying her, or causing her stress?"

There was a round of shrugs from the others present in the room; Seamus' older brother and the best friend of Carole, Seamus' late wife.

"What time did you return home last night?" asked the younger detective.

"A little after ten, I think? Maybe half-past? Sorry, I've forgotten your name, Detective."

"DC Obigwe. Call me Mercy," she said, gently. "And you said you'd been away for a few days?"

"Yeah, Manchester."

"There was a trade conference," Dominic said. "I would have gone myself, but we're in the middle of negotiating a new contract ..." He squeezed his brother's shoulder. "Maybe if you'd been here ... If I'd gone instead, she wouldn't have ..." he broke off and wiped his face. "I'm so sorry, Seamus."

Seamus shook his head but couldn't bring himself to speak.

"When did you last speak to your wife?" Freeland asked.

"The morning I left. Monday. I texted her a couple of times to let her know how things were going, then to let her know when I was due to return."

"But you didn't speak?"

He shook his head, tears forming again. "I didn't get a chance. It's the biggest conference of the year. I spent all day pitching to people, then ate out with existing clients in the evening. By the time I got back each night, it was too late ..." His voice caught. "I should have made the time. Maybe if I'd spoken to her, she wouldn't have ... maybe I could have heard something in her voice and realised she needed me ..."

"Hey, hey, stop that," Dominic said, enfolding Seamus in his arms. "You couldn't have known what she was planning on doing. And it's not just you, remember? I knew she was alone, I could have phoned or driven over to see her."

"You were her best friend, I believe, Mrs Harrington?" said Obigwe, turning to the dark-haired woman hovering awkwardly behind the sofa.

"Yeah, friends since university," she said. "Seamus and my husband were on the same course. Carole and I played netball."

"And Carole was originally from the US?" Freeland asked.

"Yes, Wyoming. She came over on a scholarship," Seamus said. "She was supposed to return, but I asked her to marry me in our final year, and she decided to settle permanently."

"Where is your husband now, Mrs Harrington?" Freeland asked.

"He's visiting a client in Glasgow." Dominic spoke up. "We're hoping to expand north of the border."

"He works for you as well?" Freeland said.

"Yes, he's our head of corporate expansion." Dominic gave an embarrassed smile. "The job titles are a bit meaningless, if I'm honest. There are only a few of us, so we all pitch in and do what's necessary."

"And what is it you actually do?" Freeland asked.

"We supply security solutions to public and private institutions. Alarms, CCTV, that sort of thing," Dominic said.

Freeland nodded. He returned his attention to Seamus.

"I'm really sorry to ask this, Seamus, but we need positive identification it was your wife in the shed."

Seamus whitened even further. His hands were wrapped in light bandages from where he'd tried to force the shed door open. It had housed his pride and joy, a petrol-powered sit-on lawnmower, and so he'd invested in heavy-duty padlocks. They'd been hanging open when he returned home, but the keys to the mortice lock had been inside the shed.

"I don't think I can face ..."

"No, no, I'm not asking you to view the ... to view your wife," Freeland said gently. "We'll make the match using DNA, or other means. If you can supply us with her toothbrush, or perhaps her hairbrush, we can get what we need from that."

Seamus nodded. The unsaid implication hung in the air. Carole's body was burned beyond recognition; only science could identify her now.

"I'll get them," Dominic offered, jumping to his feet. He squeezed his brother's shoulder again.

"I'll come with you," Obigwe said.

The two of them headed for the stairs. Harrington replaced Dominic on the couch and took Seamus' hand in hers.

Freeland cleared his throat. "When the officers attended last night, they noticed the smell of, what they believed to be, cannabis, and what appeared to be the remains of two joints in the ashtray. They took them as evidence."

Seamus stiffened, and Freeland held up a placating hand. "We're not here to investigate a bit of weed. But I do have to ask a couple of questions. There was also an empty bottle of wine. Did Carole have any substance issues? Drugs, medication, alcohol?"

Seamus was silent for a few moments. "She liked to smoke a bit of weed, now and again. We both did. She also used to drink. Not every day," he added hastily, "but perhaps more than she should have sometimes."

Freeland turned his gaze to Harrington.

"Yeah, what Seamus said. She liked a joint to chill out in the evenings sometimes. And she did drink." She looked away from Seamus. "A couple of times she stayed over at mine because she was too drunk to make it home. Sorry, I should have told you."

Seamus closed his eyes.

"Anything else? Prescription medications perhaps?"

"Nothing at the moment," he said.

Harrington shook her head.

"We've got what we need," Obigwe announced as she returned to the room, wearing blue disposable gloves. She held up two plastic evidence bags containing a hairbrush and a toothbrush. "They were taken from the en suite bathroom attached to the main bedroom. Can you confirm they are your wife's?"

Seamus forced himself to look, before nodding. How many times had he seen his wife brushing her golden hair with that brush? Or mumbling around the toothbrush last thing at night?

Freeland snapped his pocketbook closed and stood up.

"Thank you for your time, and again, I'm very sorry for your loss. We'll keep in touch."

"What happens now?" Dominic asked. The body had been removed early that morning in a private ambulance. The end of the garden was still taped off, fire specialists combing through the remains of the shed.

"Our investigators will continue to look through the debris." Freeland gave an apologetic smile. "Could be another couple of days until they've finished, I'm afraid."

"And Carole?" Seamus asked. "I need to speak to her parents. Oh God, we never decided what to do when we ... where we wanted to be buried. They'll want to take her back to the States ..."

Freeland placed a hand on his shoulder. "Don't rush, Seamus. There will need to be a post-mortem and an inquest, so it's probably going to be a few weeks until the coroner releases her body. My advice is to let her parents know what's happened, then take your time deciding what to do."

Obigwe opened her bag and removed a leaflet. "This will tell you what happens next, and the coroner service has a really helpful website."

Seamus took it without a word.

"I see you have CCTV," Freeland said. "Would it be possible for us to get a copy of it? It'll help us to piece together the events of last night, and perhaps identify any visitors who might be able to tell us about your wife's state of mind."

The blood drained from Seamus' face, and he swallowed.

"Of course." His voice caught. "But I don't think ..."

"You won't need to watch it, Seamus," Obigwe interjected, gently. "If you can show us how to operate the system, then we can retrieve what we need ourselves, and watch it back at the station."

Seamus nodded, although the colour didn't fully return to his face.

He led them upstairs to his office where the digital video recorder for the CCTV was housed.

"We have cameras over the front door, overlooking the rear garden, the drive, and above the garage door."

"Any internal cameras?" Freeland asked, pulling on a pair of nitrile gloves.

"No, I always thought that was a bit creepy," Seamus said.

"This looks like a standard system," Freeland said, half to Seamus and half to Obigwe. "Which is good, because the course I went on was only an afternoon. It means I won't have to unplug the whole unit and take it to Digital Forensics. It could take days for them to look at it."

He inserted a thumb drive into the device's USB slot and navigated to the search screen. He clicked the mouse a few times, before turning to Seamus with a frown.

"Where's the footage from last night?"

Eight Years Ago

Five Years Before The Fire

Chapter Four

"Relax, Bro', everything will be fine. It's a beautiful day, everyone's here. It'll be perfect, you'll see."

The two brothers embraced.

"I'm so glad you're here," Seamus said. "I don't think I could bear it without you by my side."

"Of course, and I'm proud you asked me," Dominic said. "Even if it's only because you don't have any other friends."

"Knob."

"Watch your language, Jesus is listening."

Before Seamus could reply, the music started.

"Show time, little brother," Dominic said, as they turned to look down the aisle.

Seamus let out a deep breath.

"Wow," Dominic said.

"That's my line," Seamus said.

As one, the congregation turned, cameras and phones flashing.

Resplendent in a white silk dress, her golden hair tied in an elaborate top knot, Carole Werner – soon-to-be Carole Monaghan – started her slow walk towards the altar, led by her bridesmaids. Her father, beaming from cheek-to-cheek, had his arm hooked through his daughter's. In the front row, her mother dabbed at her eyes.

Seamus stood and drank in the sight. Beside him, Dominic checked his pocket for the hundredth time; the rings were still there.

Finally, Carole was at the steps. Seamus grasped his soon-to-be father-in-law's hand. "I'll take good care of her, sir, I promise," he said quietly.

***

Dominic Monaghan tapped his champagne flute, and the crowded room fell silent.

"Today is the proudest moment of my life," he looked over at his brother and his new bride. "Not only am I here as best man, I'm also here on behalf of our parents, and our grandparents." His voice caught. "Who I'm sure are watching over us. And who would have loved Carole as much as Seamus does. And I do."

Seamus reached over and touched his elbow.

Dominic smiled. "I was three years old when Mum and Dad brought Seamus home from the hospital. I'll be honest, as much as I love my brother, I really wanted a sister."

A ripple of laughter ran around the room. "Because to my mind, a little sister probably wouldn't want to play with my toys."

Seamus shook his head and mouthed 'knob' at him.

"Of course, I changed my mind the first time I held him." He turned to his brother. "I know it didn't always seem like it, but I loved sharing my toys with you. Until today, playing with you in Mum and Dad's living room – even sharing a room with you at Nan and Granddad's – were my happiest memories."

"Me too, Dom, me too," Seamus mumbled.

Beside the best man, Kitty, Carole's younger sister wiped her eyes.

Dominic turned to Seamus and held his glass aloft.

"Seamus, you are my brother and my best friend, and finally, after twenty-two years you've given me what I always wanted. A sister!"

This time there was a chorus of "ahh"s mixed with the laughter. Dominic turned back to the room.

"Now enough of the soppy shit, did I ever tell you about the time I taught Seamus to shave?"

***

Dominic had lost count of how many bottles of beer he'd consumed. He sat in a chair at the edge of dance floor, his legs outstretched. He had no idea where his jacket was, and his tie had been wrapped around his forehead since the DJ had played Dire Straits, *Money For Nothing*.

Now he was watching Seamus and Carole bellowing *Wake Me Up Before You Go-Go* in the centre of the dance floor with Seamus' old flatmates.

"If you had a video camera, you'd be like that creepy guy in *Love Actually*," Andrea said, as she flopped down beside him, and handed him another beer. "You know the one? The best man they placed in charge of shooting the wedding video, but it turns out all he filmed all day was the bride?"

She slipped her shoes off with a moan, then reached over and touched his forearm. "Seamus is in good hands. Carole will look after him, I promise."

"Yeah, I know," Dominic sighed. "I know she will. She's great; we both know he's punching well above his weight."

She gave him a playful slap. "Be nice, it's his wedding day."

She settled back in her seat and watched the newly-weds, as they segued into *Come On Eileen*.

After a couple of minutes, Dominic leaned over, his voice wistful. "I guess I just got used to being the one he turned to, you know? When Mum and Dad died, it felt like it was just the two of us." He snorted. "Christ, I was eleven years old, and he was barely eight, but

I convinced myself that he was my responsibility. That I had to do Mum and Dad's job now they were gone."

"What about your grandparents?" Andrea asked. "Seamus never really talks about them."

"They did their best," Dominic said, eventually. "But Mum and Dad had us quite late, and *they* had Dad pretty late also, so they were both nearly eighty when we went to live with them. Looking back, I realise they must have been grieving as much as we were. And they were retired, looking for a quiet life, not planning on starting all over again with two broken little boys. I think that if they hadn't suddenly been lumbered with us, they may even have moved back to Ireland." He gave a lop-sided smile. "Although I don't think the Ireland of the late-nineties and early-noughties was the Ireland they left forty-odd years before. The thought of a referendum about same-sex marriage would have blown their minds."

He sighed again. "It can't have been easy for them. Money wasn't a problem fortunately, our parents had life insurance, but we had to share a bedroom for the first time. And parenting had changed." He winced. "Granddad still gave us the slipper if we misbehaved. Sundays were church and *Songs Of Praise*. We didn't even have a video recorder, let alone computer games. In the evening, Nan watched her soaps then Granddad watched the news; neither of us will ever be choosing 'popular TV shows of our childhood' as our specialist subject on *Mastermind*."

"Sounds stifling," Andrea said.

Dominic shrugged. "If I'm honest, I couldn't wait to move out, but I didn't want to leave Seamus. I decided to stay until he turned eighteen and went to university. On the plus side, I'd got myself a cracking apprenticeship at a local electronics firm and I was living rent-free, saving every penny I earned, so there was that."

"And now you're the CEO of Monaghan Security Solutions," she said. "The next Bill Gates."

"Ha! Remind me to show you our accounts someday."

"There he is!"

"Hello Markie," Dominic said, as Marcus, another of Seamus' and Carole's university friends, collapsed into the chair next to Andrea. He gave her a sloppy kiss on the cheek, before leaning across her to shout at Dominic.

"Bloody brilliant speech, mate. Don't tell anyone, but you had me in tears."

"Your secret's safe with me," Dominic assured him, although Marcus had said the same thing to practically every guest there, including him. Twice.

Marcus placed the back of his hand over his mouth and stifled a burp.

"Did I tell you I got onto the graduate training program at Barclays?" he asked.

"I think you mentioned it, yeah," Dominic said.

Andrea rolled her eyes. "Sorry," she mouthed.

"Did I tell you how much they're going to pay me?" Marcus bellowed.

"Remind me," Dominic said politely.

"With bonuses, it'll be ..." he paused, then suddenly shouted, "I love this song!" as the opening bars of *Time Warp* came over the speakers. He lurched to his feet. "Come on, this is a classic."

He held out his hand, and Andrea took it.

"You're all right, mate, I'll sit this one out," Dominic said. He winked at Andrea. "I thought I might try my luck and have a crack at one of the bridesmaids. It's traditional."

"I'd steer clear of Carole's sister," Andrea advised. "Their Dad collects guns."

Saluting the couple with his bottle, Dominic settled back in his seat to continue watching his little brother and the woman who had stolen his heart.

Now

The Morning After The Storm

Chapter Five

"SHE HAS NO ID, and is dressed inappropriately for the weather," PC Poppy Hall said. "She's also malnourished, and the doctors found something disturbing that I think you guys should see."

It was just before nine a.m., and PC Hall had stayed past the end of her shift to meet the detective who'd promised to come and have a look at the woman who'd been hit by the Seacombes the previous night.

DI Katie Stafford scanned through the email that had been waiting in her inbox that morning.

"IC1 female, blonde hair, approximately five-feet seven inches, slim-to-underweight. Currently unconscious, no ID. Have you let Missing Persons know, or run her prints through the system?"

"Yes to Missing Persons. Awaiting a warrant from the magistrate for the prints."

"OK, so tell me what's worrying you so much."

Stafford was familiar with Poppy Hall. Solid and dependable, she had twenty-odd years under her belt. If she said she thought it was worth someone from Stafford's team taking a look, then Stafford was prepared to take a look.

"First the location; Valley View Road. It's a bit out in the sticks; not the sort of place you'd be out walking in pissing rain and lightning. It's mostly farmland or private residences, but the properties are spread out."

"Could she have broken down?"

"We've no reports yet of stranded vehicles in the area," Hall said.

"What else?"

"Clothing was a thin T-shirt, a couple of sizes too big. Lightweight sweatpants, the sort you might wear in bed, again too large. Shoes were plimsoles; the type worn as slippers. You might nip out to the recycling bin dressed like that, but you aren't going to walk any distance, especially not in that sort of weather.

"She was covered in mud, and her arms and face had fresh scratches, possibly from tree branches, because there was leaf litter in her hair and stuck to her clothes."

"The report says she appeared to fall off the embankment at the side of the road into the path of the vehicle?"

"Yes, the road is cut into the hillside. On one side there's a raised embankment with a fence, and a narrow strip of mud and weeds before the treeline. The other side has a crash barrier, and then the woodland slopes down the valley. From what the Seacombes have said, the young woman appeared to be halfway up the embankment when she fell into the road. To get there, she was either climbing out of the road, or had clambered over the fence from the direction of the woods, then lost her footing."

"All right, it's definitely a concern, but what's *really* worrying you, Poppy?" Stafford asked. She'd certainly be following up; but she could tell there was more. There had to be a reason why Poppy Hall had stayed past the end of what must have been a cold, wet and busy night shift to make certain she was fully listened to.

"The doctors and I have both had a look, and we agree. There are scars on her wrists that look like she may have been shackled."

***

Seamus Monaghan burst out laughing when his brother entered the gents' bathroom carrying his kit bag. Monaghan Security Solutions rented space in a fully-serviced office block. Employees had access to a canteen, a small gym and – most importantly this morning – showering facilities. Seamus made use of them if he cycled into work.

Today they were necessary, as he and Andrea had woken to find the power still hadn't been restored, so they had no hot water. He'd dropped Andrea off for a swim so she could use the showers at the leisure centre. Without electricity her online exercise class – which he'd dubbed 'Preggers Pilates' – was a no go. Afterwards, she'd catch a cab home; hopefully the power would be restored by then, so she could do some work. She wasn't due to go on maternity leave for another couple of weeks, but she was in the final stages of a couple of commissions, and wanted everything wrapped-up.

Seamus had decided to go into work for a couple of hours to work on a presentation and have a shower. The aborted party the night before meant he didn't have the hangover he'd allowed for.

Dominic was rumpled, his eyes reddened through lack of sleep, his shoes covered in mud. Without a word, he opened one of the lockers and started stripping off.

"You don't have any electricity, do you?" Seamus crowed.

"Piss off," Dominic grumbled.

"Remind me how much you spent on that battery back-up for your solar panels?"

"The battery back-up was fine, thank you very much," he said. "What wasn't fine was my house's shitty fuse box."

"What happened?" Seamus asked.

"A power surge tripped the circuit breakers," Dominic said. "Which is annoying, but that's what's supposed to happen. But when I tried to reset them last night, I found that the high-current ring-mains for the kitchen and the bathroom were burned out. Probably from a cheap circuit breaker, or dodgy wiring from the dickhead who owned the house before me." He slammed the door to the locker. "I have lighting and plug sockets, but I can't cook anything – the microwave is integrated into the oven – or use the shower. Earliest an emergency electrician can come out is tomorrow morning, and it'll be Sunday rates."

"Ah, shit, that's rough," Seamus said. "I'll tell you what; the power company reckon we'll have everything restored by lunchtime. Come to ours this evening. I'll whack something in the oven, and you can stay over. If the power's still out, we'll all go round to yours instead, since you have lights, and we'll either boil the kettle and have Pot Noodles, or phone for takeaway."

Dominic forced a smile. "Sounds like a plan."

Chapter Six

STAFFORD AND HALL WERE stood by the woman's bed. Her face was swollen and grazed, a large bandage wrapped her head, portions of which had been shaved. Her arms were on top of the covers, the right encased in a plaster cast. They were skinny, almost emaciated. The sheets on the bed covered a frame to keep pressure off her smashed pelvis. Even with the swelling, the first word that sprang to mind when Stafford saw her face was 'gaunt'.

"She's in an induced coma," explained the neurologist. "The head injury sustained when she was hit by the car caused a bleed on the brain. We dealt with that last night, and she's currently stable. Orthopaedics will be taking another look at that pelvis tomorrow."

"How long until she's likely to regain consciousness?" Stafford asked.

The doctor shrugged. "No way to tell at this stage. She received a hell of a bang to the head. Hopefully we'll be able to remove the sedation in a few days, but I'll warn you now, there's no guarantee she'll come around. And if she does ... well you might not get much out of her. Ever."

"How old do you think these abrasions are?" Stafford asked, pointing to the welts on the woman's wrists.

"I'm not a pathologist," warned the doctor, "but there's a mix. Some are pretty well-healed, so I guess you're looking at months or years for those. These are more recent, perhaps a few weeks old?"

Stafford and Hall exchanged a glance.

"Good call, Poppy," Stafford said. "This is definitely worth a closer look."

***

Whilst Hall went to fetch them a coffee, Stafford phoned her boss, DCI Gemma Girton, her team leader in the Sexual Exploitation Unit.

"Definitely something the SEU should be looking at," Stafford said. "Obviously, I can't tell if she's been sexually abused, but everything about this is screaming people trafficking or modern slavery. I recommend we open a case and proceed as if it falls under our remit; we can always hand it back to Roads Policing if it turns out not to be anything sinister."

"I agree," Girton said. "What are you going to do next?"

"I'm heading out for a quick look at where the collision occurred with PC Hall, and then I'll pop back and brief you."

Stafford hung up as Hall returned with their drinks. They headed towards the car park.

"It's a go. Well spotted, Poppy."

"Thanks. You hear about these lone women escaping from sex-rings, but never think it'll happen on your patch."

"Don't get too excited," Stafford cautioned. "Nine times out of ten it's nothing so dramatic. Sometimes couples just like a bit of kink with handcuffs, but I won't be happy until we've worked out who she is and checked out her background."

The two women got into the car, Hall extra careful not to slop her coffee over the passenger seat. Stafford downed hers in one go.

"Asbestos mouth and hands," she said by way of an explanation. "Got it from my grandmother. That woman could pour freshly boiled water from a metal teapot without even flinching." She crushed the paper cup and placed it in a bag.

As they pulled out of the car park, Stafford glanced over at Hall. "Are you sure you're up to this Poppy?"

"I'm good." She raised her cup. "This'll keep me going for another couple of hours, then I'll crash. I'm on a rest day tomorrow, so I want it all handed over before I'm off. I won't sleep right until I'm satisfied you guys are on the case."

Evidence of the previous night's collision still existed, even though the Seacombes' car had been removed. The grass verge was chewed up, and there was paint on the battered crash barrier. Broken glass lay scattered all around. The rain had stopped in the early hours, but the road was still slick with muddy water.

Hall walked a dozen or so metres up the road from where the car had entered the verge.

"This was where we found her lying."

The brown mud on the carriageway was mixed with blood. Stafford took a series of photographs for context, then picked her way carefully over to the embankment. Clumps of scrubby grass and weeds were missing, and the soil was disturbed. It looked as though the edge of the raised bank had given way. Wooden posts a metre or so high, strung with wire, separated the road from the woodland beyond.

"The fence is supposed to stop deer or other wildlife coming out onto the road," Hall said.

Stafford looked into the woods. "I don't know how much damage the rain has done to the scene," she said, "but I'll get a team up here to see if they can figure out where she came from."

"There are a couple of houses on the other side of the woods, about half a mile as the crow flies," Hall said. She pointed along the road. "And there are properties a mile or so in either direction."

"So, she could have come from the woods, or been walking along the embankment when she fell," Stafford said.

"She'd been out in it for some time," Hall said. "The driver covered her in a raincoat, but she was still soaked through and borderline hypothermic. There are no reports yet of abandoned vehicles in the vicinity. I find it hard to imagine somebody dropped her off at the roadside; not dressed like that."

"I'll get a team up here to start canvassing the properties along this road," Stafford said. "Maybe there's CCTV, or somebody saw something?"

"It'll have been pitch black," Hall warned. "A lightning strike took out the local substation. I think the whole area is still waiting for the power to be restored."

"A dog team might pick up her scent," Stafford mused, making a note to look into it. The budget was tight, but the marks on the woman's wrists worried her. Most of the recent cases of modern slavery they'd been investigating were based in the nearby cities and towns; trafficked woman and men forced to work in poorly regulated cash industries like car washes and nail bars. There had been some instances of forced labour on farms, although none within a reasonable distance of where they were now.

A chill wind swept across the road, and she shivered. Every instinct was telling her something was deeply wrong here. Hall's worried look mirrored her own thoughts.

Chapter Seven

Power to the hillside was restored by early afternoon. Dominic returned home and confirmed he had mains power, and his solar panels and battery were working, but that he couldn't cook or shower. He insisted on stopping on the way to his brother's and buying a takeout curry meal from the local supermarket.

"The electrician will be coming between seven and eight a.m.," he said, "so I won't stay over."

Seamus handed him an alcohol-free beer from the fridge. "Then try this, I've not had this one before."

Dominic took a mouthful. "Not too bad," he said. "I've had worse. But the sooner Elon Musk fully turns on the autopilot in my car and it can drive me home after a skinful, the better."

"You are such a nerd," Andrea said as she entered the kitchen. She pecked him on the cheek. "Or is it a geek? I can never remember."

She helped herself to a swig from her husband's beer. "Mmm, I'll add this to the shopping list." She turned back to Dominic. "Well autopilot or not, I'm glad the weather has improved. Last night was horrendous. It's a good job you took the main road; apparently there was a nasty accident on Valley View Road."

"I saw it was blocked on the sat nav," Dominic said.

"Yeah, apparently some woman got knocked over by a couple driving home."

"On Valley View Road?" Seamus asked. "What on earth was she doing out there?"

"The website didn't say," Andrea said.

"Did they say anything about who she was?" Dominic asked. "She could have been one of my neighbours."

"Nothing. It was just a couple of paragraphs. They said the police were trying to contact her next of kin; appealing for witnesses, that sort of thing."

"So she's dead?" Dominic asked.

"I don't think so. The article didn't say she died; they said she was taken by ambulance to University Hospital."

The electronic timer started beeping. Seamus opened the oven and slid in a baking tray of sundries. He restarted the timer, and then stabbed at the plastic film covering the container of pilau rice, before placing it into the microwave.

"Can you get some bowls out, Dom?"

"Hmm?" Dominic looked up from his phone. "Sorry. Nothing new about that poor woman. What were you asking?"

"Bowls. Bottom cupboard. I'm worried that if Andy bends down to fetch them, she'll never get back up."

"You let him speak to you like that?" Dominic asked, as he slid off his chair.

"Unfortunately, it's true," Andrea said with a groan. "I haven't seen my feet without the help of a mirror for weeks. The sooner these two vacate the premises the better."

Dominic fetched the crockery, whilst Andrea laid out cutlery and filled a jug with tap water.

"Mmm, nice and spicy," Andrea said once they'd started. "I've no idea if my sense of taste will go back to normal after the birth, but in the meantime, Madras all the way."

"I hope it doesn't. It'll be nice to have someone who appreciates my special chilli," Dominic said. "One day I'll cook us a big pan that we can stuff ourselves with, and I'll make Seamus his own girly one that won't make him cry."

"Wow, you've insulted both of us in one go," Seamus said. "How do you do that?"

"It's a gift."

After finishing the curry, they decided to cut into Seamus' birthday cake.

"Andy and I are going to drive over to the cemetery Monday," Seamus said quietly, as they finished. "Do you want to join us?"

"Christ, three years already," Dominic said. "I'll check the calendar, but I should be free." He took a swig of his beer. "Have you spoken to her family recently?"

Seamus shook his head. "I wrote a letter at Christmas, but I got no reply. Kitty replied to an email; said her parents are OK, but that was it."

Andrea stroked his hand.

"They still hold me responsible," Seamus said quietly. "And I can't say I blame them." His voice caught. "On the day of our wedding, I promised her father I'd look after her. But I didn't, did I?"

"Hey, we've been through this," Dominic said. "It wasn't your fault. Carole did what she did for her own reasons."

Seamus said nothing.

"I take it you haven't spoken to them?" Dominic asked Andrea.

"Not since the funeral," she replied. "And even then, I left as soon as was decent." She wiped her eye. "With everything that happened afterwards and then ..." She looked down at her hand entwined in Seamus'. "You know how it is," she said eventually.

She sneezed. "Shit, I think I got curry up my nose."

She sneezed again. "No, don't laugh, I'm in a delicate condition. Three sneezes in a row, and you'll be fetching the hot towels."

She got up out of her chair. "I'm going to go and wipe my face." She sneezed again. "And give my nose a good blow." She squeezed Seamus' shoulder and gave him a meaningful look. "I'll leave you two to catch up."

"Shout if you go into labour," Dominic called after her, as he crammed the last bit of poppadom into his mouth and started collecting up the dirty bowls.

Seamus took a deep breath, suddenly nervous.

"Dom, can I ask you something?"

"Sure thing, Bro'," Dominic said, as he started loading the dishwasher.

"This last girl you were seeing?"

"Ellie?"

"Yeah. What went wrong? The two of you seemed perfect for one another."

"It was fun whilst it lasted, but you know how these things are. Sometimes you both want different things out of life. Better to end it whilst you're still enjoying being together, than wait until you are sick of the sight of each other, and everyone's miserable."

"I suppose," Seamus said. "The thing is. Well, what I wanted to ask ..." He started again. "What Andy and I have noticed, is that there seems to be a bit of a pattern here. You find a lovely woman, seem perfectly happy, and then it all ends. Why is that?"

Dominic closed the machine and set it going, before turning around.

"I told you. Sometimes you just want different things in life."

"Are you sure there isn't more to it?" Seamus persisted.

"Like what?" Dominic said, his voice taking on a slight edge. "Look Seamus, Carole was your first proper girlfriend. You got lucky right out of the gate. Then, after ... you know ... lightning struck a second time. Not everyone has that."

"I know, I know. It's just we were thinking ... well you know I love you right? That you can tell me anything. Anything at all. I just want you to be happy. And true to yourself ..." The silence stretched between them, before Dominic started to laugh.

"Seamus, are you asking me if I'm gay?"

"Yeah, I suppose I am. I know Nan and Granddad were a bit old-fashioned about this sort of thing, but you know me better than that. I just want you to find the right person."

Dominic shook his head. "No, little brother, I'm not gay. I just haven't found Mrs Right."

"Good," Seamus said eventually. He cleared his throat. "Glad we cleared that up."

He fetched another couple of beers from the fridge, despite neither of them having finished the one they were drinking.

"I guess the next question is, who is the right person?" he asked.

"Once I figure that out, you'll be the first to know," Dominic promised. He raised his voice. "Andy, you can come back downstairs now, the awkward bit's over. I'm not gay."

"Has anyone ever told you you're a knob?" Seamus asked.

Then

Three Days After The Fire

Chapter Eight

Seamus awoke Sunday morning with a hangover. Staggering down to the kitchen, he filled the kettle and placed a couple of slices of bread in the toaster, knowing he should force himself to eat. The half-full bottle of whiskey on the counter was calling out to him and for a moment, he was tempted to add a healthy slug to his coffee to get him through the day ahead, but the nausea from the night before stopped him. Instead, he dry-swallowed a couple of paracetamol. The sound of muted voices behind the drawn curtains told him that the CSI team were still picking over the remains of the shed.

The coffee table in the lounge was covered with envelopes, most hand delivered. None had been opened. The bunches of flowers sitting in the kitchen sink were still wrapped, stems held together with elastic bands.

The doorbell rang.

He was tempted to just ignore it, but his car was parked outside, alongside the forensic vans. He knew if didn't answer, they'd just keep on ringing.

The two detectives who had visited the morning after the fire were standing on the doorstep as he opened the door, squinting against the bright sunshine. He was still wearing the T-shirt and tracksuit bottoms he'd been wearing for the last couple of days. Showering hadn't been a priority, and he felt a brief flash of embarrassment. Struggling to remember their names through the brain fog, he invited them in.

"Everyone has been incredibly kind," he said. "But in the end, I had to ask them to give me some space."

"I understand," said Freeland, the older man's tone gentle and sympathetic. He and his partner – Obigwe? – had accepted a glass of water each. Which was just as well, since the milk had turned and there were no clean mugs.

"I'm sorry to tell you Seamus, but DNA tests have confirmed that it was your wife, Carole, in the shed," said Freeland.

Seamus slumped and he let out a shuddering breath.

"Of course. It had to be." He wiped his eyes. His voice became thick. "I mean there was never really any doubt was there? But still, there's that little glimmer of hope ..."

He cleared his throat. "Did she ... did she suffer?" he asked.

The detectives glanced at one another, before Freeland spoke. "We don't believe so."

Seamus took a sip of his black coffee, before starting to speak again. "You know, it's actually almost a relief? I knew in my heart she was gone, but ever since that night, I've been in limbo. Now I know it was actually her ..." He gave a sniff. "You must think I'm a right shit."

"No," said Freeland. "It's actually quite a normal reaction. The uncertainty is often the worst part. Knowing one way or the other helps start the healing process." He continued speaking, but Seamus got the impression the remarks were addressed as much to his partner as him. He looked at the detective. How old was she, he wondered? She wore her hair in tight braids and was dressed in a smart business suit, but he suddenly got the impression that she was younger than she was trying to portray.

"I've worked a number of murders where the body hasn't been immediately found," continued Freeland. "Everyone, family included, knows the victim is dead. We have evidence of the killing, sometimes we even have the murderer awaiting trial, but we haven't got a body. We haven't got 100 percent, cast-iron certainty. And without that, the family are never truly at peace. A small part of them never quite accepts their loved one is gone; that they'll never walk through the door again. You have that now, Seamus. Don't feel guilty it's a relief."

"Thank you," Seamus said.

After a decent interval Freeland cleared his throat. "Do you know if your wife had any visitors whilst you were away?"

Seamus frowned at the unexpected question, before shaking his head. "Not that I'm aware of. At least nobody has said that they came over. Why do you ask?"

"Just trying to establish what Carole's frame of mind was leading up to the fire," Freeland said. "If she had a visitor, then they might have some thoughts."

His sympathetic smile was well-rehearsed, but his kind eyes were searching. He felt the weight of Obigwe's gaze.

"Would you allow us to conduct a search of your house and vehicles," Freeland asked. "We might come across something that gives us an insight into why Carole did what she did."

Seamus' mouth became dry. He'd watched enough TV to know that in the case of an unexpected death, the police viewed everything with suspicion until they were satisfied no foul play was involved. He felt that thrill of illogical, paranoid guilt that he experienced every time he flew and the airport security locked eyes with him and asked if he had packed his own bag, and if he had any banned items. Should he demand to see a search warrant? Stall for time and phone Dominic to arrange a solicitor? He gave himself a mental shake. He was being ridiculous.

"Do what you need to," he said. "The sooner this nightmare is over, the better."

"Look, you don't want to be here while the CSIs are going through everything," Obigwe said, with a sympathetic smile. "Why don't you come with us to the station? We can get a formal statement off you there and leave them to it."

Again, Seamus thought for a moment before giving a resigned shrug. "Yeah, I'll get changed."

***

"Thank you for agreeing to see us, Seamus," Freeland said. "For the recording, can you confirm that you are here voluntarily to assist with our enquiries, and that you understand that you can end the interview at any time. You have declined the services of a solicitor, but you are free to change your mind at any time."

Seamus nodded. "Whatever you need," he said. "I just want to get this over with."

"We just need to clear up a few details about the last few days," Freeland said. He opened a blue, A4, lined pad. It looked as though he'd already filled several dozen pages. Was that normal for a suspected suicide? Seamus tried to read the man's handwriting upside down, but the angle was wrong and Freeland's scrawl was illegible.

"You say you went to Manchester on Monday to attend a security conference. How did you travel there?"

"Train," Seamus said. "I took the direct service to Manchester Piccadilly. I can't remember the exact one I took, but I arrived about half-nine."

Beside him, Obigwe was writing notes in her own book.

"And you were staying at the conference hotel? The Regal?"

"Yes, I stayed there until Thursday."

"Why until Thursday?" Freeland asked. "According to the website, the conference finished on Wednesday afternoon."

Seamus started. His throat tightened and he cleared it. "I decided to stay another day in case I needed to attend any follow-up meetings."

"And did you? Attend any follow-up meetings?"

Seamus paused – where was this going? "Not this time," he said.

"So what did you do Wednesday evening?" Obigwe asked.

"I was tired," Seamus said. "The conference is always hard-going, so I had an early night."

"Did you go out to eat?" she asked.

"Um, no. I ordered room service."

Freeland was busy scribbling. "What time did you return on Thursday?" he asked.

Seamus felt warm. Why were they so interested in his whereabouts?

"I can't remember. I had an open return. Late evening. I spent a bit of time in Manchester."

"There was a train that arrived at 21.04," Obigwe said helpfully.

"That sounds about right," he said, forcing himself to remain casual. They are just being thorough, he told himself. That's their job.

"How did you return home from the station? Did you drive?" Freeland asked.

"No, I caught a taxi."

"And you came straight from the station?" he continued.

"Yes."

"How was your relationship with your wife?" Obigwe asked.

Seamus blinked at the sudden change in topic. "OK. We've had a tough couple of years, but things were going well lately... or at least I thought they were," he added. Clearly they wouldn't be here if everything had been tickety-boo.

"Two years ago your wife suffered a miscarriage, I understand," Freeland said, his voice gentle. "That must have been very hard for you both."

Seamus felt the prickle of incipient tears. "Yeah," he mumbled, his voice thick. "It was a really difficult time. But like I said, things were going well lately." He cleared his throat. "We'd even started trying for a baby again."

Too much? That was more than they needed to know.

"I'm sorry," Freeland said. "But I have to ask. Do you think the loss of your baby could have affected your wife's state of mind? I believe the anniversary is soon."

Seamus wiped his eyes. "I don't know. She suffered from post-partum depression after the ... death. It still happens sometimes, even when the pregnancy ends ... well, you know. Her GP diagnosed PTSD and we had counselling. Carole needed anti-depressants for a while, but like I said, I thought she was doing OK." His voice caught. "Could I have missed the signs? Do you think that's why she decided to ...?"

"I'm sorry, but that's something I really can't tell you," said Freeland. "It's not my area of expertise." Again, his voice was gentle, but Seamus felt as though the man's eyes were probing his soul.

"I appreciate this is a very difficult time, and these questions may be uncomfortable," Freeland continued, "but your friend said Carole sometimes used cannabis and that she could drink to excess. Are you aware of any other drugs she may have been using?"

Seamus gave a small shake of the head. "I know that she has been drinking and has been using cannabis occasionally. In the past she's used cocaine, but I thought she'd stopped that. We were trying for a baby, so she was careful not to take anything when she might have been pregnant." He felt his cheeks flush at discussing something so intimate with total strangers. "She was doing pregnancy tests regularly, and charting her hormone levels, so she only drank or smoked when she knew she was definitely not pregnant. And made sure not to take anything before we tried again."

"I understand," Freeland said, before pausing. When he spoke again, his tone was measured, his words precise. "We ran a toxicology screen on blood taken from your wife. The results are preliminary, but they showed high levels of alcohol and cannabis in your wife's body at the time of her death."

"The morning I left, she'd just had another negative test," Seamus said; again his voice caught. That day seemed so long ago now. "It was her way of dealing with the disappointment, I guess.

I should have cancelled my trip, but she told me we couldn't plan our whole lives around trying for a baby. It could take years. She knew how important the trade conference was, so she insisted I go. Christ, I wish I hadn't now."

"We also found other drugs in your wife's system," Freeland said.

Seamus swallowed. "Cocaine?"

"No, opiates. Most likely heroin."

Seamus gave a bark of laughter. "Piss off." He sobered. "Sorry. What do you mean, heroin?"

"We found a needle beside her body, and evidence she has been injecting. Probably for some time. At the time of her death, the concentrations were enough that she was probably insensate by the time the fire fully took hold."

"Don't be ridiculous," Seamus said. "Heroin? Carole wasn't a bloody junkie. For fuck's sake, I saw her naked the day before I went away. I'd think I'd notice if my wife had track marks up her arms. There's no way she was a heroin addict. Run the tests again."

"As I said, they are preliminary results," Freeland said. "But there were injection marks between her toes. It's something a lot of users do to hide their habit."

"No, no way. Carole drank and did a bit of weed, even a little coke. But she wasn't a fucking idiot. I can tell you now, I saw no signs that she was using heroin." He started to get up. "I've had enough of this shit."

"Please sit back down, Seamus," Freeland said, his tone suddenly firm.

"Why? So you can continue trashing my wife's reputation?"

Seamus looked at the door. He was here voluntarily; they couldn't stop him walking out if he chose to.

But what would that accomplish? Like it or not, he needed to know what they had found out. To be fully prepared for the coming days and weeks.

Freeland and Obigwe hadn't moved a muscle, as if they'd seen this bluff a thousand times.

"Who did you spend Wednesday night with in Manchester?" Freeland asked.

Jesus, what do they know? thought Seamus, still half-in, half-out of his chair.

"Excuse me?" he managed.

"Wednesday night, after the conference had ended, you spent the night with someone in Manchester," Freeland said. "Who was that person?"

"Nobody, I went to my room alone." Even to his ears, his voice sounded weak.

Freeland opened a buff-coloured folder and pushed a printout across the table.

"According to the invoice charged to your personal credit card, you ordered room service at eight p.m. A twelve-ounce steak and fries with all the trimmings, and a plate of lasagne with garlic bread, a side order of chips, a slice of banoffee pie with ice cream and a slice of chocolate cheesecake with whipped cream. Plus, two bottles of Stella and a bottle of champagne. You ordered a second bottle of champagne at ten p.m. Rather a lot of food and drink for one person, wouldn't you say?"

"You also took two small bottles of vodka and two gins, plus mixers, from the minibar that night. And there were two full-English breakfasts charged to your room the following morning," Obigwe said.

Seamus collapsed back into his chair; the previous night's excesses had caught up with him again, and he felt nauseous.

"Who stayed with you that night?" Freeland asked.

"No comment," Seamus muttered.

Freeland opened the folder again.

"According to the ticket machines at Manchester Piccadilly, your open return ticket was used to access the platforms at 12.37. A train left seven minutes later, and arrived back here at Brook Street Station, on time, at 14.24. Your ticket released the barriers two minutes later. Where did you spend the seven hours before you called the emergency services just after 21.30?"

Seamus' heard the pound of his blood surging through his ears; his hands felt clammy and his stomach rolled.

"I'd like to speak to a solicitor."

Five Years Ago

Two Years Before The Fire

Chapter Nine

The journey home was horrible; Seamus had long since run out of things to say.

In the passenger seat, Carole stared sightlessly out of the window. The tears had finally stopped running down her cheeks, but he knew they were welling up behind her eyes, waiting for the dam to break again.

He pulled into the drive and was relieved to see Dominic's Range Rover parked outside the house. He wasn't ready to be alone with Carole just yet.

Only forty-eight hours previously, their little bubble had seemed perfect. Barely three months to go and the scans were good. Carole's blood pressure had settled down after a brief scare, and her blood sugars were back within the normal range, after initial worries she may be developing gestational diabetes.

He hopped out of the car and went around to the passenger side, offering his hand to his wife. She ignored it and pulled herself out.

The front door opened, revealing Dominic standing there uncertainly. A moment later, he came down the steps, giving Carole an awkward hug.

"I'm so, so sorry," he whispered in her ear, giving her hand a squeeze. She gave him a small smile, but said nothing, her eyes brimming with tears. Letting go of his hand, she walked towards the house.

"How are you holding up, little brother?" Dominic asked, once Carole was out of earshot.

"Oh, you know," Seamus managed, terrified that if he said any more, he'd breakdown. He couldn't. Not yet. He had to be strong for Carole. He'd grieve in his own way, later. In private.

"I've moved everything from the nursery into the loft, like you asked," Dominic said quietly, as they headed indoors.

Seamus nodded his thanks. The cot and the baby stuff had been stored in the corner of Carole's studio. The last thing she needed was a constant reminder of their loss, as she tried to get back to her normal routine.

"I've got the kettle on," Dominic said as they went into the living room. The air smelled of pine air freshener, and Seamus noticed it had been tidied. The carpet, which had been a little grubby, if he was honest, had been vacuumed.

"You didn't have to do this," he protested.

"Don't be daft," Dominic said. "You and Carole have enough to be getting on with."

He took their coats, and Carole sat down on the sofa. Seamus joined her and took her hand in his. It felt cool. He gave a gentle squeeze. After a moment she squeezed his in return.

The house felt different. There were three people in the room, yet it felt empty. As Dominic fussed over them with coffee and biscuits, Seamus suddenly felt like a guest in his own home.

The house never felt the same after that day. The energy had gone from it. Carole, his live-wire, American wife, who could light up the room with her smile and her rapid-fire wit, was no longer present. And Seamus didn't know how he was going to get her back.

Then

Three Days After The Fire

Chapter Ten

"Before we start, I'd like to remind you that my client, Mr Monaghan, has suffered a terrible bereavement, under the most shocking of circumstances, and that as such, his memories of the last few days might be somewhat hazy."

"Of course, we fully understand," Freeland said.

Seamus forced his hands to unclench and resisted the urge to look at the solicitor Dominic had conjured up for him. Although given the monthly retainer the company paid Oldroyd and Parker, the conjuring was nothing more than a phone call.

Angus Oldroyd had a paper-thin laptop open on the interview table, next to a lined legal pad. It was a toss-up between what cost more, the computer, the fountain pen, or the three-piece suit he wore.

"Mr Monaghan decided to spend an additional day in Manchester. Whilst he was there, he spent some time with a friend. That is all he wishes to say on the matter. You have stated that you wish to clarify the events leading up to the death of Mrs Monaghan and he has agreed to help you in your inquiries."

"Thank you, your cooperation is appreciated," Freeland said. The man's tone was professionally neutral, but Oldroyd shot him a warning glare.

"Who is this friend you spent time with?" Freeland asked.

"No comment," Seamus said.

Freeland raised an eyebrow, but Seamus kept his mouth shut.

"We know there was a gap of seven hours between your train arriving from Manchester, and when you claim to the taxi dropped you off at your home. What did you do in that time?"

Seamus cleared his throat, and his face burned. "I caught a taxi to a friend's house. I stayed there for a few hours, before catching another cab home. That was when I discovered the fire and ..." his voice petered out.

"This 'friend'," Freeland said, "was it the same person you were with in Manchester?"

Seamus nodded. There was no point denying it and Oldroyd had advised that a degree of cooperation might get this over with sooner, rather than later.

"And what were you and this friend doing?" Obigwe asked.

"I'm not sure that's relevant," Oldroyd interjected.

"Did you and this friend leave their house during those seven hours?" Freeland asked.

"No," Seamus said.

"Was there anyone else present at your friend's house?" Freeland continued.

"No."

"Can you remember the name of the taxi firm you used to travel to your friend's house?" Obigwe asked.

"Not really, but it's the one that has its own rank outside Brook Street Station."

"Metro Cabs?" she suggested.

"Yes, that's the one," Seamus said.

"Can you recall any other details?" she asked.

Seamus frowned. "It was a dark blue Toyota. A Prius, I think."

"What about the driver?"

Seamus shrugged. "A white man. Eastern European?"

"And how did you pay?"

"Cash."

"Did you use the same firm to get from your friend's house to your home?" Freeland asked.

"No, I used an Uber."

Beside Seamus, Oldroyd shifted, but he couldn't tell why.

"Was it on your own account?" Obigwe asked.

"Yes."

"I'm going to ask you again, Seamus. Who was this friend that you spent time with?" Freeland asked.

"Mr Monaghan has made it clear he does not wish to answer that question. I remind you that he is here voluntarily, and is not under arrest," Oldroyd said. The man's tone was firm, and he locked eyes with Freeland. Freeland gave him a tight smile.

"Seamus, please don't waste our time," Freeland said. "We need this person to verify what you just told us. Therefore, we *will* track them down." He raised the fingers on his left hand, folding them down as he made each point. "The driver for Metro cab will have recorded his journey, so we know roughly where you were dropped off. Your Uber app will have a pick-up address. We know what time you went through the gates at Manchester Piccadilly and exited Brook Street Station, so we can locate the CCTV. Presumably, you sat with your 'friend' on the train, so, if necessary, we can retrieve the CCTV from that carriage. The Regal Hotel doubtless has security cameras, so we can ask for footage from them.

"But all that will take time. And for what purpose?"

His voice grew kinder. "Seamus, what happened to your wife was a terrible tragedy. All we want to do is cross all the Ts and dot all the Is, so that we can present a file to the coroner. Then you can get on with your grieving."

Seamus picked at the sleeve on his jumper, before answering.

"I really don't want her name to come out," he said eventually. "It's a bit of a delicate situation."

Freeland smiled sympathetically. "I appreciate that. I promise you Seamus, we will be as discreet as we can. It's not in anyone's interest, ours included, to make a fuss unnecessarily."

Seamus nodded. When he spoke, his voice was little more than a whisper.

"Thank you," Freeland said. "I would appreciate it if you could remain available until we've verified what we've been told. We'll be as quick – and as sensitive – as we can."

Seamus nodded. Beside him Oldroyd remained impassive.

"Interview suspended."

Chapter Eleven

"Thank you for agreeing to speak to us, Mrs Harrington," Freeland said. "We appreciate this is a difficult time for you."

"Please, Mrs Harrington is my mother-in-law's name. Call me Andrea."

They were seated in an interview suite, coffee and biscuits in the centre of the table.

DC Obigwe had appeared on Andrea's doorstep without warning. The invitation to attend the police station to help with enquiries, though presented as a request, wasn't really. The uniformed officer accompanying Obigwe, and the marked police car, made it clear her compliance was expected.

Andrea had felt her face flush. *What did they know?*

With her husband out, she could think of only one person to call.

Dominic had been reassuring. Without asking why she was being pulled in for questioning – and why she thought that might be a problem – he told her she would be met in reception by Clarence Parker, from Oldroyd and Parker, the legal firm that Dominic retained.

She didn't think to ask why the solicitor would already be present at the station.

Within a few minutes of her private consultation with the rake-thin legal representative, she knew that Seamus was in a similar room just down the corridor, and it was clear the police had suspicions about exactly what had happened that night. And that despite the friendly appearances, she should be open, but not too open.

Beside her, Clarence Parker sat with his laptop open, and his pen poised over the notebook resting on his knee.

"Of course, Andrea," Freeland said, as she corrected his use of her married name. "When was the last time you saw Mrs Monaghan?"

"Last weekend. We met in town for a coffee at the *Slice of Happiness* cake shop."

"And how did she seem?"

Andrea shrugged. "Normal. We chatted a bit about the weather and plans for the garden, books we were reading, what we watched on TV. It was just a catch-up, really."

"What about any concerns or worries?" asked Obigwe.

"Nothing," she said.

"And did you speak to her at all whilst Seamus was in Manchester?" Freeland asked.

"No," Andrea said, her throat tightening.

"Mr Monaghan – Seamus – claims you were with him in Manchester. Can you confirm that."

Andrea cleared her throat. "Yes."

There was no point denying it; Parker had explained Seamus had already admitted to it. Which was why she was now sitting here.

Beside her, Parker said nothing, but he and Freeland looked at one another. Freeland looked almost disappointed. Parker ... smug?

She'd gone through the events of the previous few days with Parker before the interview commenced. Throughout her rambling account he'd referred to notes in an expensive, leather-bound notebook, occasionally stopping and correcting her to 'provide clarity'.

Now Obigwe and Freeland were the ones taking notes, in blue, A4, notebooks, as she explained how she'd travelled up to Manchester on the Tuesday afternoon, the day after Seamus arrived for the conference. She'd bought her own train ticket. Seamus had attended a drinks reception in the evening, whilst she had room service, before meeting him in a bar. They then returned to the hotel and spent the night together. She'd made her own arrangements for breakfast on the Wednesday and gone shopping in Manchester. After the conference ended, she'd met him for a massage at a luxury spa, before they returned to the hotel and ordered room service; steak for him, lasagne for her. The following morning, they had breakfast at the hotel, followed by a late check-out, before travelling back by train.

"What happened after you arrived back at Brook Street Station?" Freeland asked.

"We caught a taxi back to mine," she said. Recounting the events of the previous few days to strangers had been humiliating. It wasn't going to get any less so.

"And then what happened?" Freeland asked.

"We spent the afternoon together."

"All afternoon?"

"Yes."

Thankfully he didn't ask her to elaborate on what they had been doing. She suspected the burn of her cheeks made that obvious. Beside her, Parker had jotted down an occasional note; curiously, the notebook he was using appeared different to the one he had read from in their pre-interview consultation. For the first time, she wondered how much of this was going to find its way back to Dominic.

"What time did Seamus leave?" Freeland asked.

"I'm not sure exactly; after dark. He called an Uber, so they'll have a record," she said.

"Can I ask where your husband was at this time?" Obigwe asked.

"In Glasgow," Andrea said. "MSS are hoping to land a contract upgrading the security systems at Queen Elizabeth Hospital. He was going to do a pitch, then do a tour of the premises to find out what they needed, so they could make a formal bid. He came home Friday, as soon as he heard the news."

"And when did he go?"

"He caught the train Tuesday morning."

"That's convenient," Freeland said.

Andrea felt her blush deepen. "Seamus was originally going to visit Glasgow, and Marcus was going to do the trade fair. Seamus switched them around."

"So, you got to stay in the Regal Hotel, whilst your husband slummed it in a Travelodge?" Freeland said.

Parker cleared his throat.

Andrea could feel the tears threatening. Parker might object to the judgemental tone of Freeland's questioning, but he wasn't wrong.

"I know what you must all think of me," she said. "And you're right. I feel the same way. Carole was my best friend. She came over here from the States with nobody, so in many ways, I'm all she had. But Seamus and I ... well, neither of us were happy—"

Parker cleared his throat again.

Too much information. Parker had advised her – instructed her really – to stick to the basic facts; to avoid speculation or discussing feelings and other, less *tangible* things. But that was easier said than done when you felt the burn of judgement from everyone around you. None of them knew the reality of the situation; the complex spiderweb of emotions and reasons. The subtle shades of grey. They just saw a black and white distillation of a multilayered story: man cheats on wife with wife's best friend. Wife kills herself.

The angels and demons were clearly defined for all to see; pick your side.

Parker's advice be damned. She would not sit here and let others judge her and Seamus. And perhaps speaking about it aloud for the first time would help her justify it to herself also.

"You know all about Carole and Seamus' loss," Andrea said. "Things were never the same between them again. Carole had depression and needed medication and counselling. Seamus took it on the chin; he put on a brave face for her and everyone, but I know he was absolutely devastated. Looking back, he was probably depressed himself, but he couldn't show it," she sniffed. "He and Dom lost their parents when they were very young. A car crash. They were brought up by their grandparents. They weren't abused, or anything like that, but their grandparents took them on out of a sense of duty and necessity, and their upbringing was ... 'functional'. That was the way Seamus once described it. He and Dom learned from an early age to keep a lid on their feelings and soldier on. To be 'brave', as if that's something to be proud of in a grieving child."

"And what about you, Andrea? Why were you unhappy?" Obigwe asked, her tone one of sympathy, not judgement.

Andrea shrugged. Strangely, she felt more embarrassed about this than the actual affair. "Marcus wasn't the same man I met at university. Or rather he was, and that was the problem. It's been nearly ten years, and behaviour that was OK when we were eighteen or nineteen is less funny or appealing when you're in your late twenties."

Now that she'd said it out loud, she wondered how it would sound to others. Why had she stayed with Marcus so long? On the other hand, why had she gone behind his back? She and Seamus had betrayed two people; Marcus and Carole, neither of whom deserved it. She could have dealt with things differently.

Shades of grey again.

"When did you and Seamus get together?" Freeland asked.

"Is this really relevant?" Parker interrupted.

"Yes," Freeland said, without even looking at him.

"A few months ago," Andrea said. Given what she'd just shared with them, the additional detail hardly seemed to matter. She wondered if it was just Parker trying to assert his dominance?

"It just sort of happened. We'd had a bit of a party around Dominic's to celebrate him winning an award for something or other.

Everyone was a bit drunk, and Carole and Marcus had obviously been snorting cocaine. Seamus was really angry, as he and Carole were supposed to be trying for a baby. And Marcus can be a bit of a ... well a bit of twat, if I'm honest, when he's drunk or high. He and Carole had a big argument. I tried to calm things down, which just made things worse, then Marcus called a taxi and stormed off home. Carole was being unreasonable, and it was winding Seamus up, so Dom put her to bed in the guest room. Dom was always good at dealing with her when she was like that."

Across from her, Freeland and Obigwe were scribbling in their books.

"Seamus couldn't face dealing with Carole the next morning when he would be hungover, so Dom suggested he go home and return the next day. We could only get one cab, so decided to take me home first, but halfway to mine decided to go back to his instead." Her voice petered out, before she regained her composure. "Things kind of spiralled from there."

"Do you think Carole knew about your affair?" Freeland asked.

"No, we were very careful," her voice caught. *Was that the truth, or just what I want to believe?* She pushed the thought away. "Neither of us were proud of what we were doing. We knew it wasn't right, but we just couldn't help ourselves."

"And what about your husband?" Obigwe asked.

"No ... things would have been really complicated if he found out. Technically, Seamus is his boss, although it was Dom who head-hunted him." She paused. "Does any of this need to be made public? Dom will be really pissed off if he finds out what's been going on."

Her comments were aimed as much at Clarence Parker as the two detectives. Parker had clearly been in consultation with Angus Oldroyd, who was advising Seamus, but were they reporting back to Dominic? Wouldn't that be unethical?

"We will be as discreet as we can," Freeland said. Parker looked away.

"Did you see Carole at all between your trip to the coffee shop at the weekend and the night she died," Freeland asked again.

"No," she replied firmly.

"What I'm about to ask you next might be uncomfortable for you to hear, but we really need you to be honest with us," he said.

Andrea braced herself.

"We have found evidence that Carole may have been using heroin. Do you know anything about that at all?"

Andrea shook her head. "No, the first I hear about it was an hour ago, when Mr Parker told me about it."

Freeland scowled at the solicitor, who kept a poker face.

"And were you surprised when you heard?" he asked.

"Well, yeah. Look we've been pretty open about the fact that we smoke a bit of weed now and again. And Carole did the occasional line of coke. But heroin? That's nuts. She held down a good job, and she was into keep-fit and healthy living. She and Seamus were trying for a baby. I never saw any signs, and surely Seamus would have noticed something?"

"As I said, they are preliminary results," Freeland said. "But users can be very good at hiding things from their loved ones."

"No, Carole wasn't a junkie," Andrea said firmly. "I would have known."

"OK, just one more thing then," Freeland said. "I'd like to request a DNA sample and fingerprints, to help us eliminate you from any samples we have taken from the scene."

"Are you planning on arresting Mrs Harrington?" Parker asked, before Andrea had a chance to answer.

"No, that won't be necessary," Freeland said.

"Then I would advise my client that such tests are unnecessarily invasive and serve no useful purpose," Parker said firmly.

Trust his judgement, Dominic had advised when she'd called him earlier. *He's the best in the business.*

"I'd better not," she said.

Chapter Twelve

"Hello Seamus, sorry we kept you waiting so long. Did the custody sergeant fix you up with some sandwiches?" Freeland took a seat at the table.

"Yes, thank you," Seamus replied. He'd been sitting in the little room for what seemed like hours. Angus Oldroyd had left briefly to make some phone calls and confirm that Andrea was currently being interviewed. His partner Clarence was with her.

Obigwe set the recorder running and ran quickly through the preliminaries. Oldroyd spoke only to confirm his name.

"We've spoken to Andrea, and she has confirmed your version of events," Freeland said.

Seamus relaxed slightly. Of course she had. Yeah, it was embarrassing, but better to tell the truth than be caught in a lie. Beside him, Oldroyd remained attentive.

"How long have you worked for Monaghan Security Solutions?" Freeland asked.

It was a strange question and Seamus answered it without thinking.

"Oh, blimey, about three years, maybe?"

"Where were you working before?" Freeland asked.

Seamus felt a cold chill pass through him. Surely they weren't thinking ...

"I worked as a financial adviser," he said. "For a small firm in town."

"Doing what?" Obigwe asked.

"Advising high-value clients on investment strategies mainly."

He took a sip from the bottle of water on the table in front of him.

"And that involved managing clients' accounts?" Obigwe asked.

Seamus sighed. "Look, I know where this is going. It was all a misunderstanding. It was all sorted out in the end."

"It was a big enough misunderstanding that your employer – sorry, former employer – decided to call the police," Freeland said. "How much went missing from the client accounts in total?"

"£42,365," Obigwe supplied. "And eighty-five pence."

Oldroyd stirred. "As Mr Monaghan explained, it was all a misunderstanding. He was never charged with any crime."

"Yes, I see that," Freeland said. "I believe the CPS declined to authorise charges when your employer asked them not to, and you were released with no further action taken."

"Gambling, wasn't it?" Obigwe asked.

"Don't answer that," Oldroyd advised. "This is water under the bridge."

It was like being a spectator in a tennis match, the two sides fighting for dominance as if Seamus wasn't even there.

"Well anyway, I spoke to the officer in charge," Freeland said. "Apparently, you repaid that sum of money – with a generous amount of interest – and it was decided that there was no need for it to go any further, especially after you tendered your resignation. I imagine it was a relief to all concerned; no need for any embarrassing stories in the newspapers. The slogan on the company's website is *We Treat Your Money As We Would Our Own*. Which is ironic."

"The details of what happened are subject to a non-disclosure agreement," Oldroyd interjected.

"Yes, brokered by your firm," Freeland said. "It doesn't matter, we have all the relevant documentation here." He tapped the folder. "Where did you suddenly find £42,365—"

"—and eighty-five pence," Obigwe added. "Plus interest."

"— when your joint savings account had been systematically emptied, your credit cards were maxed out, your current account was fifteen pounds shy of its overdraft limit, and you were three months in arrears on your mortgage?"

"Don't answer that," Oldroyd warned.

"No comment," said Seamus, feeling he should at least contribute something.

Freeland shrugged. "Doesn't matter. We traced the origin of that sizeable cash injection back to Dominic's personal account. He then created a brand-new position of vice-president at Monaghan Security Solutions and employed you immediately on double your previous salary. Pretty damned generous, wouldn't you say, DC Obigwe?"

"My brother thinks a birthday card saying he spent all the money for my present paying the gas bill is funny," she said.

"Did you tell Carole what happened?" Freeland asked.

"No comment," Seamus said. Everything was moving too quickly. He needed time to think.

"Is there a point to this, DS Freeland?" Oldroyd asked.

"I don't know. Is there, Seamus?" Freeland asked.

"No comment."

Freeland opened the folder again, removing a colour photograph.

"Our forensic team has been searching your house. And they found these, hidden inside a cardboard box for some face cream, in a toilet bag in the bathroom cabinet. Do you recognise them? For the record, I'm showing Mr Monaghan a blister strip for Levest. From the expiry date on the strip, it appears to be from the repeat prescription filled by Mrs Monaghan's pharmacist a fortnight ago. Several tablets are missing."

"No comment," Seamus managed again.

"You and your wife were trying for a baby. Were you aware that Carole was using contraception?"

"No comment."

"Your fingerprints are on the strip, so I'm going to assume you knew. Were you really trying for a baby, Mr Monaghan? Or did you just think you were? Did you find her pills when you were snooping around in the bathroom cabinet? Perhaps looking for her stash of drugs?"

"No comment," Seamus whispered.

"I think now would be a good time to take a break," Oldroyd said. "Seamus, I'd like to speak to you."

"Yeah, I need a break," Seamus said.

"Don't go anywhere, will you?" Freeland said, as he reached over and switched off the recording.

***

"This is madness," Seamus said. "They think I had something to do with Carole's death."

"OK, keep calm, Seamus, we can deal with this," Oldroyd said.

"Really? Easy for you to say, you're not the one facing a bloody murder charge!"

Seamus stood up and started pacing.

"Listen to me," Oldroyd said. "They *do not* have enough to charge you. The Crown Prosecution Service will not authorise charging you based on what they have shown us so far, trust me."

"So, they aren't going to arrest me?" Seamus asked, hope flaring.

Oldroyd paused. "I'll be honest, Seamus, I'm pretty sure that's where this is heading."

"Oh my God, this is a nightmare." Seamus turned towards Oldroyd. "You need to do something, Angus. I had nothing to do with Carole's death. Jesus, how much is Dom paying you guys anyway? Earn your bloody money!"

"Seamus!" Oldroyd snapped. "Calm down and let's work through what they've got. If they do arrest you, I'm going to request disclosure. They don't have to give us everything at this stage, but we might get an idea of what they're thinking. But you've got to help me here. I can't do my job if I get sandbagged with evidence like the contraceptive pills. You need to tell me what else might come out."

"I don't know," Seamus wailed. "They're twisting everything. Making innocent stuff look bad. Like the whole thing about the contraceptive pills. I did find them, I admit that. I thought she might be using cocaine again, so I went through the house looking for her stash. I found them in that toilet bag the day before I went to Manchester."

"And did you confront her about them?"

"No, I didn't get a chance." Seamus pushed away a surge of embarrassment. Surely they were past that now? "We weren't on good terms, and I didn't have the head space to deal with it with the conference coming up. I was going to speak to her when I got back."

He sat back down. How had it come to this?

After a few seconds, he continued. "What's going to happen to Andy? Are they going to arrest her as well?"

"I don't know," Oldroyd said. "So far, they've only been questioning her about what the two of you did on your Manchester trip. But again, if there is anything that she might say that could cause us difficulties, I need to know about it now."

Seamus chewed his nail. "I told Andy I found the pills. I said I was thinking of asking Carole for a trial separation."

"Then let's hope Andrea doesn't share that with the police," Oldroyd said.

Chapter Thirteen

SEAMUS' INTERVIEW RECOMMENCED LATER that evening. He was still there voluntarily, but Oldroyd would be pushing for a resolution. One way or the other.

"DC Obigwe and I requested a copy of your CCTV. However, the cameras were turned off the night your wife died. Why was that?" Freeland started.

"I told you," Seamus said, ignoring Oldroyd's instruction not to answer the question. "The recorder has been playing up."

Surely a bit of cooperation on the simple things would stop misunderstandings later? Perhaps Oldroyd was wrong, and once Seamus had satisfied the two detectives he would be free to go?

"You work for a firm that installs these systems. In fact, I believe that Monaghan Security Solutions actually fitted the cameras," Freeland said. "Are you telling me you were unable to get one of your engineers to fix the problem?"

"We were going to get them replaced with the latest model, but the team hasn't been able to find the time to come out." Seamus shrugged, helplessly. "We're short-staffed and company policy is to prioritise paying customers."

"Seamus, you do not have to answer any of their questions," Oldroyd said forcefully.

"The thing is, there isn't a fault," Freeland said, removing a printout from the folder. "The cameras were deliberately disabled remotely, using an app. An app that was logged into using your personal account. Now why would you do that, Seamus?"

Seamus' jaw dropped. "What?" he stammered. How could they possibly know that?

"The cameras were disabled at 18:58 that night," Freeland said. "About two hours before we believe the fire was started. They weren't switched back on until the early hours of the morning. Which conveniently means there is no footage of the fire starting. We know that you and Andrea were back from Manchester by that point. You see how this looks."

"No, no, no," Seamus said. He turned to Oldroyd, his breath growing ragged. "Tell them Angus. Tell them I had nothing to do with Carole's death."

"Here's what I think," Freeland said. "We know your marriage was going through a difficult patch. You were supposed to be trying for a baby, but Carole wasn't playing ball, was she?"

"No, it wasn't like that," Seamus said.

Freeland ignored the interruption. "Carole should have been looking after herself, making sure she was fit and ready for her pregnancy, but she wasn't, was she? She was still drinking and using drugs. We've spoken to some of your friends and acquaintances and apparently, she made a bit of a fool of herself – and you – a few months ago at your brother's birthday party."

"This is crazy," Seamus said. "You're just twisting things to suit your story."

"Seamus, remember what we discussed," Oldroyd warned.

"After what happened two years ago, you'd think Carole would be absolutely paranoid about making certain she was ready to try for a baby again," Obigwe said. "But of course, she wasn't really trying, was she? She was secretly on the pill. Why was that?"

"I don't know!" Seamus shouted. How long had it been since they'd turned up on his doorstep? Twelve hours? Less? In that time they'd gone from treating him as a grieving husband to a suspect. How had everything spiralled so quickly?

"I can think of several possibilities off the top of my head," Freeland said. "First, she was scared of getting pregnant again, after what happened last time. Two, she was a drug addict, and didn't want to jeopardise the baby. Three, she was thinking of leaving you. Or four, she was worried you might leave her. Did Carole know about your affair with Andrea?"

"No, it wasn't like that. I swear."

"Then what was it like, Seamus?" Obigwe asked.

"Do *not* answer that question," Oldroyd said.

"Well," continued Freeland, "I think you were going to leave Carole for Andrea. Her best friend."

"Andrea is unhappy in her marriage, she's admitted that," Obigwe added. "The two of you have known each other since university. When did you really get together? Did you hook up back then?"

"No, we were just friends," Seamus said. "You have to believe me."

"I don't suppose the details really matter," Freeland said. "The key thing is that you're together now."

"But there was a problem, wasn't there?" Obigwe interjected.

"You're the main breadwinner," Freeland said. "Carole's design work comes and goes. You're going to end up on the wrong end of a hefty divorce settlement."

"And then there's Dominic," Obigwe continued. "He head-hunted Andrea's husband specifically. He isn't going to thank you for tearing their marriage apart, and possibly losing Marcus. Dominic's been incredibly loyal and generous to you. He's looked after you since you were kids, including sorting out that problem with the missing money, but could this be the final straw? The time he finally says, 'I love you, little brother, but it's time you learned to stand on your own two feet and deal with the consequences of your bad choices'."

"You're just trying to make the facts fit your theory," Seamus protested, his gaze flicking between his two interrogators.

"I'm inclined to agree," Oldroyd said. "You're really over-stretching here."

"Indulge us," Freeland said. "Now where was I? Oh yes, you have a big problem that you need to solve. You're trapped in a marriage you can't afford to leave. Your lover also wants to leave her own marriage. Carole has a life insurance policy that will let you and Andrea set up a new life together. You've had the policy long enough that the suicide clause has expired. If you get rid of Carole, and it comes down to a choice between you and Marcus, then Dominic is obviously going to back his grieving brother, which means Marcus is also out of the picture."

"You're sick," Seamus said. "I have an alibi. Call the taxi firms, they'll tell you I was at Andy's. I'll bet there's even CCTV of me getting into the cab at the train station. Check my phone, it'll show I was at her house until I left to go home. I know you can do it; everyone knows you can show exactly where I was all that time."

"Everyone also knows you can just leave your phone behind and go out and about undetected," Freeland countered. "It's a ten-minute drive from Andrea's house to yours – less if you put your foot down. You know those roads like the back of your hand. You could easily drive from Andrea's to yours, pump your wife full of heroin, then light that fire, before returning to Andrea's in time to hop in the Uber you ordered at 21:04 and go back out there, and raise the alarm. All after disabling the CCTV to ensure there was no evidence."

"How would I get out there?" Seamus asked. "My car was parked at home; I went to Manchester by train."

"Both Andrea's and Marcus' cars were available," Obigwe said. "The keys were hanging in the kitchen."

"The shed was locked from the inside," Seamus said. "How could I have set the fire and then escaped?"

"The shed had a large window," Freeland reminded him. "It wasn't locked."

"This is madness, where is your evidence?" Seamus demanded. "I've had enough of this bullshit, I'm going home."

He stood to leave.

Freeland also stood.

"Seamus Monaghan, I am arresting you on suspicion of the murder of Carole Monaghan. You do not have to say anything. But, it may harm your defence if you do not mention when questioned something which you later rely on in court. Anything you do say may be given in evidence. Do you understand what I have just told you?"

Four And A Half Years Ago

Eighteen Months Before The Fire

Chapter Fourteen

The car took the bend too fast, drifting across the centre line. Clutching the wheel so hard her knuckles were white, Carole Monaghan wrestled it back onto the left-hand side of the road. She was in no state to drive, but she was so angry she didn't care.

She and Seamus were supposed to have stayed over at Dominic's that night. He'd been dating a woman he'd met using some app for the past month, and tonight was supposed to be when she met his younger brother and sister-in-law, his only remaining family. Marcus had been in Ireland for the past fortnight, spending a final few days with his terminally-ill grandmother, and so Andrea had also been invited.

Dominic had cooked a roast chicken, with all the trimmings, and provided a selection of fine wines.

It was obvious what Dominic had seen in Helena. She was, frankly, gorgeous, and he'd been uncharacteristically shy as he'd made his introductions.

The meal had gone well at first. Helena had been vague about what she actually did for a living, but Carole had put that down to nerves; meeting a new partner's closest friends and loved ones could be intimidating. The wine was as delicious as the food, and Carole had enjoyed several glasses with dinner. It was a Friday night, and nobody was working the next day.

After finishing dessert, they'd retired to the living area and Dominic had produced some weed.

As they passed the joint around, the mood became more mellow. And more boring.

Helena, it turned out, was very pretty, but her conversation was rather less sparkling than her sequined top. Her very revealing sequined top. Quite how she managed to stay inside it, as she leaned forward to take a drink, or pass the joint over, was a mystery, given she didn't appear to have recruited the help of a bra.

Slumped against Seamus, Carole couldn't help noticing her husband held his breath every time Helena changed position.

Keen to involve Dominic's new paramour in the conversation, they found themselves avoiding current affairs, sport, literature and pretty much all culture. Even Andrea, who could strike up a conversation with anyone, was struggling. After almost an hour trying to summon up an interest in reality TV shows she'd never watched and dramas she'd never heard of, Carole excused herself to go to the bathroom.

She was beginning to have her suspicions about Helena. From what she had gleaned, she was even younger than she looked, and held some sort of very minor clerical position in an accountant's office. Carole didn't like to think of herself as a snob, but she was wondering what a pretty young woman like Helena saw in a wealthy man like Dominic almost ten years her senior ... She could see from Andrea's body language that she wasn't the only one with suspicions.

Rooting around in her handbag for some lipstick, her fingers closed around a small plastic bag she had forgotten was in there.

That ought to make the night more interesting she decided.

And in some ways, it certainly did.

Half an hour later, Helena was calling an Uber; Dominic was outside pleading with her to stay; Seamus was tearing a strip off Carole in the kitchen; and Andrea was trying to keep out of the way of everyone.

Ten minutes after that, Carole was in Seamus' car, driving home with the lights still off and the stereo blaring, angry tears coursing down her face. Seamus could stay the night with Dominic or catch a cab home and sleep on the couch, she really couldn't give a shit. Either way, he wasn't sharing her bed that night.

How dare he! The two brothers were as bad as each other; a flash of twenty-year-old tit and they both lost all judgement. Bloody men! Couldn't they see the gold-digging trollop was just after Dominic's money?

They should be grateful to her for looking out for him.

Sweeping around another bend, she was blinded by a pair of oncoming headlights. She fought to bring the car back to her side of the road, but it was too little too late. The vehicle just missed her as it flew past, the driver swerving hard to avoid a head-on collision. Carole felt the wheels lock as she overcompensated, and the car started to spin. For a heart-stopping moment, everything seemed to stand still, then the car crunched into the wooden fence separating the road from the woodland beyond, finishing with two wheels on the road and two on the grass verge, pointing back the way from which she had come. The car stalled and the lights and radio cut out.

The night suddenly seemed very dark and very quiet.

Clambering out of the passenger side, she half fell out of the door onto the tarmac. Without her own headlights illuminating the road, and just the barest sliver of a moon behind the thick cloud, the only source of light was a faint red glow shining upwards from the hillside below. The safety barriers separating the road from the twenty-foot drop had been torn apart, leaving a gaping, twisted hole.

Her mouth went dry, and she felt paralysed with fear.

She stood there for what seemed like an age, before a sudden adrenaline jolt shocked her sober. Pulling out her mobile phone, she instinctively dialled 911, before remembering she was in the

UK. By the time she'd deleted the three digits and pressed the nine three times, her rational brain had caught up with her instincts.

What was she going to do? Call the police? She'd drunk enough that night she probably wouldn't be safe to drive until tomorrow afternoon. And even if by some miracle she blew below the legal limit, she was full of weed and cocaine.

There was no way she'd be getting away with a fine and points on her licence; she was looking at jail time. And what if the worst had happened? Ten years? More? She cleared the number.

But she couldn't just leave them; they could be seriously injured.

She'd leave an anonymous message, she decided. She'd tell them she thought she'd seen a crashed vehicle on Valley View Road and a missing crash barrier. Her car was still driveable; by the time the emergency services arrived she'd be long gone.

She started to dial again, before stopping once more. Who was she kidding? It was the 21st century, there was no such thing as anonymous. The handset was registered in her name; the police would be banging on the door within hours.

She stood, rooted to the spot, for almost a minute.

She had no choice.

"I'm sorry," she whispered, and got back in the car.

Now

The Day After The Storm

Chapter Fifteen

*S*HE'S FLOATING, AS IF *in a warm pool. There's a light ahead of her, but she can't swim towards it, her body is ignoring her commands. Time has ceased to have any meaning for her. She could have been here hours, days or just minutes. How she arrived remains elusive. She remembers only snatches; bright lights coming towards her then an impact, before everything goes black. Her head hurts, and pain suffuses the lower half of her body and her arm, but it is dulled; muted as if somebody has turned the volume down. Every so often she becomes aware of voices, of being prodded and poked, then everything fades away and sleep reclaims her.*

***

Katie Stafford took over the early morning briefing of the Sexual Exploitation Unit from DCI Girton. On the wall screen, she'd projected a photograph of the woman's battered face.

"The magistrate signed off on the warrants for our unknown woman's fingerprints and DNA yesterday. So far, there are no matches on the system for her prints. Missing Persons have a couple of dozen potentials in the immediate area matching our rough description; they're looking through them now. DNA will be back in the next couple of days.

"A brief examination by her doctors shows no indication of recent sexual assault, so we don't have enough to justify an intimate examination without her explicit consent. However, we have retained fingernail clippings, and her clothes have been stored in case we need to do forensic analysis down the line."

"What about releasing her picture to the press?" asked one of the probationers.

"Her face is very swollen, with cuts and abrasions, and bandages from the surgery," Stafford said. "So, we've got a sketch artist in to do an e-fit. We'll release it to the press in a couple of days if we still haven't identified her when the DNA comes through." She nodded at DS Paige, the specialist Police Search Adviser. "Tracie, you're the POLSA, can you take us through the house-to-house strategy?"

"The woman was found on Valley View Road. For those of you unfamiliar with that patch, it's semi-rural and up on the hillside. A search team believes she probably came from the direction of the woods above the road, and the scratches on her arms and dirt on her clothes support that, but there was very heavy rainfall that night, so it's largely guesswork. We're hoping for a dog team, but they're short-staffed at the moment.

"There are only a few properties nearby. The majority are private residential, with a couple of small farms. It's an exclusive area, with most of the houses worth at least a couple of million. Unfortunately, that buys you privacy. Few, if any, of the houses are within shouting distance of their neighbours and all have lengthy driveways, so any CCTV that hadn't been knocked out by the storm is unlikely to show much, unless she cut directly across their property."

Stafford took over. "If we assume that our unknown woman has been living – perhaps against her will – within a few miles of where she was run over, then given the demographics, the most likely scenarios for incarceration would be as forced domestic help or working as forced labour, either on the land, or perhaps transported into town to work in cash businesses. Prostitution is another possibility, although there are no obvious signs of sexual abuse, nor are there any indications of drug use.

"We're walking a tightrope here. She's ringing a lot of alarm bells for us obviously, so we need to be careful not to tip off any captor that she's now in our care. But there could still be a reasonable explanation for her condition, and if she was out there after an unexpected mental health episode, her friends and neighbours might not even realise she's missing yet."

"What's your strategy, Katie?" Girton asked.

"We're going to do it quickly, hitting multiple properties at the same time. That way any neighbourhood WhatsApp groups won't give the game away. We'll be pairing uniformed officers with trafficking specialists to look for indicators of suspicious activity. I'm planning on starting at six p.m., to give us time to get the e-fit completed, assemble a team and try to catch people whilst they have dinner. It's a Sunday, hopefully folks will be home getting ready for work tomorrow."

Girton nodded her consent. "Sounds like a plan."

***

Andrea sniffed the bunch of peonies and smiled. They had been Carole's favourite, forming the backbone of her wedding bouquet, and it seemed appropriate they should be placed on her memorial plaque when they visited it tomorrow.

Seamus had already been gone when she woke up that morning, having left for the office to continue finishing the presentation he was preparing for prospective investors. He'd been reluctant to travel to Scotland with her due date so close, suggesting Dominic go in his place, but she'd been insistent. They still had a month to go, and it was Seamus who had done all the groundwork for the deal. He'd reached out to the investment firm a year ago, and it had been him who had pursued the relationship.

Andrea had met the firm's board at a lunch a few months previously. The fund was family-owned, and they only invested their money with clients they liked and trusted. Sending Dominic in Seamus' place risked being perceived as a snub, and there were millions of pounds at stake. With the firm's financial backing, Monaghan Security Solutions was ready to take the next step and expand beyond the UK.

Of course, that wasn't the only reason Seamus was up so early. It was the same every year. The days leading up to the anniversary were always difficult; he didn't sleep properly and even his birthday celebrations were tinged with melancholy. The last time he'd seen Carole was the morning of his twenty-seventh birthday. They'd just had another negative pregnancy test, and they'd argued before he got on the train to Manchester that Monday. Andrea still felt guilty that Carole had been expecting to celebrate Seamus' birthday when he returned on Thursday, not realising that he and Andrea had celebrated it in their own way after she'd joined him at the conference hotel.

Living in the house where Carole had died hardly helped matters. Dominic had offered to loan them some money to help them move, but Seamus refused. Whether it was his pride – his brother had been helping him all of his life, and she knew that his impending fatherhood had made him determined to stand on his own two feet – or some sort of penance, she didn't know. The remains of the shed had been disposed of long ago, and they had planted a tree and small memorial garden on the spot.

It had seemed like a good idea at the time, but now she wasn't so sure. It was another tie binding them to the house. The tree was still little more than a sapling, and could be transplanted to wherever they moved, but the memorial garden marked the actual spot where Carole had died; leaving the house would mean leaving that behind. Andrea wasn't sure Seamus could do that.

It wasn't that she didn't want to remember Carole; far from it. Feelings of guilt aside, Carole had been her best friend, and she still missed her every day. But sometimes she felt as if she was living in her shadow. It had been three years now; she and Seamus had their own lives. They were starting a family, and one day she hoped to become his wife.

Perhaps things would be different if Carole's remains were still with them. Seamus was a Catholic and had always envisaged he and his wife being buried together. Unfortunately, Carole's family were in the US. Although Seamus was Carole's next of kin, when the details of Seamus' and Andrea's affair had emerged, the pain caused had led to a bitter and acrimonious fight over what to do with Carole's body. It was a battle Seamus would almost certainly have won, but at what cost? Andrea knew Seamus still harboured hopes that he could one day reconcile with his in-laws, who he had grown to love dearly, as they partially filled the gap left by his own parents.

In the end it was Dominic who had proposed a compromise that, whilst not entirely satisfying, had at least allowed them to move on. Carole had been cremated, and her ashes divided in two, with one urn travelling back to the States with her parents. The other had been interred, along with a memorial stone, at the same cemetery as Seamus and Dominic's parents and grandparents. It was something, rather than nothing, but Andrea knew Seamus still felt that Carole should have remained complete in death, as she was in life.

For her part, Andrea still felt uncomfortable with the decision to cremate, given the manner of Carole's death, but had kept her own counsel.

Returning to the car, Andrea rubbed her belly. Whilst her taste buds had inexplicably adjusted to crave the spiciest of foods, her stomach hadn't. The previous night's curry had left her with cramps.

Just a few more weeks, she thought wistfully. As much as she'd enjoyed being pregnant, and was excited about the prospect of twins, she'd now had enough.

"You'd better not have a late-checkout, you two," she said, addressing her bump. "I want you out of there on the dot, you hear me?"

There was no response, not even a kick.

"Great, we have a pair of sulkers to look forward to," she muttered.

Chapter Sixteen

It was well after ten p.m. when Stafford sat down in DCI Girton's office to feed back on the findings from the house-to-house canvas.

"Of the fourteen properties within our initial radius, twelve answered the door," said Tracie Paige, who'd coordinated the team. "We'll try the two outstanding properties again first thing tomorrow."

"Just give me the highlights," Girton instructed, stifling a yawn.

"Not much to give," Paige said. "None of the homeowners recognised the artist's impression, nor had they heard of anyone going missing."

"That's not hugely surprising," Stafford admitted. "If the woman was employed illegally by any of the people they interviewed, then they're hardly going to admit to it. The best we could hope for is one of their neighbours remembering seeing the woman coming and going from their property."

"Unfortunately, the houses are spaced far apart," Paige said. "They're only neighbours in the loosest sense of the word. It's unlikely they'd know next door's movements."

"Do any of them employ workers?" Girton asked.

"Two of them that we could confirm," Paige said. "One of the properties is a working farm, breeding pigs. They employ two local men who don't live on site. According to both the property owner and their nearest neighbour they've worked there for years. We have their contact details, and we'll follow up with them tomorrow."

"What was the officer's opinion? Could they be employing someone off the books to help out?"

"They saw no evidence anyone else was staying there," Paige said. "DC Bishop pulled the old, 'can I use your bathroom' trick and had a quick look around upstairs. It's a three-bedroom house. The couple who own it have teenagers, and she reckons it looks like a family home. Compared to some of the houses out there, it's fairly modest in size; they haven't converted any of the outbuildings to dwellings. Unless our victim was kipping with the pigs or sleeping in the barn with the farm tools, there's nowhere they could have realistically been staying."

"We've seen worse," Girton said. "But you're right, it doesn't sound likely. Keeping someone there against their will would be risky if their two farm hands are free to come and go. Not to mention one of the kids saying something at school."

"What about the second property?" Stafford asked.

"It's a guest house, owned by an older couple. They employ a cleaner on an ad hoc basis when they have guests. She's an older woman who lives in town; again, she's been there for years. Nothing suspicious. They don't have any outbuildings."

"Do any of the property owners run businesses that might require additional workers?" Girton asked.

"We'll be doing checks tomorrow," Stafford said. "But based on the reports I've read through, none of them admit to owning nail bars or car washes or any of the usual cash-based businesses that employ forced labour."

"That just leaves CCTV," Girton said.

"Slim pickings," Stafford said. "At the time she was hit by the car, the whole area was without electricity. But even if there was footage from earlier in the evening, any cameras are there to deter burglars. None of them extend as far as the road; she'd have had to walk right across their front lawns to get picked up. We've requested what we can from the six hours before she was knocked down, but I'll need your authorisation to have the Video Analysis Unit trawl through it."

Girton shook her head. "Retrieve what you can, just in case, but from what you've told me, I don't think I can justify the expense of analysing it yet, unless we have reason to believe she may have been spotted in the area."

She rubbed her eyes. "Our hands are tied. We don't have any evidence she has been trafficked or exploited, just a suspicion. For all we know, she could have had a row with her partner and been kicked out of the car on the way home. I think our focus at the moment should be identifying her."

"The DNA test should be back in forty-eight hours or so," Stafford said. "But her fingerprints aren't on the system, so don't get your hopes up; it doesn't look like she's been arrested before."

"What about Missing Persons?"

"Nothing in the immediate area in the past six months," Stafford said. "They're expanding the search terms. If they do find a possible misper, we can do a comparison with her dental records, but we'll need a name first."

"What are the chances she'll wake up anytime soon and be able to tell us her name herself?" Girton asked.

"I spoke to the hospital a couple of hours ago," Stafford said. "Her latest CT scan showed that the head injury is healing. They hope to remove the sedation soon, but the neurology team can't say whether she'll come around, or if she'll be in any state to tell us anything useful if she does."

"In that case, we'll have to go public," Girton said. "I'll speak to the Media Relations Team about releasing the artist's impression tomorrow, after I've cleared it with the chief super." She forced a smile. "Good work, you've done everything you can so far. Let's just hope something turns up. Now go home and get some sleep."

***

She's floating again. She feels like she's drifting under water, looking up towards the sun. How much time has passed since she was last aware? She's more comfortable than before. The pain in her head is less sharp, and her hip is numb. A warm, fuzzy feeling envelops her.

But she can't lie here forever. There's something she needs to say. Something important. But she's forgotten what it is. She tries to ask for help, but she can't recall how to form words. She can't remember how to string them together in the order necessary to convey her thoughts.

Slowly she becomes aware of a new sensation; a burning in her chest as she tries to draw breath. Her heart starts to pound, and a feeling of panic sets in. Is she drowning? She tries to swim towards the light, but her arms and legs won't respond. As the need for oxygen grows, so too does the panic. It's getting darker, as if she's sinking away from the light.

"Help me!" she screams, but she doesn't know if the sound she hears is audible or is just echoing inside her mind.

She starts to gasp, but it's as if water is filling her lungs, robbing them of their ability to take in air.

It's getting darker, and the burning continues to increase. From a distance she can hear raised voices, but she can't make out the words. Then they too fade away, along with the rest of the light.

And then there's nothing.

Then

Three Days After The Fire

Chapter Seventeen

SEAMUS WAS IN SHOCK as he stood at the custody desk. He was flanked by Obigwe and Freeland. Oldroyd was a few paces away speaking urgently into his mobile phone.

The custody sergeant was repeating the grounds for his arrest.

"But I haven't done anything," Seamus said. "Everything is just circumstantial."

"I am satisfied there is sufficient reason to authorise your detention whilst additional evidence is gathered," the sergeant said patiently.

All this was bringing back horrible memories of the time three years previously, when he'd made the biggest mistake of his life. But back then, he'd been questioned at length, then bailed to return home to await his fate, placing his trust in Dominic, and Oldroyd and Parker Solicitors.

That wouldn't be happening this time.

He answered the routine questions about his mental health, medication and dietary requirements automatically, before being led to a side room, where his fingerprints were scanned electronically. Obigwe swiped the inside of his mouth with a sterile swab, then left the room whilst he changed out of his clothes into a grey tracksuit.

It was the change of clothing that finally brought reality crashing down. How many times had he watched fly-on-the-wall documentaries of custody suites and seen suspects wearing the exact same clothing?

He was a suspect.

A *murder* suspect.

He couldn't believe it. What had gone wrong?

A brisk, efficient woman in a black polo-shirt with a G4S logo on her shoulder led him down a corridor to a cell. The rear of her shirt had 'Custodian' in white writing. He wasn't even the concern of an actual police officer now. Oldroyd followed, having surrendered his phone at the desk, lest he try and pass it to Seamus.

The cell was just as they showed on TV. A small, windowless room, with a poured concrete bed covered in a blue, plastic mattress. A steel toilet and sink were bolted to the floor in the corner. A faint smell of disinfectant lingered in the air. He shuddered to think what previous occupants of the room had done whilst they were in there.

The custodian handed him a thin, pale-blue blanket and an even thinner pillow, both labelled with the police force's crest. What did they think he was going to do, steal them for the spare bedroom?

After offering them coffee, the custodian left. "Shout when you're done," she said to Oldroyd, closing the door behind her. The metal clang was exactly as he remembered from last time. In the opposite corner of the room to the toilet, an unblinking CCTV camera stared down. He couldn't even take a piss in private.

Seamus collapsed on the bed and placed his head in his hands. Oldroyd remained standing.

"I can't do this," Seamus said. He'd been in there less than five minutes, and already the walls were closing in on him. What if he was charged? He'd probably be remanded in custody until trial – that could take ages; months on remand in a prison, surrounded by other men, some of them guilty of horrendous crimes.

"Deep breaths, Seamus," Oldroyd said. For the first time since they met, the solicitor's clipped tones were replaced with something approaching kindness.

"I've asked for the evidence from your CCTV system; we have our own experts that can look at it and see if it is as watertight as the police believe. Andrea insists you were with her at the time the fire was set. We'll speak to her neighbours and see if any of them can back her up. Does her house have CCTV?"

"Yes, but there's a side gate that it doesn't cover," he gave a grim smile. "That seemed convenient when we wanted to sneak in and out of there whilst Marcus was at work. Not recording our comings and goings doesn't seem like such a good idea now."

"Then we'll attack on another front. We need to show Carole was suicidal on the run up to her death. Based on what we've been shown so far, it's still an open question as to whether she was unlawfully killed or took her own life. Do you have access to her social media accounts? Friends with whom she might have shared her worries? What about her family?"

"I don't know the passwords to her accounts," Seamus said. "But her mum and dad are coming over. I can talk to her sister as well, and I think she kept in touch with a few of her friends from high school."

"That's good. Anything the police find on her mobile phone and laptop will need to be disclosed, so that'll give us a backdoor into her social media. Now, according to the scene report, she was found with a mobile phone. It's badly fire-damaged, but they have identified the make and model. It appears to be a very cheap Huawei smartphone."

Already, Seamus was shaking his head. "She owned a top-of-the-range Samsung. She only upgraded last month. The police took that, and her laptop, the night she died."

"I suspected as much. That's good. I'm not expecting the police to find much, the chances are the heat will have destroyed the memory card, but it's evidence of a double life, especially if it is an unregistered, pay-as-you-go."

Oldroyd continued. "The syringe she was found with has been badly damaged. I doubt they'll get any useful fingerprints off it.

So that's neutral evidentially; it won't show if you handled it, or if Carole injected herself. Ideally, they'll find her heroin stash, with her fingerprints on it. If we could find out who was dealing it to her, that would be bloody useful, but I suspect her dealer's number might be in her second phone's memory, so that's probably gone."

Seamus looked up. "I might be able to help with that," he said.

***

Andrea caught a taxi home. She could have called Marcus, but she needed time alone to think. To decide what she was going to do.

Seamus arrested? She couldn't believe it. There was no way he could have killed Carole. She was sure of it. She thought back to her own interrogation – for that was what it had been. She realised that now. She'd thought Dominic had been ridiculously over-dramatic hiring that expensive lawyer, but he hadn't been. Parker's advice to keep it simple had protected Seamus as well as her. It seemed that she was his alibi.

She thought back to the questions she'd been asked, and the answers she'd given. She'd probably told them more than they needed to know about her and Seamus' relationship, but he'd already admitted they were together, so she couldn't see any harm.

As for the rest of the questions, she'd answered them truthfully, except for one or two minor details that weren't important. They didn't need to know everything, did they?

"Where the hell have you been?" Marcus greeted her. "I've been calling you all day. Why was your phone turned off?"

"I was at the police station."

"What? Why?" his anger turned to concern.

"Helping the police with their enquiries," she said. "They've arrested Seamus."

Hot tears began to flow down her cheeks.

"You are shitting me."

"Apparently there are inconsistencies that make them think Carole might not have killed herself."

Before she knew it, she was telling Marcus everything. Parker had told her to keep things to herself, but surely that didn't include from her husband?

"Carole was a junkie? That can't be right," he said.

"That's what they are claiming."

"Where does Seamus come into this, then?"

"I don't know," she said. She was exhausted and barely thinking straight. She hadn't decided yet what she was going to tell Marcus. She had hoped her and Seamus' affair might remain secret, but now he had been arrested, it was all bound to come out.

"Wait, why were they speaking to you?" he asked, his tone suspicious.

"They wanted background. I was Carole's best friend," she said. It was the truth in so far as it went.

Marcus stared directly at her, saying nothing. She met his gaze, until eventually he looked away and stood up.

"Where are you going?" she asked.

"Out," he said, putting on his long, leather coat. It had started to rain again, and he grabbed his umbrella.

"Where?" she asked.

"I need some fresh air, and we've run out of milk."

She stood open-mouthed as he walked out the front door. Things had been strained between them for weeks, months even, yet his wife's best friend – who he had known just as long as she had – had just died in the most horrible manner imaginable. And now Carole's husband, another of Marcus' close friends, had just been arrested on suspicion of her murder. Marcus' own wife had spent most of the day being questioned by police. You'd think the last thing on his mind would be sodding milk.

Oh, God, he knows, thought Andrea. He'd figured out her and Seamus' secret.

She'd been so careful. After she heard about Carole, and Marcus cut short his trip to Glasgow, she'd changed the bedding and hidden any evidence that Seamus had spent the afternoon with her.

But in that moment, she'd seen a darkness in Marcus' eyes that she'd never witnessed before.

A minute later, she saw Marcus' car go past the window.

Andrea collapsed onto the sofa. What was she going to do? Suddenly, she felt all alone. She really needed to speak to someone. Somebody who would listen and let her vent, then hug her and tell her everything was going to be all right.

Somebody like Carole.

She'd cried when Dominic had rung her at four a.m. to tell her the news. But she'd pulled herself together and driven over to support Seamus. She'd cried when she'd phoned Marcus the following day to tell him what had happened, then cried in bed that night.

But now she really cried. Loud, wracking sobs for thirty minutes solid, leaving her helpless and exhausted.

When, after an hour, Marcus hadn't returned home, she screwed up her strength and rang his mobile. It went straight to voicemail. She hung up without leaving a message, and immediately redialled. Again, no answer. "Ring me back, sweetheart, I really need you," she managed after the tone. For a moment, she debated deleting the message and trying again; trying to sound less needy. But she couldn't think what else to say, so she left it and hung up. She sent him a text repeating the same thing, followed by a WhatsApp for good measure.

No reply.

Carole was gone. Seamus was in custody. Her husband had deliberately switched his phone off. She wouldn't know where to start with her parents. Only one person remained that she could call. She should have spoken to him earlier.

When Dominic's phone also went to voicemail, she could have screamed.

There was an open bottle of white wine in the fridge. She'd have preferred something stronger, but there was nothing else in the house. Pouring a generous glass, she swallowed it in two gulps, before returning to the fridge and refilling it with the remainder of the bottle. She was about to close the door, when she stopped.

Nestled in the door was a brand-new four-pinter of milk.

She started to cry again.

Chapter Eighteen

Seamus hadn't slept. He'd lain awake, staring at the ceiling. At about two a.m., the first of the evening's drunk and disorderlies had been tossed – literally – into the cell next to him. Judging by the screams, and the range of different voices shouting over him, it had taken at least five officers to manhandle him into the room, and they'd slammed the door shut immediately. It had been a further hour before his new neighbour had finally gone to sleep, treating Seamus to his snoring.

All that was unpleasant, but the real reason Seamus hadn't slept was fear. Fear that despite Angus Oldroyd's confident assurances, he would be charged with Carole's murder and spend the next few months of his life on remand, praying that eventually a jury would believe he was an innocent, grieving husband.

He thought back to what Oldroyd had said, and what he'd gleaned from watching TV. They apparently had up to twenty-four hours to question him, before they needed to either release him, bail him, charge him, or apply for a further extension to custody. Another twelve hours could be authorised by a senior officer. He did the sums. That took him to mid-morning the following day. After that, it would require a warrant from a magistrate to further detain him, up to a total of four days. Then he had to be charged or released.

Four days.

In the cell beside him, his neighbour had woken up. Whatever hangover he was suffering from had worsened his mood, and the on-duty custodian's offer of breakfast had been met with such a torrent of four-letter abuse, that the custody sergeant had come down to support her.

"Doesn't sound like he'll be tipping you," joked the sergeant as they passed Seamus' cell on the way back to the reception area.

"I'll leave a chocolate on his pillow and fold the end of the toilet roll into a triangle for him," she said.

"I heard that you fucking twats," came a voice from down the corridor.

Four days of this, thought Seamus in despair.
I don't think I can handle it.

***

Marcus hadn't come home the previous night. Andrea's repeated calls to his mobile phone had gone unanswered. By mid-morning, she was exhausted through lack of sleep, days of grief, worry about Seamus, and now her wayward husband.

She tried Dominic again. This time he picked up. It took him almost a minute to calm Andrea down enough to get her to listen to him. Eventually, he told her to stay put, and he'd drive over to see her.

"I know everything," he said when they sat down at the dining table. "I know about the affair you and Seamus were having. I know about him arranging for you two to meet up in Manchester, whilst Marcus was sent to Glasgow."

"I'm sorry, Dominic. Really, I am."

He dismissed her apologies with a wave of his hand. "We'll deal with that later. Our priority at the moment is to get Seamus out of jail and stop these ludicrous suggestions that he killed Carole." He pinched the bridge of his nose and close his eyes. "Christ, I can't believe I just said that. This is crazy. Seamus a murderer? I mean, none of us want to believe that things were so bad that Carole killed herself, but to think that the other explanation is that Seamus stuck a needle between her toes, pumped her full of heroin and then set her on fire ..."

Andrea placed her hand on his forearm. As long as she had known him, Dominic had always been a steady presence; invariably the life of the party, yet still the dependable one. He'd visited Seamus at least once a month when he was at university. He was usually the one who instigated the drinking games or turned up with a load of cheap alcohol from a cross-channel booze cruise. His ubiquitous camera phone had captured the good, the bad and the ugly from their exploits.

Yet he was also the one who got them all into a taxi at the end of the night, or retraced their footsteps until he found Seamus' wallet under a tree in the park where he'd dropped it after going for an emergency pee.

For the first time since she'd met him, Andrea saw another side of Dominic; the worried big brother. She thought back to Carole and Seamus' wedding, as she and Dominic had sat on the edge of the dance floor and watched the couple dance. Dominic had been uncharacteristically maudlin, as he realised he was no longer the most important person in his brother's life. She had been thinking about what could have been ... until Marcus had ruined the moment. As he always did.

She gave Dominic a hug. In the space of less than a week, he'd lost his sister-in-law, and now he was facing the loss of his little brother.

"Marcus didn't come home last night," Andrea said quietly. "And he isn't answering his phone. He knows about me and Seamus, doesn't he?"

"Yeah," Dominic said.

"Oh God, this is such a mess," she said. "If Seamus and I hadn't betrayed Carole, none of this would have happened."

"Hey, you don't know that," Dominic said. "At the moment, we're just guessing why Carole did what she did. She was clearly struggling after the loss of the baby, she was obviously deeper into drugs than we thought, she may even have been homesick. When was the last time she and Seamus took a long holiday in the States with her family?"

"It must be a couple of years," Andrea said. She wiped her eyes. "Do you believe them about the heroin? That Carole was a junkie?"

Dominic sighed. "Yeah, I do."

Chapter Nineteen

Dominic parked in the visitor's bay. Locking the car, he followed the signs and headed into the main reception area. He and Andrea had spoken for an hour before they conducted a brief search of the house. Judging from the missing clothing and toiletries, Marcus had gone. Andrea had been upset, but accepting of what he told her. As he'd left, she gave him another big hug and thanked him for everything.

There was a brief queue before he presented himself at the desk.

"I'd like to see the officers in charge of the Carole Monaghan death. I have something they need to know."

***

"I'm sorry, I should have said something before," Dominic said. "But I didn't want to upset Seamus or Andrea. Or tarnish Carole's memory, I guess."

He'd spent the past hour rehearsing what he wanted to say. His brother was in a hell of a mess. Had Dominic known the police would arrest Seamus on suspicion of Carole's murder, rather than accepting it as a tragic suicide, he'd have been more open from the start.

The phone sat on the table between them. The interview was being recorded, but he was glad not to have the oppressive presence of Oldroyd or Parker in the room. They were the best in the business, and quite rightly would have had kittens if they knew what he was about to tell the police. But Seamus' life was on the line and Dominic was clear on what he had to do.

"I knew that Carole had a drug problem," he said.

"What type of drug?" Freeland asked.

"Heroin," he admitted. "She probably drank more than she should, perhaps relied a little too heavily on weed after a bad day and liked coke at parties. But it was the heroin that was the worry. That's the real bad news."

"How did you find out?" Obigwe asked.

"She told me," he said simply.

Freeland blinked. "When?"

"I can't remember the exact date, but a few months ago, she asked if she could have a word. She and Seamus had been arguing again, and I assumed it was about that. That was when she told me she'd been experimenting with heroin, and she was worried that she was developing a problem. I was ..." he searched for the right word. "... gobsmacked. I didn't see that coming."

"Did anyone else know?" Freeland asked.

"No, I was the first person she told. I promised I'd keep her secret."

"Why?" Obigwe asked. "Shouldn't your brother know his wife is a drug user?"

"I thought about telling him. Honestly, I did. I've never kept secrets from my brother, and he is always honest with me ... or at least I thought he was ..." He cleared his throat. "Anyway, Carole wanted my help. I figured that if I could get her that help, then when she was in a better place, I could persuade her to speak to Seamus. But at the time, getting her sorted out seemed more important."

"And how did you help her?" Freeland asked.

"At first it was just moral support, trying to help her kick the habit. She reckoned she wasn't an addict – she would last days without using – but it could go that way." He sighed. "She was probably in denial, but I knew Carole well enough to know that she needed to do things at her own pace. Eventually, she admitted she needed professional help. I found a private clinic about twenty miles away. Very discreet. The plan was that she would have a couple of outpatient appointments to assess her needs, and then we'd arrange a residential stay if necessary."

"How were you intending to hide that from her husband?" Obigwe asked.

Dominic looked at the tabletop, his voice a mumble. "We were going to pretend she had gone abroad as a visiting lecturer on a design course. She delivered a series of well-received talks in London a couple of years ago, so it wouldn't seem implausible. I was going to adjust our work schedule so Seamus couldn't fly out for a surprise weekend."

Freeland raised an eyebrow.

"We hadn't worked out all the details," Dominic admitted. "And I was hoping Carole would be persuaded that honesty was the best policy, and we could drop the charade. Seamus would be pissed off at first, but he'd come around eventually, and see that I was just trying to help."

"And you have evidence of this?" Freeland asked.

Dominic turned his phone around. WhatsApp was open on the screen.

"Carole bought a cheap smartphone so we could speak in private. Sometimes we sent texts, other times we used voice." He reached over and scrolled through the messages. "As you can see, she was getting pretty desperate."

"Where was she getting the drugs?" Freeland asked.

"I don't know," Dominic said.

Freeland let the silence hang for a moment, but Dominic said nothing. He'd given them enough. They had everything they needed; there was no point opening that can of worms.

"When did she start treatment?" Obigwe asked.

Dominic reached over and scrolled to the last message, sent the night she died. "She was due to have her first appointment that day. I was supposed to take her, but I had an urgent meeting." His eyes filled with tears. "She said that it was OK, she could make her own way there. She never showed up."

***

Seamus had opted for a cheese and lettuce sandwich for lunch and a banana, along with a mug of something the custodian described as coffee. He forced himself to eat the sandwich, and swallow the coffee, but in less than a minute he was throwing it back up into the metal toilet.

Oldroyd returned half an hour later.

"They were planning on interviewing you again after you finished lunch, but they've postponed it," he said.

"What does that mean?" Seamus asked. Hope flared briefly, then dimmed.

"I'm not sure. It could be they are struggling to find things to ask you, which might be a good sign." He raised his hand to quell Seamus' excitement. "Or it could mean that they're chasing down some new evidence they want to put to you."

He took a deep breath. "But what I do know, is that Dominic has just spent an hour with them."

"Why? What did they want to speak to him for?"

Oldroyd filled him in on what Dominic had just told him.

Seamus was stunned. "You mean he knew that Carole was having problems, but he didn't say anything?"

"Yes," Oldroyd admitted. "I'm afraid you'll have to ask him why he kept it a secret." His features softened. "For what it's worth, it sounds as though he was in a very difficult position. I think he thought he could help Carole, and then get her to confide in you eventually."

Seamus let out a shuddering breath. On top of everything, he couldn't process this as well. He'd deal with it later.

"I'm afraid I've got some more bad news," Oldroyd said. "Andrea thinks Marcus knows about your affair. Dominic reckons he's walked out on her."

Seamus groaned. Could today get any worse?

Four Years Ago

Nine Months Before The Fire

Chapter Twenty

As expected, Dominic's thirtieth birthday party was a raucous bash. The house throbbed with the pulse of music from his state-of-the-art stereo system, delivered throughout by individually-controlled hidden speakers. He'd set the miniature mood-lights buried in the ceiling to pulse in time with the beat, cycling through different colours so that the huge, open-plan living area was like a nightclub.

The catering company had dropped off enough food to feed twice the number of guests, and Dominic had bought some cardboard food cartons so revellers could take home some of the leftover nibbles alongside their slice of cake.

The party was brash, generous and overstated; everything that Dominic was, and Seamus wasn't.

It didn't mean Seamus wasn't having a bloody good time though.

The evening was dry and still pleasantly warm, so Dominic had thrown open the French doors at the front and the rear, and his guests had spilled out into the grounds surrounding the house. The nearest neighbours were hundreds of metres away, but even if the wind had carried the noise that far, they wouldn't care; they were enjoying the party along with everyone else.

"I tell you, Seamus, the best thing I ever did was joining you guys," Marcus said, as he drunkenly rolled a joint, half the makings spilling onto his lap. They were sitting in the rear garden. Seamus smiled tolerantly; Marcus tended to repeat himself when he was drunk. Sometimes he wondered what Andrea saw in him. He shook his head when Marcus offered him a toke; he'd already had more to drink than was wise, and he'd learned through experience that weed on top would make him feel crap tomorrow.

"This place is fucking amazing," Marcus said. "Andrea told me all about it. It's like Dominic's testing out every device we supply to our clients. CCTV, body heat intruder sensors, keypads for the doors, automatic window blinds, he's even got that bullet-proof glass we recommend to VIPs. I wouldn't like his electricity bill, though."

Seamus pointed to the roof. "Solar panels. On a sunny day, he generates so much more than he uses, he makes a profit from selling it back to the National Grid. His next plan is to fit a big battery in the garage, so he can store the excess and use it at night. That way he no longer needs to draw power from the grid when the sun goes down."

"That's awesome, he's like Tony Stark," Marcus said. "Still no Pepper Potts though. What's the name of that bird he's seeing this week?"

"Um, I'm not sure," Seamus admitted. He'd met the statuesque blonde when they'd arrived earlier. Apparently, she was a fitness instructor. He and Carole had a wager going. She figured the woman would last a month. Seamus thought she was being generous.

"Is it true he has a games room and a private cinema?"

"Well, that's a bit of an exaggeration," Seamus said. "He has a pool table in one of the rooms, and a big screen. But he doesn't really use it." The last time Seamus had seen inside there, it was being used as a storage closet, with the pool table covered in boxes of ornaments from their grandparents' home. Dominic had bought an even bigger flat screen TV, which he'd installed on the living room wall, and a pair of reclining armchairs, so their video game nights were now hosted in the comfort of the lounge, within easy reach of the fridge.

It was typical Dominic. He was laser-focused, even single-minded, in his business dealings, but outside of work it was as if he compensated by never sticking with one thing. An endless stream of women – none of whom lasted more than a couple of months – or new hobbies picked up with great enthusiasm before being dropped for something new, were how he lived his life. His latest obsession was gardening; he'd drawn up elaborate plans to landscape the whole grounds. Even his car had to have the latest gadgets – apparently, he was on the waiting list for a Tesla, despite having owned his Range Rover for less than two years. He'd decided that MSS was going to be carbon neutral within five years, and planned to lead by example.

It had been that way ever since they were kids. Where Seamus had been quietly studious, Dominic – despite being the more academically gifted of the two – couldn't wait to leave formal education. He'd done his A levels, but then drifted for nine months from job to job with no clear plan or goals. As they'd lain awake in their bunk bed, Seamus had mapped out his own future: degree in finance, a stable job with a bank, wife, kids, early retirement. Dominic had listened quietly, unable to offer more than a grunt in response.

The apprenticeship Dominic snagged with a local security firm had been the making of him. Employed as a fitter of burglar alarms and residential CCTV systems, he'd become fascinated with the possibilities afforded by the emergence of smart homes and low-cost, wirelessly-connected devices.

By the time Seamus was choosing which university to attend, Dominic was investing his share of the money their parents had left them in setting himself up as an independent security specialist. Monaghan Security Solutions had grown rapidly, expanding from fitting home systems to business premises. Then, despite still sharing his childhood bedroom with his brother, he'd snagged the contract to upgrade the recently refurbished local council offices, completing the job on time, and under budget by cutting his profit margins to zero. His financial gamble paid off. The council were so impressed that he hadn't ripped them off, they outsourced all their future work to him and sang his praises. Next came a major contract for the local NHS trust, and soon, Dominic had made his first million.

Dominic preferred to work with people he knew, so when Seamus suddenly found himself urgently in need of paid employment – and financial assistance – Dominic had immediately created the position of vice-president. A few months ago, he'd head-hunted Marcus with promises of a fifty per cent hike in salary. He'd even paid Carole to design the company's corporate branding and hired Andrea to set up its new website.

Since the day that a shell-shocked grandfather had sat two little boys down and told them that their mummy and daddy had gone to heaven after a car accident, Dominic had made it his mission to care for his little brother.

And as the years passed, Seamus' love for him grew only stronger.

***

As the clock passed midnight, the party showed no sign of slowing down. By now, Seamus was exhausted. Ordinarily, he would have been making his excuses and heading to bed, but he and Carole were staying over, so there was no point doing so whilst the music was still playing.

In typical Marcus fashion, he'd suddenly interrupted their conversation and loudly announced that he needed 'to point Percy at the porcelain' before lurching off in search of the bathroom.

"Sorry about Markie, you know what he's like after a few drinks," Andrea said, joining Seamus on the bench. She was wearing a full-length emerald-green dress, slit almost to the waist. She looked spectacular, and Seamus told her so.

"Flatterer," she said, taking a sip of wine. She looked around the garden. "This place never ceases to amaze me. I've never seen anywhere like it."

"You won't have done," Seamus said. "It's a complete one-off. The previous owner bought the land, designed it, and built it himself. Then he went bankrupt, and Dominic bought it for a song, although it's still a work in progress. The previous owner cut a few corners, so every time Dom does something, he finds some hidden bodge job. He had to re-plumb the kitchen because the silly sod joined the kitchen waste pipe to the drain at a point *higher* than the outlet on the washing machine."

Andrea blinked. "So the waste water had to flow *uphill*?"

"Yup, something water isn't famed for doing. Dom had lived here barely a month and couldn't work out why there was water leaking from his brand-new washing machine and a smell of drains."

Andrea put her hand over her mouth. "I shouldn't laugh."

"Feel free," Seamus said. "I pissed myself."

The two of them settled back into a companionable silence.

"Dominic really knows how to throw a party," Andrea said eventually. "But it's going to take an age to clean the place up. It's a good job he has wooden floors; with the amount of wine spilled, he'd need professional cleaners in for the carpets."

"He's got professional cleaners coming tomorrow anyway," Seamus admitted.

Andrea shook her head with a smile. "What's he like?"

The temperature had started to dip, and the electric heat lamps had come on. Pretty soon, it was just the two of them. Andrea shivered, and Seamus offered her his jacket, hoping to stay outside with her a bit longer.

"I'm so glad it's a bank holiday weekend," Andrea said. "I think I'll need the three days just to get over the hangover. I swear it takes longer to recover once you pass twenty-five."

"I reckon something happens to you after you graduate," Seamus said.

"God, yes," she said. "Can you remember some of the shit we used to drink when we were skint? It'd probably kill us now."

Seamus chuckled. "I remember that bottle of dessert wine you necked before Carole's birthday. You were so ill."

Andrea made a face. "How was I to know that dessert wine is basically sherry?" she asked. "Jesus, it was so sweet, I thought I'd wake up with no teeth. Still, I went out with a tenner in my purse and came back with five left, so it was all good."

Behind them, there came a crash, followed by drunken cheers.

"I'm all right, I'm fine," came a loud voice with an American accent.

"Oh, Christ, what's she doing now?" Seamus groaned, getting to his feet.

The two of them headed quickly back into the house.

Neither of them noticed Marcus watching them, his eyes narrowed.

***

Seamus and Andrea re-entered the living area to find Carole clambering unsteadily back onto the coffee table; there was a cut on her leg, although she didn't seem to have noticed. Somehow, the large gin and tonic she'd been holding had survived her tumble. In her other hand, she was clutching a beer bottle like a microphone.

Immediately finding her place in the song again, she resumed belting out a tuneless accompaniment to *I Will Survive*, to the amused appreciation of a small audience. Out of the corner of his eye, Seamus saw Dominic filming the goings on.

Seamus shouldered his way through the crowd and held his hand out.

"Come on sweetheart, let's get you down from there before you break your neck."

Carole turned towards him. "Boooo!" she jeered. "Boooo!" A few of her audience joined in, before realising who she was booing.

"Come on darling," Seamus said, forcing a smile.

"Boooo!" she shouted more loudly.

Seamus tried to slip his arm around her waist, but she brushed it off.

"You're always trying to ruin my fun," she said. "Boring, boring Seamus. Party pooper Seamus."

Up close, he could see her nose was reddened, and her pupils were dilated.

"Get down, Carole," he hissed, feeling his face flush with embarrassment.

"No," she said, turning her back and starting to sing again, She swayed to the music, the heels of her stilettos skirting just millimetres from the edge of the coffee table.

"I've got this," Dominic said, having finally pocketed his camera phone. "Hey Sis', you haven't given me my birthday kiss yet."

Carole turned and gave him a big smile. "It's the birthday boy!" she shouted, holding her arms out in an embrace.

Dominic gave her a big hug, deftly lifting, turning, and depositing her safely on the floor. He gave Seamus a half-nod, then looked over at Andrea, who joined him. They walked Carole towards the bathroom. As they left, Seamus heard her telling Andrea how much she liked her jacket; Seamus had one just like it.

Seamus ground his teeth. It wasn't the first time Carole had drunk too much and made a fool of herself, but more than half the people in the room were his and Dominic's work colleagues.

This had to stop.

"Anyone seen Pete Ludlow?" he asked.

"Out the front, I think," Anton replied.

Seamus marched towards the doors leading to the front of the house.

Ludlow was leaning against a tree smoking a joint, chatting to a dark-haired woman who Seamus didn't know.

"Hey, Boss, cracking party," he held out his joint. Seamus ignored it.

"I need a word," he said. He waited until the woman got the hint.

"I need the bathroom," she said. "I'll catch you later, Pete."

"What can I do for you, Seamus?" asked Ludlow, taking a long drag.

"Have you been supplying Carole?" Seamus asked.

Ludlow gave a lazy shrug. "Sure. Why? Does she want some more?" he started rummaging in his pocket.

"No, she's had enough. What did you give her?"

"A bit of weed," Ludlow said, now wary.

"And?" Seamus demanded.

Ludlow swallowed. "A little coke."

"It stops. Now," Seamus said through gritted teeth.

Ludlow blinked in confusion. "Why? I've been helping you guys out for ages. You know Dom's cool with it, just so long as I never bring it into work."

"I'm not talking about the weed," Seamus said. "And I couldn't give a shit what you do in your spare time, but as of now, Carole is out of bounds. No more coke. Ever. Understood?"

Ludlow raised his hands. "Sure, anything you say. You're the boss. Or the vice-boss. Or whatever."

Seamus glared at him for a few more seconds, before nodding once and then turning on his heel and heading back inside.

"We've put Carole in the guestroom," Dominic said as Seamus entered. "She's spark out."

"No need, I'm calling an Uber," Seamus said, still seething. "We can deal with it at home tomorrow morning."

Dominic placed a hand on his brother's arm. "Are you sure that's a good idea, Bro'? Tell you what, why don't we let her sleep it off? You go home and calm down. I'll drop her back at your place tomorrow. After she and I have had a chat."

Seamus was silent, his teeth grinding.

"Seriously, kid," Dominic said. "You're both angry right now, you need space to calm down. And the last thing you want is to be dealing with this with a pair of thick heads tomorrow morning. I'll get a decent breakfast down her neck before I bring her over."

Eventually, Seamus nodded, and hugged his brother. He motioned towards Ms Fitness Instructor, who was chatting to Dominic's PA. "What about her? I don't want to cramp your style, especially on your birthday."

Dominic smiled tightly. "If I'm honest, Carole staying over is giving me just the excuse I need ... the sex is great, but I don't think I can face any more pillow talk about personal bests and protein shakes. I'll let her down gently, I promise."

Then

Four Days After The Fire

Chapter Twenty-One

"Marcus Harrington's mobile phone connected to a cell tower close to your house the evening he went missing," Freeland said.

Angus Oldroyd had insisted on joining Dominic and accompanying him into the interview suite after he had been threatened with arrest if he didn't voluntarily accompany DS Freeland to the station.

So far, the solicitor had sat in silence, barely hiding his scowl. He was already deeply unhappy that Dominic had previously attended the station without him, and even more displeased that Dominic had promised to fully cooperate.

"Yeah, he came to see me," Dominic admitted.

"Why didn't you tell us this earlier?" Freeland asked.

"You didn't ask," Dominic said. His voice was defensive, but he couldn't meet their eyes. He'd been doing his best to appear open and transparent as he attempted to get his brother out of the mess he'd found himself in. His decision to avoid telling them about Marcus' unexpected visit had scuppered that, he now realised.

"Why did he come and see you?" Obigwe asked.

"It turns out he didn't go to Glasgow as he was supposed to," Dominic admitted. If he was to restore their trust in him, now was not the time to go no comment, no matter what Oldroyd counselled. "Instead, he went to Manchester to find proof Seamus and Andrea were having an affair. He wanted to show me some photographs he'd taken of them together after the trade conference finished."

"Why?" Freeland asked. "What did it have to do with you?"

"To put it bluntly, he wanted Seamus' job. Or, if that wasn't possible, he wanted a generous severance package to resign without making a fuss."

"And did he confront Andrea and Seamus first?" Obigwe asked.

"No." Dominic's mouth twisted. "I think his plan was to get the deal in place, and then hit Andrea with the evidence. I reckon he was going to demand a divorce."

"And what was your response?" Freeland asked.

"I'm not going to lie. With the fire and everything that happened in the last couple of days, the last thing I was worrying about was whether Seamus was shagging Andrea. I told him to do one."

"And how did he take that?" Freeland asked.

"Not well," Dominic admitted. "He accused me of colluding with my brother to try and lever him out of the company. He said we'd been planning to get rid of him for ages so Seamus and Andrea could be together, and that I had the choice of either letting him go with a generous payout, or he'd quit and claim constructive dismissal."

Dominic sighed. "Look, I've known Marcus for years. I consider him a friend, and I don't want to slag him off. But the fact is, he has a dark side, especially when he's drunk or high. When he turned up last night, he'd definitely had a few drinks, and judging by the size of his pupils and his manic edge, I reckon he'd snorted something.

"I guess it'll all come out anyway, but I issued him with a written warning six months ago for drinking at work and taking drugs. I'm a pretty relaxed boss; I trust my employees to use their judgement. If they want to treat a client to lunch and have a beer or a glass of wine when they're trying to land a deal, then fine. But this was more than that."

"How much more?" Freeland asked. The detective still sounded sceptical.

"He'd been working on a multi-million-pound contract for us to fit and service an integrated security system for a retail chain. They were due to sign on the dotted line, so Marcus took them for a slap-up meal at a Michelin-starred restaurant. I was fine with that, it was a lucrative deal. But the chief executive was a Muslim, and so didn't drink. Marcus had been out the night before and was profoundly hungover, so decided to cure it with the hair of the dog. And when that didn't work, a line of coke. I spent two hours on the phone that afternoon apologising and undoing the damage, and sweetening the deal to keep them on board."

"Why didn't you just sack him?" Obigwe asked. "That sounds like gross misconduct to me."

Dominic felt his face flush. "If we had lost the contract, then he'd have been out on his ear, no question. But he's a mate, and he and Seamus have known each other since their first day at university. Plus, he's actually bloody good at what he does. He's brought in some very good clients. I couldn't actually prove he'd taken cocaine, and I admit I've made a rod for my own back by allowing staff to consume alcohol during business lunches. I didn't want to end up with a legal fight on my hands, especially when we're considering taking the company public. That's confidential by the way, I'd rather you kept it to yourself," he added, before Oldroyd interjected.

"Of course," Freeland said. "So, did you know about Seamus and Andrea's affair?"

"Not really," Dominic said. "There were times I wondered, especially when they were at university, and I always thought Andy might be sweet on him, but I guess I didn't really want to think about it. I certainly haven't been colluding with Seamus to get rid of Marcus. That's the bloody cocaine talking."

"You said Marcus has a bit of a dark side," Freeland said. "Is there anything else you aren't telling us?"

Dominic chewed his lip. "He can be a real arsehole when he's drunk, and he has a bit of a temper."

"In what way?" Freeland pressed.

"He can be verbally quite abusive and a bit unpredictable. He has a great sense of humour – until he suddenly doesn't. Once or twice back at university I had to escort him out of a bar before the bouncers did, or before he got a punch on the nose from someone. He's always very apologetic the next day, but I've seen him say things to Andy after a few that I think crossed the line."

"Would you say he could be violent?" Freeland asked casually.

Dominic thought about his response; it was clear where they were going with this line of questioning. "Perhaps," he admitted eventually. "Under the right circumstances."

"How would you characterise his relationship with Carole?" Freeland asked.

Dominic took even longer to think about his answer. "It could be ... volatile at times."

"What do you mean by volatile?" Obigwe asked.

"Both Carole and Marcus have strong personalities," Dominic said. "Politics was something we tried to steer clear of, especially if we'd been drinking. Marcus is a bit of an old-school Tory. Carole was rather more liberal – it's one of the reasons she loved living in the UK. She was somewhat at odds with her parents: died-in-the-wool Republicans who live in Wyoming."

"And aside from politics?" Obigwe asked.

"Like I said, very strong personalities." He chewed his lip. The two officers weren't fools. They could see he was willing to throw Marcus under a bus if it deflected attention away from Seamus. But nothing he'd said was a lie.

"What are you not telling us, Dominic?" Freeland asked.

Dominic sighed. "Marcus can be a little ... handsy, shall we say, after a few drinks? Last Christmas, we had a work party. I didn't see it first-hand," he cautioned. "But apparently, Marcus had a lot to drink, and Carole claims he made a pass at her. She didn't spell out what had happened, but she was clearly shaken. She was reluctant to make a big fuss, she didn't want to upset Seamus and Andy, so she asked me to have a quiet word. As his friend, not his boss. He denied it, claimed she was mistaken. But he was embarrassed enough that something had obviously happened."

"Do you think this was a one-off, or could there have been more to it?" Freeland asked.

"I genuinely don't know," Dominic said. "But Carole is ... was ... a very good-looking woman, and I know Marcus has a bit of a wandering eye. Especially after a few drinks. He is a bit ... flirtatious ... towards some of the women at work. One in particular bears more than a passing resemblance to Carole.

"Raquel," he added at Freeland's expectant pause.

The detective made a note in his blue book.

"Marcus hasn't been seen since he left your house yesterday evening," Obigwe said. "Can you tell us what happened after he spoke to you?"

"I just wanted to get rid of him," Dominic said. "I needed to speak to Seamus and Andy first, before deciding what to do. I wanted to hear their side of the story. I persuaded him to leave and said we'd have a meeting later in the week."

"How did he take that?"

"He wasn't happy, but he wasn't so high he was going to push it any further. I think that by this point, he'd realised turning up at his boss's house unannounced hadn't done him any favours. He was still angry when he left, but I assumed that either he'd go home, or he'd stay at a mate's house."

"Well, he didn't go home," Obigwe said. "Do you have any idea where he may have gone?"

"I don't really know," Dominic admitted. "But there's something you should know."

"What's that?" Freeland asked.

"I went round to Andy's this morning before I came here. She said the overnight bag he brought back from Glasgow had been emptied; the dirty clothes he wore were in the laundry basket. But she reckons a load of clean clothes were missing from his wardrobe, and the bag was missing. He must have packed them before she even returned from the station yesterday."

"Do you think he's left her?" Obigwe asked. "Where would he go?"

"I don't know, but we did a search of the house, and his passport has gone. And it's a new Irish one he applied for after Brexit, so he can still travel in Europe."

Chapter Twenty-Two

By the time DS Freeland and DC Obigwe joined Andrea in the interview suite she had gone through every scenario she could think of, although Clarence Parker had advised against further speculation before they determined what information the two detectives had. Apparently, Angus Oldroyd was in another interview suite with Dominic.

"Andrea, as you are surely aware by now, the circumstances surrounding Carole's death are more complex than we initially thought," Freeland said.

She nodded, but said nothing. Beside her, Parker had his notepad out, his pen poised.

Freeland continued. "Much of what we have uncovered about Carole supports the idea she took her own life. But we can't be certain of that yet."

"You think Seamus murdered her," she said. It still sounded crazy to her ears.

"That is one possibility," Freeland admitted. "We can't be certain she was killed unlawfully, but we have to consider the possibility."

"But Seamus was with me when you say she was killed," she said.

"Are you absolutely certain of that?" Freeland asked.

"Yes. One hundred per cent." She met his gaze squarely.

"You said yesterday that you didn't think that Marcus was aware of your affair. Do you still believe that?" Obigwe asked.

Andrea gave a tiny shake of her head. "I had my suspicions yesterday evening when he left me. Then Dominic told me this morning that Marcus visited him last night and showed him photographs of Seamus and I together in Manchester. So obviously, he must have suspected something, because he was supposed to be in Glasgow. I swear I knew nothing about that until Dominic told me this morning."

"What did Marcus say to you before he left?" Freeland asked.

"Nothing. In fact, he lied and said he was going out to fetch some milk, but we already had plenty in the fridge. He must have been planning on leaving me already."

"Why do you say that?" Obigwe asked.

"He'd already been home a few hours when I got back from the station yesterday," she said. "He seemed surprised when I told him Seamus had been arrested, but he was cold. Seamus was as much his friend as mine, but he made no move to comfort me. I realised this morning that he had already packed an overnight bag before I even got home. When Dominic came around after Marcus didn't return home last night, we searched the house for a clue to where he might have gone and found he'd taken his phone charger and his passport. Dominic told me about Marcus' visit to see him and told me to keep trying his phone. If he hadn't answered by lunchtime, he told me to report him missing. I couldn't wait that long."

"Where do you think he's gone?" Freeland asked.

"I don't know. I assumed that he had either checked into a hotel, or he'd gone around a friend's house, but I've called everyone I can think of, and nobody has seen him. Dominic said he thought he'd been drinking and perhaps even taking cocaine; I'm worried he might have crashed his car. The roads around here are quite treacherous, with inadequate crash barriers. If he was angry when he drove away …"

"We haven't had any reports of any car accidents in the local area, or any patients answering Marcus' description in any of the nearby hospitals," Freeland reassured her. "I understand Marcus' passport was Irish. Does he have any family there?"

"A few relatives. Both sides of the border," she said. "Although after his grandmother passed, I wouldn't say he was close to many of them anymore."

"DC Obigwe tells me you believe Marcus has withdrawn money from your joint accounts?" Freeland said.

She took her phone out and pushed it across the desk. "I checked our online banking app. Last night he transferred a little over two thousand pounds from our housekeeping account into an account I don't recognise, and basically emptied our joint savings account." She felt a flash of anger. "The mortgage is due in three days, the bastard. I'll have to use my own overdraft facility to cover that, and the half-dozen standing orders and direct debits coming out over the next week. If you don't find him and get that money back soon, I'll probably have to take out a loan ... oh Christ, this is such a mess," she said, as the reality of her situation dawned upon her. First the loss of Carole, then Seamus' arrest, followed by the unravelling of their secret lives. And now, on top of it all, she was facing financial ruin.

Obigwe and Freeland waited patiently whilst Parker poured her a glass of water and opened another packet of disposable tissues. Eventually she had composed herself enough to continue.

"I know what Seamus and I did was wrong, and I know Marcus is upset, but surely he can't just take our money like that? Half of it is mine." *God, she sounded so callous. Why was she focusing on the money, given everything else that was going on?*

"I'm afraid I can't advise on your legal position," Freeland said. "What was Marcus' relationship with Carole like?" he asked, without a pause.

It took Andrea a moment to process the sudden change in topic.

"OK, I suppose. We've all known each other since university."

Freeland waited; Obigwe said nothing.

"They had their ups and downs," she admitted eventually. "It's weird, but for two people with such radically different political views, they were actually very similar. Perhaps a bit too similar, if you know what I mean? They both loved a good argument, and neither of them would back down."

Freeland chose his next words very carefully. "Andrea, we have heard that Marcus could have a bit of a temper at times. That sometimes he could be a little aggressive. Towards you."

Andrea's face went blank. "People talk a lot about things they know nothing about," she said.

"Andrea," Obigwe said, softly. "Was Marcus ever violent towards you?"

There was a long pause, as Andrea slowly realised where they were heading.

"Oh, no," she said. "No, you can't be serious." She placed her hand over her mouth, her eyes widening. "You think Marcus had something to do with Carole's death."

Freeland and Obigwe said nothing. Beside her, Parker was scribbling furiously.

"First Seamus, now Marcus? Please, tell me you don't think he could have been involved?" she managed.

"We just need to speak to him," Freeland said. "To clear up a few details. It would really help if you could tell us what Marcus was like."

Parker shifted in his seat and cleared his throat.

"I'd like a break," Andrea said.

***

Andrea was composed when she returned from the break.

"Marcus can be a ... difficult man," she admitted. "Most of the time he is good fun and very loving, but sometimes after a drink he can be ... unpleasant."

"In what way?" Obigwe asked.

"He's always been very witty. The first to crack a joke or make a pun. He loves to wind people up. But after a drink, it is as if he loses his filter. The jokes he cracks can be very close to the knuckle. Sometimes, they can even be a bit cruel. And when he has too much to drink, he can lose his sense of humour without warning."

She looked down at the table. "When he's high, he can be very unpredictable. All laughing and messing about one minute, argumentative and nasty the next."

"Was he ever physically abusive towards you?" Obigwe asked.

Andrea shook her head. "No ..." she paused. "But a few times, I decided it would be best if I left him alone to get his head straight."

"Do you think he could be violent towards anyone else?" Obigwe asked.

Andrea sighed. "At university, he got into a couple of fights. Drunken squabbles usually that seemed to come out of nowhere. One night he took exception to some bloke who he thought had been saying things about us behind our back. We were queuing to get into a club. I didn't hear what this guy had said – I'm not even sure Marcus heard him right – but the next thing I knew Marcus was punching him to the ground. Fortunately, Dominic was present that night, and he pulled Marcus off. If he hadn't been there ... well, I don't know what would have happened."

She wiped her nose on a tissue. "He is even worse when he uses cocaine. I've asked him not to, but he ignores me. He's been using it more and more. I'm worried he has a problem."

"Can I ask where you got the drugs?" Freeland asked. It stood to reason that Carole probably got her heroin from the same source. It would be useful to the coroner if they could find out the scale of Carole's problem.

Andrea chewed her lip. "No comment," she said eventually.

Freeland changed tack. "Going back to the relationship between Marcus and Carole. You said they could be argumentative, but that they were also more alike than you'd expect. Could there have been any more to it?"

Andrea was silent for a long moment. "I know Marcus kind of fancied her," she admitted. "I've caught him staring at her a few times when he didn't think I was looking." She shrugged. "I wasn't too worried, I just kind of accepted it. Carole was a very beautiful woman; to be honest, I'd be surprised if he didn't think she was attractive."

"And do you think there could have been more than that?" Freeland pressed.

"I don't know," she admitted eventually. "I tried not to think about it. Things have been difficult between us for a long while." She blushed. "And I can hardly take the moral high ground, can I?"

"Before we finish, do you know if either Marcus or Seamus has another mobile phone?" Freeland asked. "Other than the main one that they carry around with them?"

"I've never seen one," she said. "Seamus and I used WhatsApp, and we were both always very careful to lock our phones whenever we left them unattended. If Marcus had another phone, he kept it well hidden."

"In the light of what we've spoken about, and recent events, is there anything else you'd like to tell us?" Freeland asked. "Or perhaps anything you would like to correct?"

She shook her head. "No."

"Then let's finish the interview for now."

Now

Three Days After The Storm

Chapter Twenty-Three

"SHE'S BEEN MOVED TO a different room, and there are two uniforms guarding the door," Stafford said. "Nobody in or out unless they are accompanied."

It was barely seven a.m. and she was in DCI Girton's office filling her in on the previous night's attempt to kill the unknown traffic accident victim.

"How is she?" Girton asked, sipping from her coffee. Stafford had already drunk three strong cups since being roused from her bed four hours previously, and she dare not have any more.

"It looks like the duty nurse stopped him before he managed to finish smothering her," she said.

"And it's definitely a he?"

"Yes. Male and white is the best she can do," Stafford said. "It was dark, and the attacker was wearing full scrubs with a facemask. Unfortunately, he punched the nurse who interrupted him. Nothing too serious, but it knocked her senseless whilst he made his escape." Stafford rubbed her face wearily. "It was sheer good fortune her attacker didn't succeed. Much longer and she'd be dead."

"What actually happened?" Girton asked. "I've only heard the highlights."

"Our victim was in her own room," Stafford said. "She's still in an induced coma, wired up to an ECG, but she's not high dependency. They keep an eye on her vitals from the nurse's station, and somebody pokes their head in every so often and does a manual check. The duty nurse had just finished her latest visit, but she realised she'd left her pen in there. She returned and found someone holding a pillow over the woman's face. It sounds as though her attacker was as surprised to see the nurse as she was to see him. She acted on instinct and confronted him but got a right hook for her trouble."

"It sounds like somebody who knew the nursing staff's routine," said Girton. "Which is worrying." She frowned. "You said they were monitoring her vitals from the nurses' station – surely, they'd pick up on the sudden change and an alarm would sound? They'd be caught in the act."

Stafford's mouth twisted. "And this is where it gets really scary. The attacker had unplugged the leads from her ECG, and then plugged in his *own* leads, which were attached to his own chest. Unplugging the leads doesn't trigger an immediate alarm; there's a grace period to allow staff to replace the electrodes without everything going nuts. It's obvious when you see the trace before and after the gap in the readings; his heart rate is thirty beats per minute higher than hers, but it's still within the safe zone, so there was no alert. Presumably he was planning on switching them back after he killed her, then escaping in the confusion when they tried to resuscitate her."

"Jesus," Girton said. "How did he get onto the ward? It was one a.m., surely you can't just wander in off the street?"

"Access is via swipe card outside visiting hours, but we're having difficulty retrieving the logs."

"Great. What about CCTV? The hospital is covered in cameras."

"They went down a few minutes before the attack."

"What? All of them?" Girton asked.

"Complete system failure. Even the car park."

"Don't tell me that's a coincidence," Girton said.

"No evidence either way, yet," Stafford scowled. "But let's not kid ourselves."

Girton ran her hand through her hair.

"Who the hell is this woman, Katie? And what the fuck has she got herself into?"

***

On his way into work, Dominic stopped off at the supermarket and picked up some flowers.

Today was always a hard day. Dominic knew that things hadn't been right between Carole and Seamus for some time before her death. It was why Dominic had acted in the way he had. But Carole's death had occurred before the marriage had finally petered to its natural conclusion, and so Seamus grieved Carole as if they had still been a happy couple. She had been snatched away, rather than drifting away.

For over twenty years, Dominic had been there at his brother's side as he experienced his brightest highs and darkest lows. From the devastation of their parents' death, to the excitement of his engagement to Carole, then the hammer blow of the miscarriage, Dominic had been there. It was his self-imposed duty and he regretted nothing.

Carole's death had almost finished Seamus off, but again, Dominic had done his best to pick up the pieces. Theirs was a unique bond, and Dominic loved his brother with the same ferocity he'd felt when their parents had brought that squealing bundle home from the hospital, and he'd realised that perhaps a little brother might be even better than a sister.

At least Seamus had Andrea now; someone else to support and love him when Dominic couldn't. Dominic would never say it out loud, but that was the way it should have been from the start. Carole and Seamus had been in love; he knew that for a fact. They had got together young, and their relationship had burned brightly.

But perhaps that had been the problem? Perhaps it had burned too brightly?

With Andrea, the relationship had grown organically, out of a deep friendship. To this day, Dominic had no idea if anything had ever happened between the two of them at university. He remembered the wistful look on Andrea's face at the wedding as she watched her two best friends dancing as man and wife, and he was convinced Andrea was thinking about what might have been. Years later, that friendship meant that when they finally did get together, the relationship had a solid foundation that had allowed them to weather the storms ahead.

As far as Dominic was concerned, Andrea should never have married Marcus. Professionally, the man was fantastic at what he did. And when you got past the abrasive and sometimes dickish personality, he could be fun to be around. But even if Seamus was off-limits, Andrea could have done better. He firmly believed her acceptance of Marcus' proposal was a reaction to Seamus and Carole's marriage.

But now, it had been three years since Marcus disappeared and the recent law changes surrounding no-fault divorces meant that Andrea would be able to file for divorce, even without Marcus' consent.

Finally, she and Seamus could move on with their lives.

Shortly after Marcus' disappearance, his silver Volvo had been found burnt out on industrial ground near Birkenhead in Merseyside. There was no record of his passport being used on the ferry crossing to Northern Ireland, but the failure to fully implement the post-Brexit border checks meant it wouldn't be difficult to find a lorry driver willing to earn a few hundred quid by risking an unofficial passenger.

Carole's inquest had returned an open verdict. Due to some inconsistencies, the coroner was unwilling to declare her death a suicide; Dominic knew her family refused to accept that she would take her own life and couldn't believe she would use heroin.

On the other hand, although Marcus' sudden disappearance was suspicious, the police had been unable to find enough evidence to declare him anything more than a person of interest. Dominic and his colleagues at MSS had been questioned about Marcus extensively. The police had been especially interested in Marcus' role supervising the alarm engineers, from which Dominic surmised that they were at least entertaining the possibility he might have had access to the passwords used to disable Carole and Seamus' security system. It also looked as though Marcus had used his position as chief financial officer to disburse the money transferred out of his and Andrea's bank accounts into a number of MSS operating accounts. By the time the money had been tracked, it was long gone.

As for Marcus' family, they refused to accept that he could be involved in Carole's death and had floated all sorts of crazy and hurtful conspiracy theories, especially after Andrea and Seamus' affair had been revealed.

And Andrea ... Dominic sighed. He wished there was something he could do to lessen her pain and guilt. He knew she still clung to the hope that Carole had killed herself, because the alternative – that Marcus had killed her – was too much to bear. But if it was a suicide, then an obvious conclusion was that her affair with Seamus might have contributed to it. Dominic had done his best to convince Andrea and Seamus that Carole was blissfully unaware of the relationship, but there was no way to be certain.

Nevertheless, the future for Seamus and Andrea was finally becoming brighter. They were on the verge of becoming parents twice over and Seamus had already proposed, in anticipation of her eventual divorce.

Dominic could never say so publicly, but perhaps the loss of Carole would one day turn out to have been a blessing?

That's what he chose to believe, anyway.

Chapter Twenty-Four

At Stafford's request, the DNA lab had pushed the sample from the unknown woman to the front of the queue, promising to deliver the results within a few hours.

"Missing Persons are still drawing a blank on her identity," Stafford told Girton. "They've exhausted this county, and all adjoining counties, and have now expanded nationwide. We got a dentist in to take impressions so we can confirm any potential matches. Given the educated guesswork of the sketch artist, and the fact that she appears to have lost weight, she might not closely resemble any pictures in the database."

"Sounds sensible," Girton said.

"Any decision yet on whether to release her picture to the press?" Stafford asked.

"The risk assessment is ongoing," Girton said. "Given the attack on her, there are concerns that publishing her picture may expose her to additional danger."

"But surely the attack last night proves she is already in danger?" Stafford said. "We've been showing her picture to the residents close to where the accident occurred, so the cat's out of the bag. If she was being held against her will, they know she's in hospital, hence last night's attempt on her life." She leaned forward. "Come on Gemma, surely the best way we can ensure her safety is to identify her as quickly as possible, and then work out who might want to kill her?"

"You're preaching to the converted," Girton said. "Between you and me, the brass are just covering their arses. If something were to happen to her, then they want everything done by the book for the inquiry."

Stafford slumped back into her chair. "Bloody Standards Department second guessing everything with the benefit of twenty-twenty hindsight," she grumbled.

"Have the house-to-house team caught up with those two households that were out when we called yesterday?" Girton asked. The two women had been friends and colleagues for years, and she knew that if she didn't change the subject, Stafford would spend the next half an hour explaining exactly what she thought was wrong with modern policing. Her forthright, common-sense views – not always expressed tactfully – probably accounted for why she had been looked over for promotion to chief inspector on more than one occasion. Girton's ability to keep her mouth shut when necessary was, in her opinion, the main reason Katie Stafford answered to her, and not the other way around. Which in Girton's view perfectly encapsulated what was wrong with today's service: talent was all-too-often overlooked in favour of politicking.

"Yeah, nothing to report," Stafford said. "We also checked out the employees from the two houses that employ workers. None of them recognised her, and there's no reason to suspect they are lying."

"What about businesses in town?"

"Ongoing," Stafford said. "You know as well as I do how hard it is to get anyone to speak out about any of the businesses we have suspicions about, but none of our intelligence suggests that a woman matching her description has been giving manicures or washing cars in this area. As far as we know, most of the farms around here source their seasonal workers through reputable agencies."

Girton rubbed the bridge of her nose.

"Who is this woman?" she asked again.

***

Seamus hitched a lift with his brother to the cemetery; guilt-free motoring Dominic called it, given that the car was charged off the house solar panels. Along the way, they picked up Andrea. Seamus climbed into the back, so Andrea could stretch her legs in the passenger seat.

Her face was drawn and pale and she looked uncomfortable, clutching the peonies she'd bought the previous day.

"I see from the neighbourhood WhatsApp group that the police have been knocking on doors asking about that woman who was run over," Seamus said in an attempt to break the silence. "They obviously figure we live too far away from the scene of the accident to question. Have they been round yours?"

"Yeah, they knocked on the door Sunday evening," Dominic said.

"What did they ask?" Andrea asked.

"Not a lot," Dominic said. "They mostly seemed to want to know her identity. They showed me an artist's impression and asked if I knew her or had seen her in the local area." He shrugged. "I didn't recognise her and I'm not aware of any of my neighbours having a woman that age staying with them."

"I heard she was dressed in almost nothing," Andrea said, "and she was soaked through. It makes you wonder what on earth she was doing out there on a night like that? And why nobody has reported her missing yet?"

"Probably had an argument with her boyfriend and stormed off," Seamus said.

"Or girlfriend," Dominic countered. "I thought you were open-minded about these things?"

"Knob," Seamus said.

Dominic smiled at the brief moment of levity. Sometimes he wished there was something he could do to make days like this easier on his brother. But he knew there wasn't. What was done was done, and there was no going back and changing it.

Pulling into the cemetery car park, he jumped out of the driver's seat and opened Andrea's door.

"See," she said to her fiancé. "That's how a real gentleman acts."

"I did try to teach him ..." Dominic said.

"Knob," Seamus mumbled again.

Andrea winced as she climbed out.

"You OK?" Dominic asked.

"Fine," she said. "Just the tenants playing up."

Three And A Half Years Ago

Six Months Before the Fire

Chapter Twenty-Five

WITH A SHUDDERING GROAN, Seamus rolled off his wife, and lay back in bed. He slipped his arm around Carole's shoulders and pulled her close. She gave a tired smile and kissed him on the cheek, before turning onto her side, her back to him.

"Sorry, sweetheart. I have a really early Skype call tomorrow with that Aussie design team," she said, reaching over to the turn off her bedside lamp. "Sweet dreams."

"Love you," he managed, concealing the frustration in his voice. He kissed the back of her neck, before getting up and heading to the en suite.

After emptying his bladder, he gave his teeth a quick clean. The toothpaste tube was pretty much empty, so he binned it and retrieved a fresh one from the bathroom cabinet, ready for the morning.

Neatly stacked next to the spare toothpaste boxes were several similarly-sized boxes. He sighed. In a few days' time, Carole would be taking one of those cartons from the shelf, removing the plastic device inside, using it, and then waiting nervously for the result. Then, if the last six months were anything to go by, she would return disappointed to the bedroom. Forced platitudes would be exchanged, and the two would then act like everything was right with the world, until the next month.

It had been a year and a half since the miscarriage. To the outside world, the couple were dealing with their loss in a quiet, dignified way. The way that society expected them to. After all, it wasn't as if they'd lost a real baby, was it?

"At least you never got to know *it*," or "You're young, you've plenty of time to try again," were just some of the things that well-meaning friends had said, unaware of how painful they were.

Amelie wasn't an *it*.

Had things gone to plan, six months ago they'd have celebrated their little girl's first birthday. There would have been cake and balloons. Friends that Carole would have made in her birthing group would have brought their own bundles of joy. Uncle Dominic would probably have showered her with over-priced gifts, whilst her honorary Aunty Andrea would have bounced her on her knee and sung to her. Perhaps Carole's parents would have made the journey from Wyoming. They were retired now, so they could have made a proper holiday of it.

But none of that happened. Instead, they had a different date that they would forever mark. One that would slowly fade from everyone's memories, except for his and Carole's.

The days and weeks after Amelie died had been painful and filled with tears and recrimination. First, Carole had blamed herself. She'd eaten the wrong things. She'd done too much exercise. Or not enough exercise. Her occasional small glass of red wine had been foolish and irresponsible. Her raucous twenty-fifth birthday party, with its attendant two-day hangover – the night Amelia was conceived – had started the pregnancy off on the wrong foot.

And then it had been Seamus' fault. He'd never really wanted a baby anyway. His callous decision to ask Dominic to strip the nursery without consulting her first, had proven that. He'd exuded negative vibes all the way through the pregnancy until he got what he wanted.

It was when she'd openly started suggesting that he'd been slipping black-market abortion pills into her food that he and Andrea had managed to persuade her to visit her GP. She'd quickly been diagnosed with the early signs of a rare form of post-partum depression and referred to a specialist before it developed into a full-blown psychosis.

Now, almost eighteen months later, Carole had stopped taking her antidepressants, and they'd been trying for a baby again.

But things weren't the same. Their lovemaking had become, if not a duty, then at least an appointment not to be missed. The spontaneity had left. Their first pregnancy hadn't been unplanned as such, rather it had been left open to chance. They were young, and wanted a family, but were in no rush. That positive test when it came had been a joyous surprise.

But now things were different.

For his part, Seamus was scared of what would happen if Carole became pregnant again; he'd read up on post-partum depression, and he knew that a dose of baby blues, or worse, was more likely in women who had suffered a previous episode. Yet equally, he was frightened about what would happen if Carole *didn't* become pregnant. Would the repeated disappointments tip her over into a different kind of depression?

Then

Four Days After The Fire

Chapter Twenty-Six

Dominic picked Seamus up from the police station after he had been given bail. Oldroyd had tried to get him Released Under Investigation, with its far less rigorous stipulations, but Freeland had stood firm. Seamus would need to return to the station the next morning with his passport, and would be expected to return twice each week to sign in. It gave the team a further twenty-eight days before they would have to decide whether to charge him or de-arrest him with no further action.

Dominic took Seamus' release as a positive sign that the police were starting to realise that any evidence pointing towards his brother was just coincidence. Furthermore, a conference between Oldroyd and Parker where they compared notes from the various interviews they had attended had concluded that the police's attention was shifting focus towards Marcus.

The journey back to Seamus and Carole's house was tense; the two brothers barely saying a word to one another.

"We need to talk," Dominic said firmly, once they pulled into the drive.

Seamus said nothing, just unfastened his seat belt.

"Please," Dominic said.

Eventually, Seamus gave a curt nod and Dominic followed him into the house.

The CSIs had finished their search that evening. The kitchen curtains were open again, and Dominic pulled them closed, blocking the view of the blackened carcass of the shed where Carole had died, just four days before.

"I'm so sorry," Dominic said. "I should have told you about Carole's problems."

"Yes, you should have," Seamus said. His jaw was clenched, and he forced the words out.

"She begged me not to," Dominic said. "She was ashamed."

"She was my wife," Seamus managed. "I had a right to know." He filled the kettle with water, his back to his brother, turning the tap to full so water sprayed everywhere. He swore and started mopping up the mess with a tea towel, his violent strokes making things worse.

"I know," Dominic said. "I told her you would want to help her, but she was in denial, I just wanted her to start the treatment programme. I figured that once she was in a better place mentally, I could persuade her to speak to you."

Seamus retrieved a jar of coffee from the cupboard, slamming its door shut harder than necessary. He took two mugs off the draining board, his back still towards Dominic. His brother had cleaned the house after the search teams had left, but Seamus refused to acknowledge the unsolicited kindness.

"We argued the morning I left for Manchester," Seamus said eventually, his voice catching. "We had another negative pregnancy test. I knew she was back on her pill but wasn't ready to confront her about it."

"Shit," Dominic said. "I had no idea. She never said anything ..."

"She phoned me that evening, but I let it go to voicemail," Seamus said. "She hung up before the beep. I'll never know what she was going to say to me."

He started to cry, his body shaking as he sobbed silently. Dominic moved around the island in the middle of the kitchen and placed his arm awkwardly around his younger brother's shoulders. Seamus turned toward him, and Dominic enveloped him in a big hug.

It was as if they had been transported back in time over twenty years to that dreadful night. The night that their grandparents had broken the news that nothing would ever be the same again. Seamus had been so young, he hadn't quite understood what it all meant at first. The death of their beloved rabbit a few weeks earlier had been his introduction to the impermanence of life. But this time there would be no trip to the pet shop to find a replacement. And the comforting cuddles from his parents that had helped him cope with that loss had been replaced by the stilted hugs of his grieving grandparents.

It had been Dominic's warm embrace that provided the security he needed that night, and every other night for the next six months. The day after their parents' death, they had moved to their grandparents' cold, austere farmhouse. They had never slept in their old beds again. An uncle had donated a bunk bed for the small bedroom that had become their new home. Little Seamus had slept on the bottom, Dominic on the top. That first night, when their grandmother had switched the light off, and Seamus had started quietly sobbing, Dominic had clambered down and into his bed. Holding him tight, repressing his own tears, he'd stayed until the sun started to force its way through the thin curtains and Seamus finally drifted off; then he'd returned to the top bunk.

He'd done that every night for months, until Seamus could finally sleep through the night without help. Their grandparents never knew.

Now, two decades later, it was Dominic that Seamus turned to once again.

***

"I'm going to fucking kill him," Seamus said. His voice was slurred. After the past few days, Dominic had decided they needed something stronger than coffee. Between them, they had polished off half a bottle of Irish whiskey. Seamus had barely eaten all day, and it had hit him hard.

"No, let me deal with Pete," Dominic insisted. "You're in enough trouble as it is. Besides, you don't want to be in work; you know what it'll be like. Everyone will be awkward and tiptoeing around you, not sure what to say. They must know about your arrest and Marcus' disappearance by now. And the police have interviewed everyone; if they haven't figured out what was going on between you and Andy yet, it's only a matter of time."

Even through his drunken haze, Seamus could see that he was right. "Don't let the slippery little bastard give you any bullshit," he said. "Then drag him down the police station. He got her hooked on that shit. *He* killed her," he said, stabbing the air for emphasis. "Just as surely as if he stuck the needle in her himself."

"No argument from me, Bro'," Dominic said. He drained his tumbler.

Despite his angry words, Seamus' eyes were starting to droop, the last few days catching up with him. For the past two hours, the men had sat opposite one another across the coffee table.

"Why didn't you speak to me?" Dominic asked. "Why didn't you tell me how you and Carole were struggling? Or how close you and Andy had become? I could have helped. You know, arranged marriage counselling. Or if that didn't work, a bloody good divorce lawyer. You know I would have."

"But that's the problem, don't you see?" Seamus said. "I'm not eight-years-old anymore. I'm a grown, fucking adult. I shouldn't have to go running to my big brother every time life gets hard. I'm not your problem anymore."

"How can you say that?" Dominic asked. "You're my brother. You'll always be my problem," his voice grew quiet, "because you're all I have."

Seamus looked at him anew. "What do you mean?"

Dominic drained his glass, then slopped in another generous measure as he searched for the words.

"When we lost Mum and Dad, I was suddenly more than a big brother. Everyone always said how brave I was, stepping up like that. But the truth is, when I was worrying about you, I wasn't worrying about myself. By focusing on helping you cope, I could pretend that I was OK. Displacement is what my therapist calls it."

"You have a therapist?" Seamus said.

"I've had at least five," Dominic admitted. "I've been seeing them for about ten years."

"Why didn't you tell me?" Seamus asked.

Dominic smiled bleakly. "For all the reasons I've just given." He chuckled bitterly. "Despite their best efforts – and many thousands of pounds – they still haven't managed to persuade me to stop focusing on you and sort myself out."

"I had no idea ..." Seamus said. "Jesus, I am such a self-absorbed prick. There I am wallowing in grief, or doing fucking stupid things, and it never even occurred to me that you were hurting just as much as I was." He looked at Dominic across the table. "I am so sorry. All these years I've been letting you down ..."

"No!" Dominic said. "You've never let me down. Don't you ever think that. You're the best brother – the best friend – I could ever have asked for." He smiled weakly. "Even though I'd still prefer a sister."

"You're a knob, you know that?" Seamus said, his eyes filling with tears again.

"So you keep on telling me," Dominic said.

The two men lapsed into silence, both of them staring into their drinks. The ornate clock that had once belonged to their great-grandmother chimed.

Two a.m.

Dominic was in no state to drive home. He could phone for an Uber, but he didn't want to leave Seamus alone. It was too late to call Andrea; besides which, she was still waiting for Marcus to return, although Dominic knew he wouldn't. And it looked as though the police had also made their mind up about that.

"You go to bed, I'll crash on the sofa," he said. "You're running on empty." He stifled a yawn.

Seamus matched him a few seconds later.

"Yeah, you're right." He struggled to his feet, then paused. "Thanks, Dom. For everything. I know you did your best."

"It wasn't enough," Dominic admitted. "I should have handled things differently."

"It wasn't your fault," Seamus said. Dominic joined him and they embraced again.

"We'll get through this," Dominic whispered in his ear.

Unable to say anything else, Seamus lurched towards the stairs.

Halfway up, he turned, and watched Dominic rearranging the cushions on the sofa.

Twenty years ago, Dominic had shared his bed, and hugged him until he went to sleep. He'd grown beyond that need, but somehow just knowing his big brother would be downstairs was comfort enough.

Chapter Twenty-Seven

SEAMUS HAD BEEN SOUND asleep when Dominic roused himself from the sofa. Forcing a black coffee down his throat, he'd helped himself to two paracetamols from the bathroom cabinet, before showering and driving into the office.

Pete Ludlow was an early starter, but Dominic was waiting for him when he arrived.

"Hey, Boss. How's Seamus?" Ludlow asked, as he chained his bicycle up.

"Bearing up," Dominic said. "Can I have a word?"

"Sure," Ludlow said, following him into the conference room. Dominic pressed the privacy button, and the integrated venetian blinds closed, shielding them from the rest of the office.

"Woah, what's the problem, Dom?" Ludlow asked, as Dominic turned on him, pushing him into the wall.

"What the fuck were you supplying Carole with?" Dominic hissed.

"Nothing, man," Ludlow stammered. He was taller than Dominic by three inches, with the build of a triathlete, but at this moment he wouldn't have rated his chances against his boss. Dominic's suit was rumpled, his eyes red-rimmed and he stank of stale whiskey. Anger radiated off him.

"Bullshit," Dominic snapped. "Carole was addicted to heroin. Now where is a nice, middle-class woman, living outside a leafy little town like this, going to get shit like that? She wouldn't have a fucking clue where to even look."

"Not me man, I swear," Ludlow said. "You know me better than that. I have a couple of mates who can score some weed and a bit of coke for a party, but heroin? Fuck that, they'd never touch that shit in a million years."

"You expect me to believe that?"

"Yes! For crying out loud, who do you think I am?" Ludlow's tone of voice had turned from surprised to indignant. "I haven't supplied Carole with anything for months. Seamus told me not to."

Dominic eased the pressure on Ludlow's chest.

"When was the last time you gave her anything?" he asked, his voice still suspicious.

"The night of your birthday party," Ludlow said. "I sold her some weed and a couple of lines of coke. But after she embarrassed herself, Seamus told me not to sell her anything else, even if she asked."

"And did she ask?"

Ludlow licked his lips. "Once or twice. She rang me a couple of times, asked if I could score her a bit of coke. I told her my mate wasn't selling anymore, and eventually she stopped asking."

Dominic searched his face for the truth.

"Did she ever ask you for heroin, or anything else?"

Ludlow shook his head. "No. Just the coke, and a bit of weed. Again, I told her that I couldn't get it anymore. I'm not sure she completely believed me, but like I said, she stopped asking."

"Did you point her towards anyone else?"

Ludlow shook his head vehemently. "No. Look, Seamus is a mate, not to mention my boss. I'm not a dealer; I just know someone who can get hold of something if we're having a party. It's just a bit of fun, you know? It was obvious Seamus was a bit worried, and from what I heard about the way she was behaving, maybe he was right to be. I never made any money out of it; I just rang my friend now and again to see what he could get hold of. He's not even a proper dealer, he just has a dodgy neighbour."

His voice became more earnest. "Seriously, you've got to believe me. The last thing I'd want is for it to become a problem for someone. Christ, Dom! Heroin? Carole? Are you sure? Do they think that's why she killed herself?"

Dominic ignored the questions. "This doesn't go any further," he warned. "If I hear even a whisper you've been shooting your mouth off, you're gone. I mean it. And you can forget about a reference."

Ludlow raised his hands. "I hear you, mate. I hear you. Not a word, I promise."

Dominic searched his face for a few more seconds, before stepping back, and giving a curt nod.

Ludlow took his cue and scuttled out of the room without so much as a backward glance.

Two Months Before The Fire

Chapter Twenty-Eight

CAROLE'S HEAD POUNDED; IT felt like someone was driving knitting needles into her eyes. Clutching her stomach, she leapt out of bed, staggering to the en suite, where she deposited the contents of her stomach in the toilet.

She swilled her mouth out with tap water, trying to erase the taste of tequila and bile. She looked in the mirror, then averted her gaze. Her eyes were bloodshot, and she'd been too far gone the previous night to remove her makeup; it was now smeared across her face and the pillow.

Refilling the tumbler with water, she swallowed two paracetamols then returned on wobbly legs to the bed. It was eleven a.m. and Seamus was long gone, his side of the bed cold.

Flashes of the previous night returned; disjointed images and half-formed memories of music and laughter, turning to arguments and shouting. A feeling of shame washed over her.

It had been Marcus' and Andrea's wedding anniversary. The plan had been to have a meal and a few drinks at the Italian restaurant down the valley. But it was a Sunday, and when Francesco called time, none of them were quite ready to call it a night. It hadn't taken much persuasion for everyone to return to hers and Seamus' for a nightcap.

Dominic was with them, mourning the end of yet another short-lived romance, so everyone had happily followed the boss's lead when he fished out the bottle of genuine Mexican tequila he'd gifted Seamus and Carole after his summer holiday.

After an initial round of slammers, Pete Ludlow had produced some weed and they'd passed the joint amongst themselves, becoming progressively more mellow.

As always, it was the coke that caused the problems. After a third round of slammers, Marcus had raised an eyebrow in Carole and Pete's direction, and making her excuses, she'd slipped away and joined them in the bathroom. It was better than the crap Pete usually sourced, and when they returned to the living room, they were all buzzing hard.

Seamus immediately cornered her in the kitchen. Carole could remember little of what was said, but when they returned to the living room, they'd retreated to opposite ends of the room in moody silence.

She'd thought Seamus was going to have it out with Pete there and then, but she convinced him that it was all Marcus' idea and he left it.

Lying back on the bed, Carole closed her eyes, the sunlight working its way through the gap between the curtains piercing her skull.

More of the evening was coming back. The tequila had been followed by vodka, and she'd half-listened whilst Marcus, Pete and Dominic argued over which superhero franchise had transitioned to the big screen more successfully, Marvel or DC? Marcus was firmly in the DC camp, preferring the dark, grounded reality of Batman. Dominic advocated the more light-hearted fare produced by Marvel. Pete flip-flopped between the two. Carole could never remember if Superman was Marvel or DC, so kept her own counsel.

Seamus and Andrea were scrolling through Spotify on Seamus' phone; Carole's eyes narrowed, as she noticed his arm draped casually across her shoulders. Marcus shot occasional glances in their direction.

By now, the combination of booze, weed and coke was making her feel hot and jittery, and she could feel her face burning. She needed fresh air. Without saying a word, she headed for the kitchen, opening the French doors, then stepping outside. They were still enjoying summer, and the night was cool but pleasant.

She was still angry with Seamus. He was her husband, not her keeper. She was an adult, and if she wanted to blow off a little steam that was her business. What right did he have to judge her?

Bright light spilled from the kitchen windows, so she walked further down the garden, to the shadowy area behind the shed. This was one of the things she loved most about their house. Shielded from the light pollution from the town below, on a clear night the Milky Way was absolutely glorious. It reminded her of the open skies of Wyoming, and she felt a pang of longing. How long had it been since she'd last been back?

As a little girl she had been able to name all of the major constellations, but time and the night's revelry had robbed her of that ability.

No matter. Just the sight of them relaxed her.

The minutes ticked by, and she drank in the peace and quiet.

Eventually there came the quiet scrape of a shoe on the path, and she felt a flash of irritation. Was ten minutes to herself too much to ask? Couldn't Seamus just leave her alone?

"I thought I might find you out here," a voice said quietly.

A hand slipped around her waist.

It wasn't Seamus.

***

Carole scrubbed herself vigorously in the shower, the water almost too hot to bear. Tears of shame coursed down her cheeks. What had happened the night before?

Her memory was still fragmented; parts of the night were clear, but others were muddled or missing. She remembered the warm breath on her neck, the hands sliding under the waistband of her jeans, the fingers probing. She could recall the hard press of his erection and then the feeling of him inside her.

She remembered how she had been angry with Seamus. His preaching about her cocaine use, followed by his arm resting comfortably across Andrea's shoulders. Perfect Andrea. Sensible Andrea, who knew her limits and never crossed that blurry line between party girl and angry drunk. Beautiful Andrea, who was pretty and slim despite never having set foot inside a gym. Blessed Andrea, who could eat whatever she wanted without ever gaining an ounce. Had she ever even had a zit?

Yes, she'd been angry with Seamus, but was she angry enough to have wanted to get her own back? She'd been drunk, stoned and high. How capable had she been of making rational decisions? She wasn't bruised. She knew she hadn't been forced. But had she actually agreed? Or had she been taken advantage of?

She just couldn't remember.

Twenty-four hours ago, she'd have taken the position that if she couldn't remember whether she had actually consented to sex or not, then clearly, she hadn't been in a fit state to give that consent. It was an argument she had put forth vigorously in numerous social media debates.

But now, in the cold light of day, she felt her resolve wobble. Because she did find him attractive. She had fantasised about him repeatedly. There had even been moments when something could have happened.

Had she, in that moment, given into that attraction? Had she been angry enough with Seamus that she had decided to punish him by giving herself to someone else?

Where was the line between her succumbing to a moment of weakness and having her vulnerability exploited?

Had she been raped last night? She truly didn't know.

Now

Three Days After The Storm

Chapter Twenty-Nine

THE DNA LAB PHONED Katie Stafford shortly after lunch.

"We can't give you a name, I'm afraid," the technician said.

"Damn," Stafford said. It wasn't a big surprise; the accident victim's fingerprints were not in the system either. If she had been arrested previously, then both a DNA swab and prints would have been taken, so it was unlikely one would be on there and not the other.

"However, the DNA does come back to a match on a previous case."

That was something. It might mean they could work back from that incident and identify her that way.

Stafford took the case number and hung up.

Entering the reference into the database, she found a single record.

"That's interesting," she said to herself. She remembered the case, although she hadn't been involved in the investigation.

Making a note of the officer in charge, she picked up the phone and dialled the central number for CID.

***

The tyres on Seamus' Toyota squealed as he rounded a bend in the road, and he forced himself to slow down. Beside him, Andrea let out a gasp of pain. He reached over and squeezed her hand.

"Not far now, sweetheart," he said, his voice tight.

The phone call had come at two p.m. Andrea had sounded almost matter of fact as she told him she had found blood spots when she went to the toilet. He'd told her to call an ambulance, but the dispatcher said the waiting time could be over an hour, and that she'd be better off making her own way to hospital if she was able. Seamus had broken records as he drove home.

The cramps had started the previous day, but she'd said nothing. There was still a month to go, and they weren't how she imagined contractions would feel, so she'd dismissed them as an aftereffect of the eye-watering curry she'd had when Dominic had visited.

Seamus was already stressed enough as it was with the upcoming pitch he was preparing for the Scottish investors, so she'd taken some antacids, made some of the herbal tea a woman in her NCT class swore by, and gone to bed early, leaving Seamus in the office.

Again, Seamus was gone by the time she awoke. The cramps were still there, but she convinced herself that was all they were. She'd felt a few twinges at the cemetery but had ignored them.

The visit to Carole's memorial stone had been brief, with Dominic and Seamus laying the flowers, whilst she directed proceedings. She'd never make it back up again if she bent down herself. They'd dropped her home on their way back to the office. They'd raise a proper toast to Carole that evening.

It was just after lunch when she'd found the blood spots.

"It's probably nothing," she said for the third time, as Seamus joined the main road towards the hospital. "There were just a couple of dots really."

Seamus said nothing; his eyes were fixed on the road, but in his mind he was screaming. *Please, not again.*

You always assumed that when a woman lost her baby, something had gone wrong with the pregnancy. Carole's problems appeared to have started *after* the loss of Amelie, but perhaps she had already been dabbling with drugs?

No! He would not blame her for the loss. It was far more likely to have been caused by a cruel twist of fate. Even at the stage they had reached, a small but heart-breaking percentage of pregnancies didn't quite make it.

Andrea had been doing everything right so far. They'd started planning months before she even came off her pill; a whole shelf of the bookcase had been given over to healthy pregnancy guides. Now, eight months in, he'd finally dared hope that everything would be OK. He'd even started decorating the back bedroom as a nursery, painting the walls a neutral colour, and applying transfers of Disney characters that Andrea had bought online to the ceiling.

Which left the possibility that the problem actually lay with Seamus. It took two sets of genes to make a baby, and he was the common denominator. What if there was something wrong with his side of the family? Losing his parents at such a young age meant he'd never had a chance to speak to his mother about her own experiences. His grandparents didn't discuss those sorts of things willingly, and neither he nor Dominic had ever thought to ask. His mother's parents were also no longer with them. For all he knew, his family history could be filled with sad tales of lost babies.

Another gasp from Andrea jerked him out of his thoughts.

"Two minutes," he promised her. They'd just passed the sign for the hospital. The speed limit was thirty, and he was pushing fifty, but at this point in time, the last thing he cared about was a fine and points on his licence. Besides which, he was sure Oldroyd and Parker, whose services Dominic retained at great cost, could get any conviction overturned.

Ignoring the already-full drop-off bays outside the maternity ward, Seamus headed for the multi-storey. Snatching the ticket from the machine, he almost scraped the roof of the car as he drove under the slowly rising barrier. This time of day there would be no spaces on the bottom four floors, so he headed straight for the roof, the concrete structure echoing with the squeak of his tyres.

"Can you walk?" he asked Andrea, when he helped her from the car.

She nodded but said nothing, clutching his arm for support, as they waddled slowly towards the bank of elevators.

The eventual ding that signalled the arrival of the lift was accompanied by a groan from Andrea and his own stifled yelp as she dug her fingernails into his hand.

Finally, they arrived at the reception desk in the maternity ward and Seamus felt the tension ease slightly. A month early, especially for twins, wasn't a disaster these days. Now they were at the hospital he could breathe easier.

Fortunately, the ward was expecting them, and a nurse appeared as soon as Andrea gave her name, whisking her off to see her midwife and an obstetrician.

Within a few minutes, Andrea was settled, and Seamus briefly excused himself. He had two missed calls and a text from Dominic asking how they were.

Seamus returned the call, and Dominic answered immediately. Seamus could hear the sound of traffic in the background. Aware he was babbling, but unable to help himself, he filled his brother in on what was happening.

"Hang tight, Bro', I'll be there in a few minutes," Dominic said.

With a shuddering sigh, Seamus hung up.

Dominic was on his way and Andrea was being treated in the best hospital in the area. For the first time in an hour, Seamus felt the pressure in his chest ease.

Chapter Thirty

"DS Obigwe, I have a message for you," the civilian support officer said.

It had been just four weeks since the promotion, and Obigwe still felt a slight thrill every time she was addressed as sergeant. It was silly she knew, but there were precious few places on the fast-track scheme, and securing one would have been beyond her wildest dreams the first time she'd strapped on her stab-proof vest and gone out on patrol as a newly-minted constable.

"Thank you, Alison," she said, taking the telephone number. She recognised the name, although she'd never worked with them before.

"Stafford," came the brisk reply.

"DS Obigwe, Murder Investigation Team. Sorry I missed your call, I was in a briefing. What can I do for you, ma'am?"

"Are you free for a chat? We're trying to identify the woman run over on Valley View Road Friday night. We've run her DNA through the system, and it's come back as a hit on a case you dealt with three years ago. Do you remember the Carole Monaghan suspected suicide?"

***

Obigwe had never been to the Sexual Exploitation Unit before, although she knew who Katie Stafford was from briefings.

The room on the third floor was a smaller version of the CID office where the Murder Investigation Team were based, even down to the irritating rattle of the air conditioning unit.

The table in the meeting room had been covered in printouts, and both women had their laptops open.

"It says that DS Freeland was the lead investigator, but I know he retired a couple of years back, I was at his leaving do," Stafford said.

"That's right," Obigwe said. Stafford was a white woman in her late-thirties, with a short blonde bob. She had something of a reputation for plain-speaking, and had immediately insisted that Obigwe call her Katie. Obigwe liked her already.

"Patrick was my mentor," Obigwe grimaced slightly. "I always felt bad that this was one of his last cases. Neither of us were satisfied with the open verdict at the inquest; we felt we'd let the family down."

Stafford smiled sympathetically. "I've had more than my fair share of those types of cases. The victims we deal with are often so traumatised they refuse to cooperate in any prosecution, so the people exploiting them are free to walk away and continue abusing other vulnerable people. You feel you've failed everyone."

She pushed a printout of the case file across the table. "Our mystery woman's DNA is a match for an unknown sample found at the Monaghan scene."

"We found a couple of joints in an ashtray," Obigwe said. "They were too crushed to give us any fingerprints, but the techs retrieved female DNA from the saliva on them. It didn't match Carole, and her husband, Seamus, was adamant they weren't in the ashtray before he left on his business trip. We believe she had a female visitor sometime between him leaving and the night of the fire. We assumed her best friend Andrea had come over, before she joined Seamus in Manchester. The two of them were having an affair," she added. "Unfortunately, she lawyered up and as we never had reasonable grounds to arrest her, we were unable to persuade her to give us a DNA sample, or obtain permission to source one clandestinely."

"Could this be Andrea?" Stafford asked, pointing to the artist's impression of their unknown woman, and the rather more graphic photograph of her badly swollen and battered face taken in the hospital.

Obigwe shook her head. "No, Andrea has darker hair and skin than this woman, and the nose is all wrong. It's been a few years, but I'm confident that's not her."

Stafford sighed. "That would have been too easy."

She tapped the pictures again. "I don't suppose there's any chance you recognise her?"

Obigwe studied the two pictures again. "No, sorry. Maybe if I saw the woman in the flesh without all the swelling and the bruising, I might recognise her from some of the women we interviewed, but I'll be honest, she isn't ringing any bells."

"Do you know if Seamus Monaghan still lives locally?" Stafford asked. "I'd like to see if he recognises the woman. If she was visiting his wife when he was away, then maybe he knows her."

"I don't know. We eventually released him with no further action, since he had an alibi for the night she died. Besides which, the autopsy on Carole was inconclusive; we could never be certain she was unlawfully killed. Not to mention the shed was locked from the inside. There was too much damage to determine if anyone entered or exited through the window. Then the disappearance of Andrea Harrington's husband shortly after the death meant that even if Carole was murdered, Seamus was no longer our primary person of interest."

Obigwe brightened. "I'll tell you something though, if we can identify your unknown woman, I'd love to interview her. There's a list of questions that were never answered she could help us with.

We never did figure out where Carole was getting her heroin from. Perhaps this woman was her dealer?"

"I wouldn't get your hopes up," Stafford cautioned. "It's far from guaranteed that she will ever be in a fit state for you to interview her." She then filled Obigwe in on the previous night's attack, which whilst announced to the press, had not yet been linked to their victim.

"Bloody hell. What was she involved in?" Obigwe asked.

"That's what we've been asking ourselves," Stafford said.

"And how did she know Carole Monaghan?"

Then

Three Days Before The Fire

Chapter Thirty-One

"Come on Carole, the taxi to the station arrives in five minutes."

Seamus was impatient, and she felt a flash of guilt. It was his twenty-seventh birthday, but they'd already argued that morning. It was always the same. Today was marked on the calendar, and the nervous anticipation every twenty-eight days had long given way to resignation and resentment.

She looked at the window on the pregnancy test. Negative. As she'd known it would be. She'd already taken her pill, retrieving the strip of tablets from where they were concealed at the bottom of a toilet bag filled with lotions and beauty treatments that Seamus had no interest in.

Like most men, he had no clue about just how much effort went into her daily routine. Head & Shoulders 2-in-1 and supermarket shower gel was pretty much all he kept in the shower caddy, with a can of deodorant, a toothbrush and some aftershave for special occasions in the medicine cabinet. He'd even switched to an electric razor. He had no idea what most of the tubes and pots contained, and had no interest in finding out.

Six months after the death of Amelie, Seamus had started dropping hints about trying again. The terrifying episode of post-partum psychosis she'd experienced was behind her, and with her GP's support she'd stopped taking the anti-depressants.

Yet she couldn't just move on. She'd been shocked at the feeling of relief that she'd felt when they had their first negative pregnancy test. Seamus had mistaken her reaction for disappointment and made a huge fuss of her.

The same thing had happened the following month. Seamus had hidden his disappointment well, but she had again felt relief.

By the time the third test was due, she found herself praying that it too would be negative.

It wasn't that she didn't want a baby — quite the opposite — but she was scared. And she wasn't alone, she soon found out. There were numerous forums on the internet that were home to people like her. Women who were still scarred and traumatised by the loss of a pregnancy, a horrendous labour, or crippling post-partum depression.

She took hope from the stories of survivors; women who had eventually overcome the fear and were now proud parents. She knew she should tell Seamus how she felt, but she couldn't bring herself to. They were, she realised, a product of their upbringings. Seamus had been raised by his grandparents, traditionalists who struggled to communicate their feelings. She had been brought up in a conservative community, where one just didn't speak about such things. For some reason she couldn't articulate, she couldn't bring herself to burden Andrea with her worries.

At the urging of members of the support forum, she'd spoken to the nurse at her local clinic about counselling, but the NHS waiting list in their area was many months. She could have gone private, but Seamus managed the household accounts. He'd have immediately noticed any payments to a clinic.

So, she'd joined the waiting list, and in the meantime had gone back on the pill to buy herself some time.

At first, she'd hated the deception. But that soon passed, replaced by a feeling of empowerment. Amelie had been a joyous surprise; they'd not used contraception in months, but otherwise hadn't really been trying. The first trimester had been plagued by morning sickness but had been exciting. But as the pregnancy wore on, and her body continued to change, she'd started feeling a sense of powerlessness. It was as if she was sitting behind the wheel of a vehicle whose controls were being manipulated by somebody else. And when the miscarriage happened, she'd felt like a passenger trapped aboard a crashing plane. For the first time in her adult life, she was no longer part of the decision-making processes concerning her own body. The calm professionalism of the medical staff dealing with her should have been reassuring, but instead she'd felt helpless.

She remembered little of the days and weeks following the miscarriage. She knew from what she'd been told afterwards that she had spiralled quickly into depression and started showing signs of psychosis. She knew her mother had suffered from the 'baby blues' after she and her sister Kitty had been born, but it hadn't occurred to her or Seamus that she may experience them after losing Amelie. Why would she? After all, she hadn't actually given birth.

The thought of being so completely out of control again scared her; the little pill she took each day to ward off pregnancy felt like she was finally in charge again.

And she liked that feeling.

Outside, she heard a car horn, followed by Seamus swearing.

"The taxi's here," he shouted, unnecessarily.

Taking a deep breath, Carole flushed the loo and emerged from the bathroom. Seamus had his coat on. He was carrying his overnight bag in one hand, with a suit carrier draped awkwardly over his other shoulder. Seeing him standing there, she was reminded again of the doubts she had about the trip to Manchester. He'd originally been due to visit Glasgow to pitch for the contract to install a new security system at the main hospital. But he'd switched at the last minute with Marcus, opting instead to go to the annual trade conference in Manchester. He'd said it was so he could be back sooner to celebrate his birthday with her, but he'd avoided her gaze. She'd accompanied him to the conference one year and been impressed by the opulent hotel. It hadn't escaped her notice that the timings now meant Marcus would be away in Glasgow whilst Seamus had an extra night in Manchester to conduct additional meetings. She wondered what she might find if she dropped in on Andrea unannounced for a coffee ...

She pushed the thought away; she was just projecting her own feelings of guilt onto him, she decided. Weeks after the incident behind the garden shed, she still couldn't remember exactly what had happened. She still couldn't be certain she hadn't had sex willingly. Since that night, she'd tried to limit contact with her ... assailant? She'd left WhatsApp messages from them unanswered, and rebuffed offers to go for a drink; whatever the truth of what had taken place, she was determined it wouldn't happen again.

"Sorry, it took a little while for me to pee," she lied. She rearranged her features appropriately. "Negative again."

Seamus' face was blank as he absorbed the information. She crossed the room and pecked him on the cheek.

"Let's hope for better luck next month," he said, his tone dull.

"Have a good trip," Carole said, as he turned and left the room. "I'll phone tonight," she added.

Seamus nodded but said nothing.

After he had left, Carole collapsed onto the bed. It was the first time he'd reacted like this to the news. It was almost as if he'd been expecting it. She felt a shiver pass through her.

He couldn't know, could he?

Now

Four Days After The Storm

Chapter Thirty-Two

NOTHING TO WORRY ABOUT. That was the assessment of the obstetrician who'd discharged Andrea that morning.

Seamus had spent an uncomfortable night on a plastic hospital chair whilst Andrea was given the full works. Carrying twins was hard work, especially for a woman with Andrea's slight build. The ultrasound had picked up two heartbeats and no evidence that the babies were in any distress.

The cramps Andrea had been experiencing were probably Braxton Hicks contractions, possibly from dehydration. She admitted that she'd been urinating more frequently than usual and might have been subconsciously drinking less to compensate. They'd hooked her up to a drip to rehydrate her and kept her in overnight for observation.

"I'm cancelling the Scotland trip," Seamus announced as he led Andrea to the car; Dominic had rejoined them that morning and he hovered worriedly.

"That's probably a good idea," Dominic said. "I'll call them and explain. We can reschedule the meeting; I'm sure they'll understand. And if push comes to shove, I can pick up the ball and run with it."

"That would be great," said Seamus as he helped Andrea into the car. "The pitch is ready. The consultant said Andy needs to take it easy for the next couple of days, by which time we'll be coming close to the due date anyway."

"Excuse me, I *am* still here," Andrea said. "Perhaps I could take part in this discussion?"

Seamus blushed. "Sorry sweetheart."

"Yeah, sorry, Andy," Dominic said. "I didn't mean to talk over you."

Andrea turned in her seat and pointed at Seamus. "You have been trying to land this deal for a year." She switched her focus to Dominic. "And you haven't even met them. The consultant said I needed to take it easy, and make sure I drink plenty of fluids. The babies are doing fine. *I* am doing fine."

"But what if something happens when I am away?" Seamus asked.

"You're going for forty-eight hours," Andrea said. "And there are regular flights back. It's the twenty-first century; I have a mobile phone and I can drive."

"But what if you are too ill to drive?" Seamus protested. "There's no way you could have got yourself here yesterday."

"Then there are ambulances and failing that, taxis. I can even call one of the neighbours."

"I'll keep my phone on in meetings, just in case," Dominic said.

Seamus glared at him. "I don't want Andy to be alone in the house," he said firmly.

Andrea turned to Dominic with a smile. "In that case, perhaps the uncle-to-be could offer his spare bedroom?"

"Um, I'm not really sure ..." Dominic stammered.

"What are you afraid of?" Andrea asked. "I thought you said you'd watched how to deliver babies on YouTube? I seem to recall you saying that it doesn't look that difficult."

"Give me some time to get the spare room ready," Dominic muttered.

Seamus gave a sigh. He knew when he'd lost the battle.

"Brilliant," Andrea said. "I could really do with soaking my ankles in your hot tub."

***

"Seamus Monaghan still lives in the house he shared with his wife three years ago, now with Andrea Harrington," Obigwe said. She was drinking coffee in DCI Girton's office. Stafford was with her.

"That's cosy – and a bit weird," Girton said. "Imagine living in the house your best friend – who was also the late wife of the man you were cheating with – died in."

"I can't say I'd want to," Obigwe admitted. "Mind you, they might not have much choice. Andrea's husband, Marcus, did a bunk with all their savings. If their house was jointly owned, she might not have been able to sell it, so she'd be stuck with the mortgage payments."

"Oof. Good job Carole had life insurance, eh?" Girton said.

"So, what happened when you tried to visit Seamus?" she asked Stafford.

"No luck. We figured it might spook him if we started asking about Carole after all these years, so Mercy sat this one out and I took a colleague with me on the pretext of widening our house-to-house inquiries about the road accident. They live at the far end of Valley View Road, so our story would have sounded plausible. But there was no one at home, and his car was gone. We tried again this morning; same result."

"That's interesting," said Girton. "Do we know when they were last seen?"

"The neighbours are too far away to see regular comings and goings," Stafford said. "However, the owner of the closest house reckons both their cars were there a couple of days ago when she walked past with her dog. She can't be certain exactly which day."

"I'd say we definitely need to speak to him," Girton said. "Presumably we still have his mobile phone number on file from the investigation three years ago? Why don't you give him a call and invite him to chat to us? Get him to look at that sketch of her and gauge his reaction. We should also speak to Andrea, given that she was her best friend.

"Mercy, I want you to continue staying in the background for the time being, but get ready to reopen the Carole Monaghan investigation if either of them recognises the woman, or if Katie gets a strange vibe."

Dismissed, the two women left the DCI's office and headed to Obigwe's desk.

"I recognise that look," Stafford said.

"What look?" Obigwe asked.

"That you're finally getting to scratch a long-standing itch."

Obigwe smiled. "Is it that obvious?"

***

"Bugger, number not in service," Stafford said. She cradled the phone.

"So, Seamus Monaghan has not been seen recently, and his phone number is no longer in use," Obigwe said.

"Could be something, could be nothing," Stafford warned, although a frown creased her forehead.

"Try Andrea's number," Obigwe suggested.

Stafford dialled again. After a few seconds, she hung up. "Also out of service."

"Maybe he's at work?" Obigwe suggested. She checked the file. "Monaghan Security Solutions. Three years ago he was vice-president, alongside his brother, Dominic."

Stafford raised an eyebrow. "We know Dominic is still around, he was on the list of homeowners that my team already visited.

Monaghan is such a common name, I didn't make the connection."

"Now I think about it, I remember that the two brothers lived at opposite ends of Valley View Road; a good few miles apart though," Obigwe said.

Stafford checked her own notes. "Yes, Seamus lives at the expensive end of the road, and Dominic lives at the *really* expensive end."

"Well, he is the boss," Obigwe pointed out, as she opened the MSS website. "Here we are, Dominic Monaghan, CEO and founder. Seamus Monaghan, vice-president and Chief Financial Officer. It looks as though he inherited Marcus Harrington's job title, along with his wife. So perhaps Marcus wasn't just a paranoid coke fiend?"

Stafford dialled the number for the main MSS switchboard and this time it was answered by a receptionist. She switched to speakerphone, then introduced herself and explained that she needed to speak to Seamus.

"I'm sorry Inspector, Mr Monaghan is away on business. Would you like me to take a message?"

Obigwe shook her head; Stafford agreed.

"No, it's a private matter, I need to speak to him directly. I tried to call him, but the mobile phone number I have listed for him isn't working. Do you have an alternative number I could use?"

The receptionist suddenly sounded wary. "I'm very sorry, Inspector. Our company's data protection policy is not to give out personal information to callers over the phone."

Stafford mouthed an obscenity that looked suspiciously like *fucking GDPR*, before continuing in a polite but firm voice.

"We need to speak to Mr Monaghan urgently as part of an ongoing investigation. He's not in any trouble," she added.

There was a silence at the end of the phone, before the receptionist replied, sounding slightly hesitant. "I could take your number and get him to ring you back?"

Stafford bit her tongue. If Seamus was dodging her calls, who knew when he'd return them? And ideally, she didn't want to give him time to practise his response.

"How about if we visit you? You could check my warrant card and ID, even phone the station to confirm my identity, then give me his number?" she suggested. "I really need to speak to him."

After a few seconds hesitation, the receptionist agreed. Obigwe noted down the address that she read out.

"By the way," Stafford said before she ended the call. "Did Ms Harrington accompany him on his business trip?"

"No, he went alone."

"Oh, that's strange. We actually tried visiting their house, but neither of them seems to be there at the moment."

"No, she wouldn't be," said the receptionist. "Dominic is looking after her whilst Seamus is away."

Stafford thanked her again and hung up.

"What's all that about?" Obigwe asked.

"No idea, but at least we know where she is. I think maybe I should take a drive out there, before that helpful receptionist calls her and Seamus to tell them the police were asking after them."

Chapter Thirty-Three

ANDREA MOANED WITH PLEASURE as she dangled her swollen ankles in the hot tub. When the twins were born and things got back to normal, she was going to persuade Seamus they needed one themselves.

Seamus had driven her in her car over to Dominic's once she'd packed an overnight bag. There were three guest rooms on the first floor of Dominic's house, each with its own en suite. Dominic's own bedroom took up a whole quarter of the ground floor. She and Seamus had stayed a few times over the years, and Dominic had decorated the largest guest room with pictures of them together to make it feel more like a home-from-home. It was typical Dominic; thoughtful and generous. She was lucky to call him a friend and looked forward to the day when he was her brother-in-law. And she would always be grateful for the way he looked out for the man she loved.

Dominic had driven Seamus to the train station half an hour ago. It would have been quicker, and probably cheaper, to fly to Scotland, but MSS had signed a net-zero carbon pledge, and Dominic was keen to minimise flying.

After the drop-off, Dominic was going to pop into the office for a couple of hours, and then he was going to cook them both a lasagne. Andrea suggested she should cook, but Dominic wouldn't hear of it. She gave in without a fight; Dominic's signature lasagne was legendary. It was just a pity she couldn't enjoy a glass of red with dinner.

She'd decided to pamper herself for the rest of the day, before taking out her laptop the following morning and finishing the website she had been building for a chain of exclusive boutiques in London and New York. They were paying her generously for her expertise, but they could afford it. She'd been uploading images from their catalogue and was astounded by how much they charged for clothes that Andrea was pretty sure she could buy in Marks and Spencer for a tenth of the price. She doubted the seamstresses in their Bangladeshi factories benefited from the vastly inflated prices.

After the uploads were complete, she would be handing the finished project over to a third-party web hosting company who would maintain it on the client's behalf.

She was just starting to drift off when the distinctive chime from the smart doorbell echoed through the house.

She groaned and tried to ignore it. The bell rang again.

Cursing quietly, she heaved herself back to her feet, donned a dressing gown, and padded back into the house. The gown barely covered her bump, and she struggled to tie the belt. The doorbell sounded a third time.

"I'm coming, damn it," she called, although she doubted her voice would carry through the triple-glazed windows. The video screen next to the door showed a smartly-dressed woman and a uniformed male police officer with a turban waiting on the doorstep, and Andrea felt her pulse jump. *Had something happened to Seamus or Dominic?*

She pressed the release on the electronic door lock and greeted her visitors.

The woman blinked in surprise at Andrea's appearance. "I'm very sorry to disturb you," she apologised.

"It's fine. What's happened? Is everyone OK?"

The woman smiled reassuringly. "It's nothing to worry about ... Ms?"

"Harrington. Andrea Harrington. I'm sorry, you must be looking for my partner's brother, Dominic. He's not here at the moment."

"I'm DI Stafford, and this is PC Singh, and it's actually you we were looking for."

Now it was Andrea's turn to blink in surprise. She'd only been in the house an hour or so, how on earth did they know to look for her here?

"Do you mind if we come in to ask you a few questions?" Stafford asked

"Of course, I'm sorry about the way I'm dressed," Andrea said stepping back.

Stafford smiled. "We would have called ahead, but I'm afraid the number we have for you is out of service."

"What is this about?" Andrea asked as she led the two police officers into the main living area.

"As I'm sure you're aware by now, there was a serious accident a mile or so up the road on Friday night."

Andrea felt herself relax. It was obvious they weren't here to impart bad news.

"Yes, a woman was run over, I believe? How is she? I haven't seen anything on the news."

"I'm afraid she was very badly injured. Unfortunately, we've been struggling to identify her, so we've been contacting residents along this road, and in the local area in the hope they can help us. We actually called here on Sunday and spoke to Dominic Monaghan. We've now widened the area we're canvassing and have made it as far as your end of the road. We called at your house, but you and your husband were out."

Andrea felt herself relax even more. She sat down on one of the sofas. Stafford and Singh took the matching seat opposite.

"Yes, we were at the hospital," she glanced reflexively at her swollen belly.

"I'm sorry to hear that," said Stafford. "I hope you're well?"

Andrea gave a small smile. "Nothing to worry about, it was just my two guests calling reception for room service. They've hopefully agreed to stay another month before settling the bill and checking out."

Stafford chuckled. "Two of them. Rather you than me."

"It's not as bad as you think it'll be," piped up Singh, the first time he'd spoken. "My wife and I have twins. Once you get into a routine, things settle down eventually."

"I hope you're right," Andrea said.

The officer had kind eyes and he gave her a sympathetic look. "My advice? Don't be afraid to ask for help. Everyone loves twins, you'll have no end of volunteers. Oh, and take the opportunity to sleep whenever you can. Be shameless about it. Hand them straight over to whoever's popped by that day and go for a nap, they'll be fine."

"Thank you," Andrea said.

Stafford took over, her tone casual. "I found yours and Seamus Monaghan's mobile phone numbers on our system, but they wouldn't connect."

Andrea stiffened, before giving a big sigh. "Well, if you've been looking at our file on the computer, then you probably know what happened three years ago."

"I only scanned the highlights, as I'm in a different department, but the whole thing must have been a terrible shock," Stafford said. "Please accept my condolences."

"Thank you," said Andrea again. "I'm afraid we had to disconnect our numbers after the fire. Seamus and I were in a relationship when Carole – that's his wife – died." She looked ashamed. "It all got a bit messy. Her family were very upset when they found out about our affair. Unfortunately, Carole's mother especially took it very hard. The poor woman has a bit of a drink problem, and she started sending nasty text messages and calling us when she was drunk. Carole was from the US and with the time difference between here and there, we were being woken up at all hours. We tried blocking the number, but she got wise to that, and kept borrowing other people's handsets." Andrea shuddered at the memory. "In the end, it was just easier for both of us to disconnect our numbers and start afresh."

"How awful for you," Stafford said. "Well anyway, I don't want to take up too much of your time." She manipulated her phone and passed it over to Andrea.

"This is an artist's impression of our unknown woman. Unfortunately, her face is pretty battered, so they've had to use some educated guesswork."

Andrea looked at the picture and her blood ran cold.

***

"She claimed not to recognise the woman, but she was lying," Stafford said. "PC Singh agrees."

Stafford was sitting with Obigwe in Girton's office.

Girton scratched her chin with a pen. "That's certainly interesting. The question, therefore, is what connection your woman has to Andrea Harrington. Any ideas?"

Stafford shrugged. "I've no idea. Apparently, Seamus is away in Scotland. I'd really like to see his reaction. Dominic claimed not to recognise her either. I've spoken to the officer that visited him on Sunday evening, but they said they didn't see anything unusual in his reaction. They couldn't tell if he was telling the truth, or just a very skilled liar."

"What about you, Mercy? Any thoughts?"

Obigwe had plenty, but she shook her head. She needed to spend some time sorting through them, before she voiced them. The ink had barely dried on her promotion, the last thing she wanted was to start airing crazy conspiracy theories.

"OK. I want you to run with this, Mercy," Girton said. "I'll clear the reassignment with DCI Squire. Katie, I know it's a cheeky ask, but would you be willing to work with Mercy? It looks as though you may share a common interest."

"Sounds good to me," Stafford said. "This is our best hope for identifying our victim and working out what the hell she's got herself involved in." She looked at her watch. "Unfortunately, my shift ended an hour ago and I have to go to the pharmacy for my mother before it shuts."

"Of course. Everything seems to be in hand for the time being. Pick it up again first thing," Girton said. Seamus Monaghan was hundreds of miles away; they wouldn't be able to speak to him yet anyway.

After saying goodbye to Stafford, Obigwe headed back to the desk she had been using. An idea had formed, but it was too ridiculous to share yet. She wanted to do a little digging around first.

Opening the Carole Monaghan file, she read through it again, focusing particularly on the images. She was in two minds. Part of her wanted her hunch to be right, but an even bigger part wanted to be wrong. The repercussions could be embarrassing and ugly.

"Shit," she muttered eventually; there were no easy answers to be found in the file.

There was only one thing for it. She dialled an internal number.

"DNA services," came the voice at the end of the line.

"It's DS Mercy Obigwe from the Murder Investigation Team. I wonder if you could do me a favour?"

Then

Night Of The Fire

Chapter Thirty-Four

Marcus Harrington pulled his Volvo into the lay-by and killed the engine. A hundred metres away, around a bend in the road, was the smart, detached house where his boss – and supposed friend – Seamus lived, with his wife, Carole.

He'd been trying to decide what to do since his trip to Manchester.

He'd suspected what was going on of course – he'd seen the way they looked at each other. He had no idea whether the two had slept together at university and he'd never asked; he'd never felt the need to (or so he told himself). Andrea could be quite tactile with those she felt close to, especially after a few drinks, so it was hard to be certain how much of their flirting and affection was just that of two old friends enjoying each other's company.

To be fair, after university, once Carole and Seamus had got engaged – and he and Andrea had become more serious – that behaviour had lessened. He'd assumed they had all grown and matured, becoming more adult.

But that changed when Carole lost the baby. The couple had been devastated, and Andrea had been more upset than he realised at first. It was to be expected, he supposed. Carole and Seamus were the first of their close friends to get pregnant and Andrea was a shoo-in as godmother. She was almost as excited as they were.

Of course she would be the one to comfort Carole. The poor woman had no family in the UK; without Andrea, she would be all alone. And it had seemed only natural she would also become Seamus' confidante. He and Dominic were close – who wouldn't be after their childhood? – but Marcus couldn't imagine his own brother comforting him after such a terrible loss.

No, there were some things that women were just better at than men. Although he'd never dare say that out loud.

It was the way Seamus had placed his jacket around Andrea's shoulders at Dominic's birthday party that had reignited the old suspicions. It just seemed too ... natural.

He understood where Seamus was coming from of course. Carole had changed. They'd all witnessed it. She just seemed sad all the time. And angry. He'd always enjoyed a bit of banter with her, playing to his Tory Boy image to wind her up. She was a bit of a whinging leftie, but privately he agreed with her more often than she realised. He only bought the *Daily Mail* when he knew she was coming around, and chucked it in the bin unread as soon as she left. He much preferred *The Times*, and even the occasional *Guardian* article. And who he placed his cross next to, in the privacy of the polling station, might have surprised her.

But since the miscarriage, all that had changed. A couple of times he'd thought she was going to slap him, and he'd vowed to steer clear of certain topics. Although he had to admit he found it hard not to revert to type when he was drunk or stoned.

And objectively speaking, he could hardly blame Seamus. On a scale of one to ten, Carole was a solid nine, no doubt (he and Pete Ludlow had discussed it in detail). But Andrea was an eleven at least. He smiled as he mentally compared them, before remembering why he was here.

Bastard.

He'd rehearsed what he was going to do and say in his mind on the way over. But now he was here, he felt his resolve weakening. Fumbling in his pocket, he took out the small plastic bag. Just a little pick-me-up, he decided. Not that he had much choice. He'd need to speak to Pete again; he'd used a bit more than he'd realised over the past few days.

He tapped the remainder of the powder onto the back of his plastic gym card and managed to snort it without spilling any on his lap. In the rear-view mirror he caught sight of a man fighting a losing battle with an over-excited terrier, and he quickly pushed the envelope and card into his pocket, and wiped his nose on his sleeve.

He'd known from the outset the real reason why Seamus had insisted they trade places this week. It was a choice between staying in a Travelodge and traipsing around a hospital in the arse-end of Glasgow, or a couple of nights in a luxury hotel in Manchester, *fucking my wife*, he thought angrily.

And of course, that prick Dominic had gone along with the plan, backing his little brother, as he always did. Not for the first time, Marcus wondered what Monaghan Security Solutions' clients would think if they knew that the company's vice-president had only got the role after his brother had paid hush money to stop his thieving ways becoming public knowledge. Or what prospective investors might think.

He could have blackmailed Dominic into giving him what he wanted by threatening to reveal Seamus' financial misconduct before they took the company public, but he was uncomfortably aware that with no charges ever brought, he was playing with a weak hand.

And then the events of the past week had happened.

The trip to Glasgow was easily switched for a series of video calls; frankly it was a waste of money trekking all the way up there, when he had already heard on the QT that they had preferred-bidder status. The blurred background setting meant nobody could tell he wasn't at home bravely doing his duty despite a nasty case of the flu. And even if that failed, he'd been careful to choose the same chain of cheap business hotels both in Manchester and back home, so nobody would suddenly wonder why the wall in his office had changed colour between meetings.

His phone was full of pictures of Seamus and Andrea together; there was no mistaking their relationship as just a close friendship. He felt bad about what he was about to do to Carole, but the impact on that cheating bastard Seamus would be devastating and he knew that when the initial shock wore off, Dominic would capitulate to his demands.

Mentally, he'd already moved on from Andrea; there were plenty more fish in the sea as they say, including at least one at work. Having Andrea cheat on him was a kick in the balls, but then if he came out of this looking like the victim ... well some women found that attractive.

By now, the cocaine was coursing around his system. The dog owner had buggered off, and it would soon be dark. It was time.

He locked his car and headed up the lane, rehearsing in his mind what he'd say when the door opened. He was just turning the corner when he saw the car coming. Instinctively, he turned away, not wanting to be seen.

But he'd already caught a glimpse of who was in the vehicle.

Shit.

Immediately, he felt his plan start to crumble. There was no way he could do what he had planned with them here.

Turning around, he headed back to his car. By the time he'd clambered back into the driving seat he'd had a new idea. He'd just have to hope the timings still worked.

Now

Five Days After The Storm

Chapter Thirty-Five

Andrea hadn't slept. DI Stafford's visit had shaken her to the core and left her confused. She'd got dressed as soon as the two officers had left, the hot tub no longer appealing.

Dominic had arrived home from the office and set about making dinner, but despite the mouth-watering aroma, Andrea had lost her appetite. After pushing the delicious food around her plate, she'd eventually apologised and pleaded exhaustion.

Dominic had been concerned, but she'd reassured him that it was just the stresses of the past day or so catching up with her. He'd placed the uneaten lasagne back in the fridge; it always tasted better reheated the next day anyway.

Andrea spent the night staring at the ceiling. Her thoughts were a jumbled mess; nothing made sense. But a cold feeling of foreboding had settled over her, and no matter how much she tried to convince herself that what she was thinking was impossible, the result of hormones and stress, she couldn't dismiss her worries.

It was the little inconsistencies that she'd ignored that weighed on her mind. Things she'd shrugged off. Things that she'd lied about.

Dominic was an early riser, and as soon as she heard him leave for work, she went downstairs. Turning on the TV news, she made herself some cereal and toast.

The national news gave way to the regional bulletin, and she half-watched it as she forced herself to eat. By now she was almost convinced she was imagining things. After an item about an ongoing planning argument over a new residential development in town, and an announcement by the local MP that he was planning on standing down at the next election, there came a brief update on the intruder at University Hospital two nights ago. A joint statement by the hospital and the police insisted there was no reason to believe that there was any danger to the public.

Frowning, Andrea searched for more information on the internet. The story had completely passed her by; she'd had other things on her mind the previous day.

Apparently, someone had attacked a patient in the hospital in the early hours of Monday morning. They had been disturbed, and the patient was left unharmed. Further down the article, there were unconfirmed reports that the patient who had been attacked was the woman injured in the road accident the night of the big storm.

Andrea's breath caught in her throat. All her worries from the previous night came flooding back. A wave of fear washed over her.

Tears prickling at the corner of her eyes, she collapsed on the sofa. Surely not? Surely what she was thinking couldn't be true?

After a few moments, her breath steadied. Yesterday she'd lied about not recognising the picture that DI Stafford had shown her. Three years ago, she'd told an even bigger lie.

Could she have been wrong all these years? She felt a kick from the twins, as if they sensed her distress. It wasn't just her she had to think about, she realised. One way or the other, she had to know if her suspicions were correct.

***

Andrea unlocked her front door and went straight upstairs. The office was next to their bedroom, and after a moment's hesitation, she went in. Seamus kept his paperwork in a metal filing cabinet next to hers. The spare key was attached with a magnet to the underside of his ergonomic office chair.

What was she doing?

Seamus was the love of her life.

Sure there were things he'd never told her. But then there were things she'd never told him.

Small things.

Things that didn't matter.

Everyone had secrets, and she trusted him.

And yet ...

Before she could change her mind again, she retrieved the key, and opened the cabinet.

Seamus could be a bit of a slob at times; his desk looked like a bomb had hit it, and she was forever picking up random items of clothing from the bathroom floor. However, he was meticulous about file-keeping. It took only a few moments to locate what she was looking for.

After Carole had died, her life insurance had paid out enough to clear most of the mortgage on the house. It had been a financial lifeline and was the only reason she and Seamus were still able to live there.

On the other hand, Marcus' disappearing act had left Andrea in a financial quandary. The mortgage to their house was in both their names, and with the sometimes erratic nature of Andrea's freelance web design business, he had paid the lion's share of it.

Unfortunately, with him classed as missing rather than deceased, Andrea had been unable to sell the house. She had petitioned the bank to convert the mortgage to an interest-only one, with a view to renting the property out, but they had been reluctant to do so without Marcus' agreement. It currently sat empty, and she still paid the mortgage on it whilst her solicitors tried to find a solution.

A brief wave of guilt washed over, and she went to replace the file unopened. She trusted Seamus. As far as she was aware, he'd never outright lied to her. He was the father of their unborn children, and had promised himself to her in marriage as soon as she could secure a divorce from the absent Marcus. Her conscience was telling her she shouldn't be snooping around behind his back. But another voice was telling her she needed to be certain. That she needed to know, if not for her, then for the future of their children.

She opened the file and skimmed through the legalese. Her breath caught in her throat. She knew exactly how much Seamus had cleared on the mortgage. Even allowing for funeral expenses and legal fees, the life insurance payout was much bigger than she'd been led to believe. In fact, he could probably have paid off the whole mortgage, and a chunk of hers also.

He'd lied to her.

Why had he done that? And equally importantly, where was the rest of the money?

***

Still reeling from the shock of what she'd found in Seamus' office, Andrea found herself driven to find answers. Surely there must be a rational explanation? But Seamus was in Scotland, and she needed to know now. To find out if her darkest fears were true.

Returning to the hallway, she retrieved the aluminium loft ladder from the airing cupboard. Taking a deep breath, she kicked off her shoes and clambered up it. Never a fan of heights at the best of times, her mind was filled with images of her falling. What would happen to the babies? If Seamus knew what she was doing ...

Pushing up the hatch, she squeezed through the tiny entrance to the attic space, then fumbled for the pull cord that operated the bare bulb hanging from the roof. She sneezed as dust tickled her nose.

She found what she was looking for in a plastic crate: bulging lever-arch files and boxes of digital evidence on DVDs. Oldroyd and Parker had requested copies of the evidence disclosure when Seamus had been arrested. When the case against him had been dropped, Seamus had insisted on taking custody of it, 'just in case'. Had he been worried the open verdict at the inquest wouldn't be the end of the matter, or was he just being cautious?

The lamp was bright enough to read by, so Andrea carefully lowered herself to the floor, and opened the files.

She wasn't really sure what she was looking for, but she hoped she would recognise it when she saw it.

The files were neatly organised, with a crude table of contents at the front, and she decided to start with the transcripts of the interviews conducted. She knew much of what had emerged during the investigation, but it still made uncomfortable reading. Her and Seamus' transgressions were laid out in black and white, and she felt the hot burn of shame. She and Seamus loved each other, and she wouldn't have changed a thing. But there was no escaping the fact they had both been married, and their actions had hurt those around them.

Seamus had been interviewed several times during his period of detention. He'd told her much of what he had been asked, but some of it had been too upsetting for him to talk about. Or so he'd said. She'd respected that, and hadn't pressed him, just grateful it was finally over.

The interview transcript she had in her hand was new to her. It was typed out like a script, and she could hear each of the participants voices in her head as she read through it.

Apparently, the detectives had just finished looking at Carole's computer and found that she had posted to an anonymous message board on the internet called BetweenUandMe.com. It seemed to be a forum where anonymous participants could unburden their darkest secrets; a digital confessional of sorts. Carole's computer had saved her password, so they had been able to identify everything that she'd posted.

The revelations were a shock. First of all, Carole admitted to having had sex with someone in the back garden of her house after a party. She claimed to have been too high to remember if it had been entirely consensual, but admitted she had fantasised about this person for a long time and so had decided not to go to the police about it.

Andrea would have to watch the video footage of the interview, recorded on the accompanying DVD, to see his reaction, but the transcript appeared to suggest Seamus knew nothing of this.

Next, the detectives seemed to be interested in something that had happened eighteen months before the fire. The date was vaguely familiar, but she couldn't be certain why. Accessing the calendar on her phone, she found the evening in question, and it all came flooding back.

Again, Seamus claimed to know nothing about it, but her blood ran cold. Because she knew, without a shadow of a doubt, that he was lying.

***

Andrea's hands shook as she sat at the kitchen table. She'd made herself a mug of a herbal tea blend that was supposed to be soothing, but it wasn't working.

Seamus had lied to her about the money, and he had lied to the police about Carole's car accident.

A few days after the disastrous dinner party, when Marcus had returned from Ireland, her husband had been late home after work. He'd dropped Seamus off at a garage downtown to pick up his car. Seamus claimed Carole had slid off the road swerving to avoid a deer, and he'd needed to take it in for some minor repairs. Andrea had wondered if that was the same night Carole had driven home dangerously drunk and high, but had decided to let things lie, just relieved that nobody had been hurt.

But according to the confession Carole had posted online, nothing could be farther from the truth. She claimed to have run someone off the road, then left the scene. The police had linked the story to a fatal accident some months previously. A thirty-year-old father of two, working extra shifts as a security guard, had inexplicably failed to take a bend on Valley View Road, crashing through a safety barrier and sliding down the hillside. He'd died on impact when a tree branch had impaled him through the windscreen.

He had no alcohol or drugs in his system, the car was in sound mechanical condition, and there was no evidence of excess speed. There had been tyre tracks further up the road, but no way to tell if they were related. The coroner had ruled the most likely explanation was he had fallen asleep at the wheel. Andrea remembered the accident, as there had been vocal public demands for the ageing crash barriers on the road to be upgraded to stop cars leaving the road in future. Her calendar confirmed the date of the dinner party.

In his interview, Seamus had denied any knowledge of the accident, and then further denied taking the car in for repairs.

Had Seamus known what had really happened that night? Or had he later found out? Carole had been so wracked with guilt that she had unburdened her conscience onto an online forum months later. What if she'd also confessed to Seamus? How would he have taken the news that he had helped his wife cover up a fatal collision she was responsible for? Especially given how his own parents had died?

And what about the missing money from the life insurance pay out? A horrible idea was starting to form in her mind, but surely it was too crazy?

***

Mercy Obigwe had been at her desk since before the rest of the day shift started. She'd lain awake most of the night. Her idea from the day before seemed even crazier the more she thought about it. Yet she just couldn't put it aside.

Obigwe checked her email again. Still no message from the DNA lab. She fished around in her desk drawer for her mug. She'd need to be a little more generous with the coffee powder than usual, to ward off a mid-morning slump.

Her phone rang and she snatched it up eagerly, before feeling disappointment when she recognised the desk sergeant manning reception.

"Mercy, I have a visitor for you."

"Who is it?"

The sergeant told her.

All thoughts of coffee evaporated, and she raced to the stairs, too impatient to wait for the lift. Entering reception, she saw Andrea waiting by the main desk, in an otherwise empty reception area.

Almost three years had passed since Obigwe had last clapped eyes on the woman. Aside from a very swollen belly, she had barely changed. She looked tired, but otherwise, pregnancy seemed to be treating her well.

Inviting Andrea to join her in an interview room, Obigwe exchanged forced pleasantries with her as she organised some water. The last time the two women had spoken, it had hardly been under the best of circumstances.

Andrea took a deep breath. "You are going to think I'm mad …"

***

Obigwe didn't know what to make of Andrea's story. At first glance, it seemed fantastical. Anyone else would have listened politely, then reassured Andrea that she was imagining things, before gently dismissing her.

Except Andrea's story fitted what Obigwe had started to suspect herself. Nevertheless, she'd been reluctant to encourage Andrea until she had something concrete. The story would be a hard sell. She forced herself to make another coffee before returning to her desk, using the time to let her thoughts settle.

When she woke up her laptop, there was an email notification waiting for her.

The report from the DNA lab left her feeling light-headed and paralysed with indecision. DCI Girton and Katie Stafford were in a meeting, but Obigwe needed someone else's perspective. There was only one person she could think to call.

Hand trembling, she dialled his number.

"Mercy, what a lovely surprise."

Obigwe ignored the pleasantries. "Are you free to meet up?" she asked him.

"Of course," he said. His voice became concerned. "Is everything all right? You sound worried."

The words when they came sounded crazy, even to Obigwe's ears.

"The dead woman from the fire three years ago wasn't Carole Monaghan."

Chapter Thirty-Six

Retirement was treating Patrick Freeland well. He'd lost at least two stone in weight, and whilst his hair had turned completely grey, the healthy tan had taken years off him. He looked five years younger than when he'd left.

They sat in his conservatory, drinking coffee. His wife was out, so they had the house to themselves.

Obigwe had spread a pile of printouts across the small table between them. Freeland was skimming the DNA report, a pair of reading glasses perched on his nose.

"One hundred per cent match, or as near as damn it," he said. "Shit. Why didn't we pick this up three years ago?"

"The lab never ran the DNA from the burned body through the database," said Obigwe. "We just asked for a match between the sample extracted during the autopsy and the DNA taken from Carole's hairbrush and the toothbrush. I fucked up."

Freeland looked up sharply. "No, you didn't. You – we – had no reason to suspect the items you bagged from the en suite weren't Carole's. We were just confirming that the woman burned to death in the Monaghan's shed was Carole Monaghan. Once that match was made, why would we waste resources running the samples through the DNA database? Besides, she'd never been arrested, she wouldn't even be on there, which is why the DNA on the joints didn't come back as a match."

He picked up another sheet.

"This Angelica Carshalton is the same height and build as Carole Monaghan. Her hair is the same colour, and she had no tattoos or distinguishing marks. She's even about the same age."

"She's on the system for soliciting and possession of Class A drugs," Obigwe said. "The Sexual Exploitation Team had a file on her, but the street team hadn't seen her for months before the fire. They figured that either she had cleaned up her act, moved out of the area or, possibly left the streets to do more upmarket escort work or porn. She was an intravenous drug user, but she'd largely kept her looks."

"And I'll bet she was careful to keep her injection sites hidden," Freeland said. "So she could charge the punters more."

"She injected between her toes," Obigwe said. "Which was observed during the autopsy."

Freeland took a long swig of his coffee, before refilling it from the cafetiere.

"So this poor woman was picked up, presumably injected with enough heroin to knock her senseless, and then set alight in the Monaghan's shed. The lab report found only her DNA on the toothbrush and hairbrush, so Carole's items must have been swapped for replacements."

"The toothbrush was pretty new," Obigwe said. "And there were only a few strands of hair caught in the bristles of her hairbrush. I took them straight from the bathroom sink and bagged them at the scene."

"I'm sure you did everything correctly," Freeland reassured her. "In which case, did Carole stage her own disappearance? And if she did, why, and where the hell has she been for the last three years?"

"We don't know," Obigwe said. "She's still unconscious. But her marriage to Seamus was clearly breaking down. Perhaps she knew Andrea and Seamus were having an affair?"

"You think she just decided to walk out and leave everything behind? But why kill this poor woman? Why fake her own death?

Why not just get a divorce? It's not as if she'd benefit from the life insurance pay out; that all went to Seamus."

"Andrea says that almost half the life insurance payment is missing," Obigwe said. "Seamus paid off most of his and Carole's outstanding mortgage, but according to the document Andrea found, the rest is unaccounted for."

"You think he went halvsies with Carole?"

"Maybe. Andrea seems to think so."

"But why?" Freeland asked. "Why did she want to leave so badly? I'm guessing the whole heroin addiction was a smokescreen. She wouldn't be the first person to fake their own death to claim life insurance, but as far as we can tell her business was doing OK. Divorce is never cheap, but this just seems so extreme. And she had family and friends who loved her. Why would she walk away from all of that? And why would Seamus let her?"

"Perhaps she was scared she would go to prison?" Obigwe said. "She confessed on that website she was responsible for a fatal traffic incident whilst heavily under the influence. Andrea confirms Seamus lied to us about having the car repaired, and if you remember we stopped pursuing that angle when Marcus Harrington became a person of interest. Perhaps Carole felt she needed to confess in person, and told Seamus about what had happened? He might not even have known at the time that was why his car ended up in some backstreet garage."

"In that case, did Seamus know that it wasn't his wife who burned to death in that shed? No, wait, he must have done if he gave her half the insurance pay out." Freeland rubbed his chin. "The question is whether he was in on this from the start, or if Carole magically reappeared after the money was paid out and demanded half the cash?"

"Andrea also admitted that she lied about Seamus' whereabouts the night of the fire," Obigwe said.

"You mean he *wasn't* with her?" Freeland said.

"Not all night. Apparently, they went straight to bed after returning from Manchester that afternoon and shared a bottle of champagne. She fell asleep after they had sex. She's a heavy sleeper and didn't wake up until she got the phone call in the early hours about the fire. He was gone. She has no idea when he left, but realised it looked bad, so told what she describes as a 'little fib'."

Freeland frowned. "If I remember the timeline, he could easily have got from Andrea's to the house, set the shed alight, then returned to hers and caught a cab from there back to his own house in time to 'discover' the fire."

"Andrea's car keys would have been hanging on a hook in the kitchen," Obigwe said. "He could have taken her car to his own house and then returned it without her realising it was gone."

"There are no traffic cameras between Andrea's house and where the Monaghans lived," Freeland recalled. "And I seem to remember there was no useful CCTV retrieved from Andrea's street."

"And the CCTV at Seamus and Carole's house was turned off by an app registered to Seamus," Obigwe said.

"So where does Angelica Carshalton come into it?" Freeland asked.

"I don't know," Obigwe admitted. "If she was involved in escort work, he could have booked her services."

"Or Carole could have," Freeland said. "In fact, a lone woman would have been less threatening than a man. Perhaps that's why she let her guard down?"

"That could work," Obigwe said.

"The next question is why Carole Monaghan suddenly reappeared three years later, soaked to the skin, in the middle of a thunderstorm? And why did someone try to kill her Sunday night?" Freeland asked.

They lapsed into silence, and eventually Freeland picked up their mugs. "This is going to need more coffee, and some decent biscuits," he said heading back into the kitchen.

Whilst he boiled the kettle again, and replaced the grounds in the cafetiere, Obigwe checked through her emails on her phone. There was a message to call the Financial Crime Unit at her earliest convenience. She flagged it to deal with later.

Freeland returned with the brewing coffee and a packet of custard creams. He paused. "Don't look at me like that, these are the king of biscuits, and supermarket own brand taste as good as more expensive varieties."

"Could be worse," Obigwe said, "DCI Girton likes Rich Tea."

Freeland gave an exaggerated shudder. "One of my few regrets was that I never convinced Gemma that a person's choice of biscuit says a lot about them. Rich Tea sends the wrong signal; they're bland, inoffensive and fall apart as soon as they meet hot water."

"So what do custard creams say about a person?" Obigwe asked.

"Easy. They are no nonsense, popular with everyone and filled with goodness, surrounded by a robust shell capable of withstanding prolonged periods of dunking."

Obigwe smiled. She'd missed Freeland's banter.

"So, do we think Seamus tried to kill Carole in hospital that night?" Freeland asked.

"He may have had the opportunity," Obigwe said. "Andrea claims she had an early night, and that Seamus has been getting up early to go into work. She was sound asleep until mid-morning. He could have sneaked out of the house and gone to the hospital, and she'd be none the wiser. It's quite a risk though, pregnant women tend to get up to pee in the night."

"OK, what about the means and method to do it?" Freeland asked. "I confess I haven't really followed the story on the news."

"The nurse who disturbed the person who tried to kill Carole was unable to describe the attacker. And rather conveniently, the hospital CCTV suffered a complete system failure. It also looks as though the attacker may have cloned a swipe card; the doors to that ward were unlocked using a card registered to a staff member that multiple witnesses have placed on the other side of the hospital when the attack occurred."

"I wonder who installed their security?" Freeland asked meaningfully. "Presumably there are codes to allow engineers to access the system if needs be?"

"I'll check that," Obigwe said.

"Which just leaves motive," Freeland said. "Why would Carole come back after all this time? And why would Seamus – or someone else – try to kill her?"

"Maybe she wanted more money?" Obigwe suggested. "Monaghan Security Solutions has grown enormously over the past few years. Seamus is a vice-president with stock options; on paper at least, he's a very wealthy man now. Perhaps Carole figured he could afford to be a bit more generous?"

"And he could hardly say no," Freeland mused. "He helped Carole cover up a fatal car accident, and he was involved in Angelica Carshalton's death. As far as the world knows, Carole Monaghan is dead, and of course Carshalton was cremated.

"She's a very clever woman; I bet she kept some sort of insurance she could dangle over Seamus. Perhaps something that implicates him in setting that fire? He can hardly admit it wasn't Carole in there, rather some other poor woman, and even if he did, who the hell would believe him?"

"But she didn't foresee getting run over in the middle of a thunderstorm," Obigwe said. "And nor did he. Carole's currently in a medically-induced coma, but he was probably terrified that she'd wake up and start talking, and we'd figure out who she really is. But if he did manage to kill her, as far as he knows, Carole's DNA and fingerprints aren't in our system. He probably figured we'd never work out who she really is."

Chapter Thirty-Seven

Andrea drove back to Dominic's. Her mind was in turmoil. All she knew was that she couldn't face returning to the house she'd shared with Seamus. The house that he'd bought with her best friend. A best friend that she'd grieved the loss of for three years, but who had now come back from the dead.

She'd prayed that Obigwe would laugh in her face when she told her of her suspicions. That she'd have immediately explained why Seamus couldn't possibly have helped Carole fake her own death. That Seamus and Carole couldn't have been involved in murdering the poor woman who died in the fire.

For three years, she'd clung to the hope that Carole had killed herself. Because the alternate hypothesis was that Marcus had killed her. She had reason enough to be angry with him; their marriage had been faltering for ages before she and Seamus got together. And if he was alive, he'd deliberately left her in the lurch financially. But she still loved him. She still loved the man who had swept her off her feet at university, even if she had a secret longing for someone else. There was room enough in her heart for two men. But over the years, the thought that she'd once shared her bed with a man capable of murder had chilled her. Was she really such a bad judge of character? And now it looked as though she may have been even more wrong.

But Obigwe hadn't laughed at her. She had a good poker face, but Andrea could see that what she was hearing wasn't a total surprise. Seamus had been released without charge three years ago, but the inquest into Carole's death had recorded an open verdict. Did that mean the investigation had remained active? Did Detective Constable – now Detective Sergeant – Obigwe and DS Freeland still believe Carole was murdered? Had they even suspected that the body in the shed wasn't her? And who was that poor woman? Had they identified her?

For a brief moment, Andrea entertained the hope it was all a big coincidence. That some poor homeless person had snuck into the shed and used the petrol for Seamus' lawnmower to set herself on fire. Carole and Seamus had then seized the opportunity to reinvent a new life for Carole. One where she would no longer be at risk of going to jail for killing that poor driver.

But she dismissed it immediately. The body in the shed had been positively identified as Carole using DNA from her toothbrush and hairbrush. That must mean they had sourced DNA samples from the dead woman and planted the items in the bathroom – how could they have done that in the short time between the fire being reported and those items being seized? Which meant Seamus must have planned it.

Andrea clambered out of the car and headed to the house. She input the code for the front door and disabled the alarm, before collapsing onto the sofa. At times like this, she would usually speak to Seamus, but she could hardly call him now, could she? Besides, even if she wanted to, she couldn't.

Laird Finlay Ballenbrooke, the wealthy investor Seamus had travelled to see, was an eccentric character. Living in the Highlands of Scotland, he ran his whisky distilling business the way his father, and generations before him had. He refused to own a mobile phone and delegated what he liked to call 'the modern side' of the business to his sons.

Seamus had been invited to his sprawling country estate. Due diligence had already been performed by his sons, so this final meeting would likely be held over dinner and out on the Laird's private golf course. Even if there was a signal out there, Seamus would have precious few opportunities to use his phone. Should he need to be contacted urgently, a message would need to be sent to the Laird's private secretary, who would then deliver it to them, wherever they might be.

The trip had sounded like a fantastic jolly when Seamus had first described it, and Andrea had been jealous she couldn't join him. Now it didn't seem like such a good idea ...

Andrea looked at the clock. Dominic would probably be back soon. He'd said he would work from home that afternoon so he could look after her. She'd bristled at the suggestion; she was pregnant, not ill. But that was the only way she could persuade Seamus to take the trip. Now she was faced with an evening trying to make small talk and avoiding giving away her suspicions.

Dominic would be heartbroken and horrified if he caught wind of what she was thinking. Yet how could she sit here, like nothing had happened?

Then there were those nagging suspicions. What, if anything, did Dominic know about what had happened? Carole had been sending him WhatsApp messages in the run up to her death. He'd arranged for a place in a private drug rehabilitation clinic. That much had been confirmed. Was Carole duping him as she set up her alibi, or had he been going along with their plan?

Dominic had helped Seamus out in the past. She wasn't clear on the details, but she was aware Seamus left his previous job under a cloud and that Dominic had stepped in with a new role at MSS. Seamus had been reluctant to talk about it, and she hadn't pushed. She and Seamus were starting a new life together, trying to forget the past.

Suddenly, Andrea didn't feel safe. Perhaps she should leave? There were several small hotels in town, and in the surrounding cities. Maybe she should just write Dominic a note thanking him for his hospitality and saying that she needed some space?

Her mind made up, she opened a booking app on her phone. She and Seamus shared a user account so they could both manage any holidays they had booked. She didn't want anyone knowing where she was going, so she logged out and set up a new account, using her personal credit card, not their joint one.

The next town over had a Holiday Inn. The rooms boasted free Wi-Fi, there was a restaurant and complimentary breakfast, and guests had free parking. She booked three nights.

That done, she went up to her room and quickly re-packed her overnight case. She had a couple of changes of clothes, but there was a large supermarket on the way she could use to buy any underwear and other items she needed; she just hoped they had sizes that fit pregnant women.

Carrying her bag downstairs, she found a pen and paper and wrote Dominic a short note. There was no way to make it sound like anything more than a brush-off, but when this was all over, she'd blame it on hormones. She doubted Dominic was any more clued up on the mysteries of pregnancy than any other single man without an expectant partner.

The hum of the door to the attached garage opening made her jump. She'd been so engrossed in trying to devise the right wording to her note she hadn't noticed that damned electric car gliding silently up the driveway.

Suddenly she had cold feet. It was one thing to sneak off, leaving a note, and entirely another to explain to her friend, and future brother-in-law, face-to-face that she was about to leave his luxurious house and go and stay in a business hotel in the next town.

She hastily shoved the note in her pocket, then grabbed her bag. She heard the connecting door from the garage open as she reached the top of the stairs.

"Hey, Andy, I'm back," he called out. "I'm going to put the kettle on, do you want a cuppa? I picked up some herbal tea on the way back."

Catching her breath from the sudden exertion, she forced herself to sound normal.

"Hi Dom. I'm upstairs, I was just about to have a nap. Thank you for buying some tea."

"No sweat, Sis'. Do you want me to wake you up for dinner? I was going to reheat that lasagne."

"No, it's fine. I'll set an alarm."

Sitting down on the end of the bed, she closed her eyes and waited for the adrenaline to subside.

Dominic's house was a fortress. It was probably the safest place for miles around.

So why did she feel so uneasy?

Chapter Thirty-Eight

Despite what she'd told Dominic, sleep was out of the question. The box from the loft had contained more files she had never seen before. One of them was sitting in front of her. She took a sip from the glass of water on the bedside table, wishing it was something stronger, and stared at the file divider. A wave of nausea passed over her. For three years it had been sitting in the loft. For three years she'd tried not to think about what was contained within it. Taking it with her as she left her house had been a spur of the moment decision, and she'd almost returned it unread.

If someone had asked her twenty-fours ago if she wanted to read Carole's WhatsApp communications with Dominic, she'd have thought them mad. Over the years, Dominic had shared only snippets of those desperate conversations. What little he had told her and Seamus had been enough. Carole had been in tremendous pain; a pain that she'd ultimately been unable to deal with. Andrea had no need or desire to see her friend's soul laid bare.

But now things had changed. She needed to read them for herself. The horrible, crazy idea that had formed in her mind had taken hold and she wouldn't be able to rest unless she knew the truth.

She opened the folder. It was filled with page after page of screenshots taken from Dominic's mobile phone. The burner phone found with Carole was too badly damaged for the data to be retrieved, but both sides of the encrypted conversation were visible on his phone. Somebody had annotated each message with initials: DM for Dominic, CM for Carole.

It was even worse than Dominic had said. Most of the messages were sent late at night, filled with self-loathing and hatred at her weakness. Dominic responded within minutes each time. Andrea felt a rush of love for him; he must have gone to bed each night with the volume on his phone turned up high, ready to wake up and comfort his brother's wife if she had a crisis. Had he set a specific alert so he knew when Carole was reaching out?

Carole's battle was laid out over the course of several weeks. Sometimes she'd go for days without indulging her habit, her reply to Dominic's regular check-ins upbeat and positive, then something would happen and her next message would be pitying. Throughout it, Dominic tried to convince her to speak to Seamus, or to Andrea. To seek help.

Finally, a fortnight before the fire, she sent a message, heart-breaking in its simplicity.

I can't do this on my own. Please can you help me?

It was what Dominic told them he had been waiting for. Within twenty-four hours he had sent her a link to the private clinic he'd found weeks before, along with an appointment. The morning she was due to have her first consultation was the day she died. They knew from the inquest that she had never attended it.

From then on, the messages were more positive. There was light at the end of the tunnel. Dominic was now acting as her cheerleader. He knew all he needed to do was keep her focused on her goal. He even sent her a couple of cheesy jokes, her response more like the Carole of old.

The day Seamus left for Manchester, she'd messaged Dominic, telling him how she was feeling low. His reply had been upbeat, telling her to focus on their visit to the clinic, or their 'road trip' as he'd taken to calling it.

Which one do you want to be? He'd asked. *Thelma or Louise?*

She'd replied with a rolling eyes emoji.

Has anyone told you what a knob you are?

And then the day before the appointment, the hammer blow that Dominic still blamed himself for.

I am so, so, sorry. The investor's meeting has been postponed until tomorrow morning. With Marcus and Seamus out of the office, I absolutely have to go to it. Can you get yourself to the clinic?

There was no response for almost two hours, before she replied. *Sure.*

Andrea blinked away her tears. Dominic had told her about the day of Carole's appointment. How she hadn't responded to his increasingly frantic messages. How he'd finally rung the clinic to find that she hadn't arrived. And then how, knowing Seamus was due back that evening, had decided to take what he insisted on calling 'the cowards way out' and letting Carole deal with Seamus on her own, hoping to avoid having to own up to their deception.

And then the late-night phone call that had changed everything.

Andrea wiped her eyes. The transcript had confirmed everything that Dominic had told them about the weeks preceding Carole's death.

And yet, something wasn't quite right.

She scanned back through the messages, looking for what was bothering her.

And then she spotted it.

Has anyone told you what a knob you are?

Her breath caught in her throat.

Carole was American. In all the years they'd been friends, she'd never heard her use the British term 'knob'.

In fact, only one person called Dominic by that insult.

Seamus.

Chapter Thirty-Nine

"Do we know where Seamus Monaghan is right now?" Girton asked. Heeding Freeland's advice, Obigwe had returned to CID and arranged for Girton's meeting to be interrupted. The DCI had made her excuses immediately and raced back.

Katie Stafford had also joined them. By the time Girton arrived, Obigwe had brought the inspector up to speed.

"He is supposed to be up in the Scottish Highlands, meeting some eccentric Laird to discuss investing in his and Dominic's company," Obigwe said. "The place is in the middle of nowhere; little or no mobile phone signal."

"Brilliant," Stafford said. "Ninety-nine per cent of this country has mobile phone coverage, but our suspect manages to find the one per cent that doesn't."

"We've applied for warrants to track his phone as far as we can," Obigwe said. "And British Transport Police are sourcing CCTV from the various train stations he may have passed through. Unfortunately, he bought an open return ticket by any permitted route, which gives him multiple choices, and there's no way to tell when he actually left."

"Ticket barriers?" Girton asked.

"Not if he didn't use Brook Street Station, and he may not have; there's a more direct route avoiding London if he got on the local train from Timberbridge," Stafford said. "You can just show your ticket and walk through."

"So, there's no proof he actually got on the train yesterday," Girton said. "Have we managed to contact this Laird Whatshisname to see if Seamus actually arrived there?"

"Not yet. His secretary says that he doesn't carry a mobile phone, and that it was just going to be Seamus, the Laird and his wife. She's left messages on the house phone, but he could be anywhere on the estate. She'll drive out there if necessary."

"Let's see if we can prove he actually caught that train first," Girton said. "Then we'll arrange for someone from Police Scotland to accompany her." She grimaced. "From what you've told me, the shit could really hit the fan if we go in mob-handed and interrupt some Scottish Laird when he's two under par on the eighteenth hole."

She turned to Obigwe. "Have Seamus' financial records come in yet?"

Obigwe handed over a printout with several entries highlighted.

"Andrea was correct. You can see here the life insurance payout going into his account. Until that point, he was on his overdraft limit, and he had several maxed-out credit cards he was barely making minimum payments on. He used the money to clear those debts. Then, almost half the remaining balance was withdrawn as cash. He did it in several instalments, presumably to avoid triggering any alerts. He's worked in finance long enough to know the thresholds for a transaction to be flagged as suspicious."

She turned to the next page. "And here he uses the remaining money to pay off a chunk of his and Carole's mortgage."

"So where did that cash go?" asked Stafford. "Carole?"

"That's our working hypothesis," Obigwe said.

"It was certainly a tidy sum," Stafford said. "And you could live on that for a couple of years if you're very careful. But something doesn't feel right here."

"In what way?" Girton asked. She had her own misgivings but wanted to hear what Stafford was thinking.

"First of all, I get why she might have faked her own death," Stafford said. "It's clear she was full of guilt over that road accident, and was worried she might end up going to prison if they realised she was responsible. But killing some poor woman to cover it up is hardly going to ease her conscience any, is it?"

"People do desperate things if they feel they are backed into a corner," Obigwe said.

"True, but where is Seamus' incentive?" Stafford said. "I can understand him feeling under pressure if Carole revealed that not only had she accidentally killed someone, but he had unwittingly helped her cover it up. But, this is a huge escalation. He now goes and helps murder an innocent person to help cover up her mistake? That makes no sense at all."

Obigwe nodded glumly. She and Freeland had come to the same conclusion.

"What are we missing here?" she asked. "There has to be a better reason."

"And where has she been for the past three years?" Stafford asked. "She was found on a remote country lane a few miles from where she once lived, underweight, and dressed completely inappropriately. Plus, there are indications that sometime in the past she was restrained. Why reappear now?"

"We thought she may have appeared asking Seamus for more money," Obigwe said. "Which would give him a potential motive to kill her in the hospital that night. Another night where he doesn't have an alibi."

Girton placed her hands on the table. "You're right, both of you," she said. "It doesn't make any sense, and I agree that we are missing some big pieces of the puzzle. At the moment, this is all speculation, backed up by precious little evidence. Hopefully, when Seamus is brought in for questioning, he can supply a few more of those pieces."

"I wouldn't bank on it," Obigwe grumbled. "If Oldroyd and Parker have any say in the matter, he'll answer no comment if the custody officer asks him how many sugars he wants in his tea."

"Then what about Carole?" Girton asked. "What do the doctors say?"

"Still too early," Stafford said. "Fortunately, it doesn't appear the attempt to suffocate her caused any more damage. They have started reducing the sedation, but there's no guarantee she'll regain consciousness anytime soon. Or that she'll be much use to us even if she does."

"Then we need to start widening the circle," Girton said. "Katie, I realise it's been a long time, but see if anyone on the Sexual Exploitation Team can track down any of Angelica Carshalton's friends and acquaintances. Maybe one of them saw her with Seamus or Carole? Mercy, if Carole was planning this for a while, then perhaps there were things missed the first time around? Go back through the case file with that in mind, rather than looking for indicators she was planning to kill herself. Re-interview witnesses and also get the Financial Crime Unit to go back through all of their accounts again. Maybe one of them got sloppy and didn't fully cover their tracks. Now we know Carole has been alive all this time, we need to work out where she's been. It's the twenty-first century; even with a bag full of cash, three years is a hell of a long time to remain invisible."

She smiled tightly and looked at her watch. "In the meantime, it's now a civilised hour in Wyoming and I have a delicate phone call to make, and some DNA samples to request. This will be a career first."

***

Hunger brought Andrea back downstairs at dinner time. Dominic had reheated the lasagne in the microwave and made some fresh garlic bread. This time, she wolfed down the whole plate and had seconds. Despite Dominic's best efforts, the silence stretched awkwardly between them.

"What's the matter, Andy?" he asked, worry etched on his face.

She managed a smile. "Nothing, I'm just tired." She patted her belly. "These two are either practising their kickboxing or learning a jig."

"That'll be the Irish genes from our side of the family," Dominic joked, although his eyes still held concern.

Twice during the meal she'd almost broken down and told Dominic her suspicions, desperate for somebody to tell her she was wrong. But she couldn't. She already felt like she had betrayed her husband by visiting DS Obigwe earlier. Dominic would be horrified she was even contemplating such a thing. Worse, what if he didn't dismiss her concerns immediately …

Refusing her offers of help, he gathered up the dirty plates and loaded the dishwasher. "If you want to make yourself useful," he said, "open the fridge. There's a little something in there for dessert."

Andrea opened the huge, double-width American refrigerator.

"Banoffee pie!" she squealed.

"Thought you'd be pleased," Dominic said with a grin.

"Where's yours?" Andrea teased, hugging the container to her.

"It feeds four. Since you're only eating for three, I thought I might have any scraps left over," he said, fetching bowls and spoons.

"This was Carole's favourite as well," Andrea said quietly, as they tucked in. "Our flatmates played football on a Wednesday night. We used to sit in the living room in our pyjamas watching old *Friends* episodes and scoff a whole tub between us."

"Yeah, I remember," Dominic said, his tone subdued also.

"Do you ever think about what you would say to her if you could go back in time?" Andrea asked, watching him carefully. "If she was standing here in front of you?"

"Umm, I guess so," Dominic said. "I suppose I'd tell her how much we all love her. That no matter what her problems were, we'd help her through them."

"And what do you really think about me and Seamus? As a couple?" she asked.

Dominic's face flushed red.

"This is getting rather intense," he said.

"How did you feel when you found out Seamus and I had been having an affair behind Carole's back?"

"Bloody hell, Andy, that's a biggy," he laughed, blushing still further.

Andrea waited until he started talking again.

"If I'm honest, I'm conflicted. I was disappointed in Seamus for what he did to Carole. She was a wonderful woman. She deserved better," he paused. "But on the other hand, you and he are just so right. You should have been together from the start," his voice grew quiet. "I just wish it finally happened under happier circumstances."

"And what about Marcus?" Andrea asked, before she could stop herself.

"He was a dick."

Chapter Forty

THE CALL FROM THE Financial Crime Unit came first thing. The analyst on the other end of the line sounded irritated.

"Is this DC Mercy Obigwe, the officer in charge of the Carole Monaghan suicide?"

"It's DS," she told the caller, cringing at how that made her sound. "But yes, that's me." She cursed herself silently. She'd seen the email asking her to call the previous day, but it had slipped her mind. She was working another case involving possible finance violations and she'd assumed it was part of that investigation and so wasn't urgent. Her priority at the moment was tracing the whereabouts of Seamus Monaghan. They had teams scouring CCTV from train stations but had yet to find him travelling up to Scotland. The movements of his mobile phone had helped narrow down the train he must have taken, but it had left the network as the signal faded on Laird Ballenbrooke's estate. Police Scotland had agreed to send a team to the estate to bring him back for questioning, given that he now had no alibi for the night of the fire, or the night Carole was attacked in the hospital. Assuming he hadn't vanished of course. He had to know by now that his attempt on Carole's life had been a failure; did that mean he'd have another go? Or was he going to try and escape?

"Finally," said the analyst. "The OIC listed is a DS Freeland, but apparently, he's no longer available. I eventually found your name on the bottom of some of the reports."

"Sorry, DS Freeland retired just after the verdict was delivered at the inquest," Obigwe said. "I was a probationer at the time, but it should have been reassigned to me after he left. What can I do for you?"

"There are flags against some bank accounts associated with the case. We're supposed to contact the OIC if there is any activity on them. We sent an email to DS Freeland, but it bounced back."

Obigwe's mouth became dry. "Who's account?"

"I'll send over the details. There has been no activity since it was flagged three years ago, but four days ago, there were two contactless purchases on Marcus Harrington's debit card."

***

"Marcus Harrington's bank card was used in a corner shop less than a mile from University Hospital, an hour before the attack on Carole Monaghan," Obigwe told the briefing. "It was used again at eight a.m. the following morning at a different store, up on Ridgeway Road. We're working with both businesses to identify his purchases and will be interviewing any witnesses who might have seen him, but we already know they don't have CCTV."

"Not a surprise," Stafford said. "I'll bet he checked out half the shops in the area until he found ones without cameras."

"Isn't there a Premier Inn on Ridgeway Road?" Girton asked.

"Yes," Obigwe said. "We're looking at their guest list and interviewing staff just in case, but if he did stay there, he must have booked it using a different method of payment."

"Why was he using that card?" Stafford asked. "It's been dormant since he disappeared, yet out of the blue he makes two purchases the night Carole is attacked. Why would he do that?"

"Perhaps he was short of money?" Girton said. "That money he pilfered from his and Andrea's joint bank account won't have been enough to keep him solvent for three years. And if he did skip over to Ireland, he'll have been earning money – probably cash-in-hand – in Euros."

"He emptied his personal bank account when he disappeared," Obigwe said. "But he has an overdraft facility, which he's now dipped into. But I think you're right, Katie. He must have known we'd be watching his bank accounts. It does seem like a hell of a risk."

"It makes you wonder if he even went to Ireland?" Freeland said.

Obigwe had phoned her former mentor as soon as the call came in from Financial Crime. After her visit to him the day before, it hadn't taken much to persuade him – or Girton – to employ his services as a consultant. Three years ago, he'd started the investigation convinced it was a tragic suicide. But despite his outward professional caution, he'd eventually come to believe Carole had been unlawfully killed. Because he was never able to definitively prove that, it had always bothered him. He'd leapt at the chance to help close his final case.

"Marcus' car was found near to where the ferry crosses to Northern Ireland," Obigwe pointed out. "And we have a paper trail showing he did withdraw some money over there, and across the border in County Louth, but his relatives swear blind he never contacted them. The *Gardai* spoke to some of their neighbours, and they claim not to have seen him."

"The question now is, where is he?" Girton asked. "Is he still in the area, waiting for another opportunity to attack Carole? Or has he disappeared again?"

"The hospital has confirmed that MSS did install and maintain its security system. They've reset all the cameras, changed their passwords and blocked that cloned swipe card," Stafford said. "So he won't be able to pull that stunt again."

"Pretty sloppy of them not to do that before," Freeland said. "How many years ago did they install that system? I can't believe Marcus Harrington still had access."

"Well, that's not our concern," Girton said. "Let's focus on Harrington's role in this affair."

"Back when we were still treating Carole Monaghan's death as a potential homicide, he was the one that made the most sense," Obigwe said. "A car similar to his was spotted by a neighbour walking his dog, close to the Monaghan's that night. ANPR placed it in the vicinity, and his phone pinged the nearest cell tower to their house. Obviously we know he was lying to us about going to Glasgow. We could prove that he followed Seamus and Andrea to Manchester, but we never got to question him about that. The night of the fire, he checked into a hotel on the outskirts of town, but turned his phone off. He was seen on CCTV leaving the hotel, then returning a few hours later apparently the worse for wear, but we never figured out what he did in that time.

"Then there was the creepy stuff. If you remember, we found all of those pictures of Carole on his computer, and we assume it was Marcus that she had sex with in the garden which she confessed to on that tell-all website. We thought at the time he was obsessed with her, perhaps to the point he had killed her. But who's to say the feelings weren't mutual?"

"So, Seamus hooks up with Andrea Harrington, whilst Marcus Harrington stages a disappearing act with Carole?" Freeland rubbed his eyes. "In thirty years, I've seen most things – and frankly the things that the monied middle-classes get up to behind closed doors no longer shock me – but this is like an episode of *Wife Swap*."

"Except an innocent woman was killed to cover up what they had done," Obigwe said. Whatever else had taken place, Angelica Carshalton had been murdered in a horrific manner.

"But again, why go to all the trouble?" Girton asked. "I just can't see what they would gain from all this deception. This was very well planned. And let's not forget Carole Monaghan suddenly turned up again on Valley View Road, underweight and under-dressed, in the middle of a stormy night. What the hell was she doing out there?"

"And why did somebody try to finish her off in the hospital Sunday night?" Stafford asked.

Freeland tapped his teeth as he thought; the gesture reminded Obigwe of their time spent working together years before.

"OK," he said eventually. "Let's assume Marcus and Carole were having an affair. First of all, we need to decide why they went to all this trouble to fake Carole's death and kill an innocent woman. There must have been a reason. Let's look at the usual motives for murder."

Freeland's eyes were shining as he slipped back into his familiar role of mentor. This was why Obigwe had called him that morning. She was an experienced detective in her own right and had just been promoted to sergeant, yet whenever she had a problem to solve, she still found herself asking, 'what would Patrick do?'.

Freeland waited as his colleagues voiced the possibilities.

"Crime of passion, in the heat of the moment," Obigwe said.

"Too well planned," Freeland said.

"Revenge," Girton suggested.

"For what?" he countered.

"Marcus could have been jealous of Seamus taking his wife?" Girton continued.

"Possible. What else?"

"Financial gain," Stafford said.

"In what way? Seamus – and by extension Andrea – received Carole's life insurance. Marcus emptied his and Andrea's shared account, but that was what? Fifteen grand? Hardly seems worth it, given that he also walked away from a nice expensive house, a very well-paying job, and stock options in a rapidly growing company."

Obigwe thought for a moment. "Drugs?"

"Expand upon that," Freeland instructed.

"We know they dabbled," Obigwe said. "We don't know if Carole actually had a heroin problem, but I doubt it. Those WhatsApp messages to Dominic were probably part of the cover story, and he certainly seems to have bought into it, booking that exclusive clinic. But we know they used cannabis and cocaine. What if Carole and Marcus bit off more than they could chew?"

"You mean they were actually dealing?" Girton suggested.

"Sure. Marcus was a finance expert, remember," Obigwe said. "He won't have been standing on street corners, selling wraps to the local junkies; he'll have been far higher up the ladder. But by all accounts, he was also erratic, especially when he was high. He and Carole could have been doing something stupid like skimming money off their suppliers and been rumbled. So, they decided they needed to disappear. Pretending Carole was dead would have got them off their backs."

Freeland's face twisted. "I can see what you mean, but it still seems very convoluted. And if they did decide to go to ground, why did Carole come back to the area? And why did somebody try to kill her? More to the point, *who* tried to kill her? Marcus?"

Obigwe thought again. "If Carole and Marcus had a falling out, Carole could have returned to the area to beg forgiveness and seek Seamus', or perhaps even Dominic's help? Remember, she's from the US originally, so her family and most of her support network is thousands of miles away. She didn't take her passport with her, so she'd have found it difficult to return to the States. What she didn't plan on was getting knocked over by some poor couple driving home late at night."

"That still doesn't explain why she was dressed like that," Stafford reminded them. "Or why someone used a pillow in hospital to try and finish her off."

"I can't explain the clothes," Obigwe admitted. "But Katie's team have been showing this artist's impression to everyone in the area. Word could have got back to her suppliers, or perhaps Marcus?"

"You know what I'm going to say, Mercy," Freeland said.

"Lots of theory, very few facts," she said.

"I couldn't have put it better myself," Girton said. "If Marcus Harrington has suddenly returned to his old stomping ground, then we need to find him and interview him. We also need to speak to Seamus Monaghan; we need to rule him in or out once and for all."

"I think we should also visit Andrea Harrington again," Freeland said. "She may have seen or heard something she hasn't shared with us. If Marcus and Carole were dealing drugs, then perhaps she knows something about that? Maybe she had suspicions about their relationship? And failing that, she might be able to give us some suggestions as to where he's holed up."

"And if she does know something, she might even be in danger from Marcus," Obigwe said.

Chapter Forty-One

Andrea Harrington looked pale and worn-out when Stafford and Obigwe arrived unannounced at Dominic Monaghan's home. She had been shocked when she heard that her estranged husband was back in town, and that he was the prime suspect in the attempt to kill Carole Monaghan. And that they now believed he and Carole had planned the whole thing.

"So, you no longer think Seamus was involved?" she asked, her voice hopeful.

Obigwe and Stafford exchanged looks. "He remains a person of interest," Obigwe said. "Have you spoken to him since he went to Scotland?"

Andrea shook her head. "He texted to say he had arrived safely, but I already knew he was likely to be out of mobile phone range once he went to Laird Ballenbrooke's estate. He is due back today; I'm expecting him to message me to say when he's on the train."

"You admitted previously that looking back on it, you realise Marcus must have figured out you and Seamus were having an affair," Obigwe said. "Do you think Carole might have suspected anything?"

"Perhaps," Andrea allowed. "There was the occasional look, or ambiguous remark. At the time, I just thought it was my own guilt making me paranoid. With the benefit of hindsight ... maybe she had her suspicions?"

"And what about Marcus and Carole?" Obigwe asked. "Did you or Seamus ever spot anything?"

Andrea was silent for a long moment, before she sighed. "I knew Marcus fancied her. But then so did everybody. She was gorgeous and fun. They argued like cats and dogs over politics, and he loved to wind her up. But they were still very close. And then there were the drugs. Marcus liked cocaine. A little too much I think, looking back on it, and Carole used to snort it at parties as well. None of the rest of us used it, we'd just have a bit of weed now and again to chill out. Seamus never approved, and I think that set her and Marcus apart a little."

The team had discussed at length what information they should share with Andrea, and had decided to lean towards full disclosure.

"Were you aware Marcus had dozens of pictures of Carole hidden on his computer, alongside pornographic images?" Obigwe asked.

Andrea put her hand to her mouth. "Oh, no. Don't tell me he was into …"

"There was nothing illegal," Obigwe reassured her quickly. "As best we can tell, all of the models are of legal age. However, his tastes did lean towards bondage and more violent imagery, and I'm sorry to say, but most of the models bore more than a passing resemblance to Carole."

Andrea swallowed and her face flushed bright red. "Early in our relationship, Marcus and I tried … well he wanted to be a little more adventurous. I was never comfortable with it, and eventually he stopped asking. I guess he was using porn to satisfy himself."

"You were Carole's best friend," Obigwe said, her tone gentle. "Do you know if Carole—"

"I have no idea," Andrea interjected. "We never talked about that sort of thing. We discussed men we fancied, especially back in the early days at uni, but I have no idea what went on in the bedroom between her and Seamus. And I'd rather not know," she added hastily.

"Of course," Obigwe said. "And I'm sorry if this is uncomfortable for you, or I have offended you."

After a few seconds, Andrea nodded her acceptance of the apology. When she started speaking again, her voice was firm, although she struggled to meet either woman's eyes. "Now I've read the interview transcripts that Seamus chose not to share with me, I know she confessed on that website to having sex with somebody in the back garden. I only vaguely remember that night, but Marcus was at the party and I kind of lost track of him."

"You think he could have been the one in the garden?"

"It would make sense," Andrea admitted. She was surprised at how bitter her voice sounded. Given her own behaviour with Seamus, it was hypocritical of her to feel jealous, or betrayed. But she still felt a stab of hurt. And then there was the fact that Carole wasn't entirely sure if it had been fully consensual. Had Marcus allowed his obsession with Carole to take over and taken advantage of her to enact his darker fantasies? Had she ever really known the man she'd married and shared her bed with for so many years?

Sensing Andrea's distress, Stafford asked if she could use the bathroom. By the time she returned, Andrea was demonstrating the complicated-looking coffee machine to Obigwe.

"You know boys and their toys," she said, as she added coffee grinds. "Apparently the filters are fully compostable, Dominic is trying to go net-zero." She gestured towards a row of neatly labelled jars. "He's found a shop that lets you bring your own containers to reduce plastic waste. It's expensive, but he says that if wealthy people like him don't support them, then they'll never flourish to the point they become cheap enough for everyone else."

"I should introduce him to my daughter," Stafford said, accepting a cup of freshly brewed coffee. "It's like living with Greta Thunberg sometimes."

The three women retook their seats.

"We really don't know if Marcus helped Carole fake her own death," Stafford admitted. "But we do need to speak to him. Do you have any idea where he may be?"

"No," Andrea said. "Until you showed up today, I thought he had either gone on the run or perhaps he'd killed himself and his body hadn't been recovered." Her voice caught, and she masked it with a sip of decaff coffee; the rocket fuel favoured by Dominic would have the twins turning cartwheels.

"We questioned his acquaintances and friends when he disappeared," Obigwe said. "Is there anyone else you forgot to tell us about?"

"Nobody," Andrea said. "I went through his address book, and as far as I know you spoke to everyone in there."

"And anything else you want to share?" Stafford asked. "Perhaps something that seemed irrelevant at the time, but might have more meaning now?"

Andrea chewed her lip, thinking back to what she'd discovered when reading the WhatsApp messages between Carole and Dominic. Finally she shook her head. They'd all but said Seamus was off the hook now; that Marcus was almost certainly the one who'd colluded with Carole. Why complicate matters? Seamus had been through enough; hopefully he'd never find out about how she had doubted him.

"Andrea, we have to ask," Obigwe said carefully. "You've admitted that both Marcus and Carole used cocaine and cannabis. We suspect the heroin addiction was a red herring, but do you know where they got their drugs from?"

Andrea was quiet for a long while, her face full of conflicting emotions. Obigwe and Stafford said nothing.

"There's a guy who works with Seamus and Dominic," she said eventually. "He has a couple of dodgy mates who can get hold of stuff for parties."

"And does he have a name?" Obigwe asked.

Andrea took a slow sip of her coffee. "I would really rather not say," she said eventually. "He's a friend and he's never been in any trouble before. He just does us a favour now and again, he's not really a dealer."

"I understand that," Obigwe said. "But the fact is, Marcus must have been living off something for the past three years; the cash he took from your joint account wouldn't be enough."

"And we also don't know why Marcus would up and leave," Stafford said. "If he did decide to go with Carole, then faking her death and walking away from everything seems extreme. He had a well-paid job and owned a house. We feel he must have had another reason. Perhaps he felt he was in danger?"

Andrea could see how their minds were working. "You think this might be to do with drugs?"

"It's one hypothesis," Obigwe said.

"Christ," Andrea said. "This just gets worse and worse."

"You said that this friend supplies the drugs as a favour. Are you certain that's all?" Obigwe asked. "Could he be more involved in the drugs business than you believe?"

"I don't know," Andrea said. Tears started to form at the corners of her eyes. She'd been in shock ever since the two officers had arrived on her doorstep. Now the shock was giving way to fear. And anger.

"Andrea, we really need to know who this friend is," Obigwe said. "Hopefully we can eliminate him from our enquiries. If not ... do you really want to shield someone like that?"

Andrea bit her lip again. "Pete Ludlow," she said eventually. "But I can't see him as a high-level drug dealer. He's a triathlete. He doesn't even smoke weed during the race season in case he fails a urine test."

"What was Marcus' relationship like with Pete?" Stafford asked. "Were they especially close? Did you ever see anything that made you suspicious?"

"It's so long ago," Andrea said. "I haven't even thought about it in months. I know Marcus got on well with him, they'd go for a drink sometimes, and play the odd game of badminton. But that's not unusual. Dominic believes close-knit teams work better together, and he encourages staff to socialise. Pete has been with MSS since the early days, so he's usually invited to any parties or get-togethers; he was with us at Seamus' birthday meal last week."

"You supplied us with Marcus' address book back then," Obigwe said. "But what about other acquaintances? People he was friendly with, but perhaps wouldn't be in there? Or at least in the address book that he shared with you?"

Andrea shrugged helplessly. "I guess there must have been, Marcus was pretty popular." She grimaced. "He could be a bit of a dick when he'd had a few, but otherwise, he was good fun to be around."

She felt a wave of sadness. Marcus *had* been fun. They'd enjoyed several happy years together. It was only as they got older, and she started to look to the future, that she began to realise Marcus still hadn't moved on from his university days. To outsiders, he appeared to be more grown up than he really was. He was married, with a mortgage, a respectable job and a pension. But after a few drinks, it was as if he was twenty again. And after a line of cocaine, he could be down-right unpleasant.

"What about unexpected wealth?" Stafford asked. "You must have had a fair idea of what he was earning. Was his spending consistent with that?"

Again she shrugged. "To be honest, I never really knew what he earned. We used his base salary and my freelance earnings when we applied for a mortgage, but I know he received performance bonuses from MSS. We had a joint account for bills and we both put aside some money each month to build up a pot so we could get an extension on the house. He was generous, but not excessively so. His biggest extravagance was his car, but even then, that was on finance."

They were getting nowhere, Obigwe finally decided. She wasn't 100 per cent certain that Andrea was telling them everything but doubted they would force any more out of her. She could tell by Stafford's body language she felt the same.

At least they had Pete Ludlow's name. Even if he was just a fixer with a dodgy mate, he might have been Carole and Marcus' gateway into the drugs world.

Taking their leave, Obigwe surveyed the house one more time.

"I'm sure there is nothing to worry about," she said, "but whilst the whereabouts of Marcus are still unknown, I think it might be a good idea if you were to stay here. This place looks pretty secure."

"You think I might be in danger?" Andrea said. Her hands cradled her bump instinctively.

"Perhaps keep a low profile," Stafford said. "Lock the doors, make sure you have your phone handy. If Marcus tries to contact you, phone 999 immediately. I'll arrange with the force control room to have your call given priority."

Obigwe smiled reassuringly. "We're just being cautious."

Summoning up her own smile, Andrea escorted them to the door.

As Obigwe and Stafford returned to Stafford's car, they heard an electronic beep, followed by the metallic clunk of deadbolts.

"Do you think she is in any danger?" Stafford asked, as she slid into the driver's seat.

"I don't know," Obigwe admitted. "But there's nothing to justify patrols, or bringing in the Domestic Violence Unit. We don't even know that Marcus is actually in the area. Besides, she's at a different address and that place is probably even more secure than one of our safe houses."

She stared thoughtfully at the house as Stafford executed a three-point turn. There was something she wanted to look at when she got back to the station.

***

"Pete Ludlow was interviewed as an acquaintance of Carole Monaghan's during the initial investigation," Freeland said. It was remarkable how easily he'd slipped back into his old role. "Sneaky bugger denied any knowledge of Carole's drugs problems. Admittedly, by this point we were looking into a potential heroin addiction, but he had plenty of opportunity to corroborate that she liked a bit of weed and cocaine."

"Hardly surprising," Girton said. "Andrea thinks he was Carole's supplier."

"Along with half the rest of the company, by the sounds of things," Freeland said. "He was also questioned again when Marcus Harrington went missing. Several people had said he and Marcus were good buddies, at least at work, so he couldn't really deny that."

"No mention that he also supplied Marcus, I take it?" Girton said.

"Nope, not a dicky bird. Which I don't believe for one second, but there you go." Freeland sighed. "I'm sorry, Gemma. This is my fault; I was so convinced at first that it was just a suicide that we never really pursued the drug angle. Mercy was keen to dig deeper and find out who Carole's dealer was, but I said we just wanted it wrapped up. If Drugs Squad were interested, they could come and take a look at what we had, but you know how it was back then; they had bigger fish to fry."

"What's done is done, Patrick," Girton said. "What have you uncovered?"

"Ludlow has a record. He received a caution for possession of Class B when he was a teenager. Then he nearly got done for letting himself be transported in a stolen vehicle, but again he was just a kid and got a caution. But he does come up on the system as a known associate of a couple of small-level dealers, who in turn are known associates of folks that Drugs Squad are a lot more interested in."

"Presumably that's how he was supplying his co-workers," Girton said. "Any indication he may have been more involved?"

"Nothing on their system," Freeland said. "But there are some other markers against his name on the PNC and they're not good. Back in his university days, he was arrested for assault on his then girlfriend. It was serious enough for the university authorities to temporarily ban him from campus whilst he was investigated. He was released with No Further Action when his former girlfriend withdrew her cooperation.

"A year later, she reported he was stalking her. Again, she withdrew her cooperation, and he was never charged. There was then a further allegation that he'd taken advantage of another woman, who claimed to be too drunk to have given consent. Again, dropped when the alleged victim changed her mind."

"Connections to drug dealers, previous allegations of violent and obsessive behaviour, not to mention a worrying attitude towards vulnerable women." Girton ticked them off on her fingers. "Not only that, but he's also a good friend of Marcus Harrington, and he's an engineer at MSS, the company that fitted both the Monaghan's security system and that of the hospital where Carole was attacked.

"I think we need a word with Mr Ludlow."

Chapter Forty-Two

Marcus was back! Andrea felt light-headed and nauseous. She staggered over to the sink, and steadied herself on the countertop, breathing heavily. After a few moments the dizziness passed, and she no longer felt the urge to vomit.

Twenty-four hours ago, she had been struggling to process the fact that Seamus, the man whom she had loved since she first saw him talking to Carole in the Students' Union, might have helped her best friend fake her own death, and been involved in the murder of an innocent woman.

Now it appeared that he might not be responsible at all.

For three years, she'd clung to the hope that Marcus had simply run away. Yet it seemed he had not only reappeared, but he might have been the one who killed the woman in the shed, and that furthermore, he had been involved with Carole.

For three years, Andrea had hoped he would return. It wasn't that she wanted to rekindle their romance – far from it – she just wanted to know he was safe and hadn't done anything wrong. And, if she was being mercenary about it, she had a pile of documents she really needed him to sign, so she could move on with her life and be with the man she truly loved.

But now he was back, she was scared. She'd never really thought that Marcus could harm her. Not really. But DS Obigwe's and DI Stafford's parting advice to 'keep a low profile' had unnerved her. If Marcus really was capable of the things they thought he had done, then maybe he was a danger to her as well? He'd killed an innocent woman, and then turned on Carole, a woman they'd been friends with almost their whole adult lives. Who knew how he would react to her being pregnant with Seamus' twins?

Suddenly, she felt exposed. The house was kitted out with the latest security technology; a showcase for the products MSS installed. Yet the whole downstairs of the house was glass-fronted, fitted with floor-to-ceiling windows that left the entire ground floor visible to any onlookers. Privacy wasn't a big concern for Dominic; the house was two hundred metres away from his nearest neighbours, surrounded by hedges and nestled at the end of a long driveway.

The windows had motorised blinds, controlled by an app on a mini tablet that Dominic used to run all his smart devices. She knew they automatically closed at the same time the lights came on, but she had no idea how to override that. She didn't even know the tablet's password. Not for the first time she reflected on how it was possible to over-engineer things.

And what about her car? It was sitting on the driveway. She hadn't changed it since before Marcus disappeared. Surely he'd recognise it?

Should she move it? The house had a double garage, but she had no idea if there was enough space for her car. Dominic had a sit-on lawnmower, similar to the one Seamus used to have. Was that in there? Plus, the charging point for Dominic's Tesla was inside the garage. Did that mean he had to park in there to top up his battery?

In the end, she decided to leave her car where it was until Dominic returned home. The idea of going outside alone, no matter how briefly, scared her.

Breathe, she told herself. Nothing's going to happen. Why would Marcus come and look for her here? Not for the first time, she wondered if this was just her hormones stoking her paranoia.

But despite her best efforts, she couldn't relax. How did the old joke go?

Just because you're paranoid, doesn't mean they aren't out to get you.

If she was Marcus, the first place she'd look for her is at their house. The next logical place would be Seamus and Carole's. And if she wasn't there, then Dominic's place. In fact, hadn't the last confirmed sighting of Marcus been when he'd turned up, ranting and raving at Dominic about her and Seamus?

If she wanted to keep out of sight of those damned windows, then she could hide upstairs. But if Marcus did manage to get inside the house, then the obvious place to look was up there. The guest rooms had locks on them, but they were just flimsy things, designed to stop someone wandering in accidentally; she needed somewhere more secure. But where?

The garage had an interconnecting door just off the kitchen. But motorised roller doors were notoriously easy to breach. She could end up trapped in there.

Casting her eyes about the spacious living area, she spied the former games room. She'd completely forgotten about it; now it was nothing more than a supply closet. Dominic had grown bored of playing pool – yet another hobby fallen by the wayside – and since he'd bought his massive new TV and reclining armchairs, he played video games with his brother in the lounge. She couldn't remember even seeing inside the room, although she was confident it didn't have any windows.

Even better, Dominic had fitted it with a high-security lock, similar to the ones that prevented entry to the house. Maybe she could hide out in there until Dominic came back?

Crossing the room, she keyed in the guest code. The keypad gave a discordant beep, and flashed red. She frowned and tried again. Same result.

That was odd. All the locks to the house had fingerprint scanners and keypads. Dominic just pressed his thumb against the scanner to gain entry, but he had programmed the locks with a code he'd given to Seamus and Andrea years ago. If he was expecting a delivery when he was out, he would programme the side door to the garage with a temporary code which he'd give to the delivery driver.

Seamus and Andrea had free reign of the house, just as he had spare keys to theirs. Why would he give the door to the storeroom a separate code?

Her phone was on the kitchen counter, and she heard the buzz of an incoming message from across the room.

Picking it up, her heart froze as she saw the caller ID. It was a number she hadn't seen for years. A number that had been copied across automatically the last time she upgraded her handset.

"It's Marcus. We need to talk. It's not what you think. Please don't tell anyone until I've had a chance to explain. I'm coming over. Mxx"

***

"Pete Ludlow has been off work for the past two days," Freeland said. "Stomach bug apparently."

"Can anyone confirm that?" Girton asked. By now she had almost forgotten Freeland was only there in an advisory capacity. And he was having so much fun, she hadn't the heart to reign him in.

"We're working on it," Freeland said. "His phone is currently turned off. Last location was his girlfriend's house, yesterday evening. He divides his time between her and her kids and his flat."

"Get teams out to both locations," Girton said. "Where's Mercy?"

"Last I saw, she was checking out some CCTV," Freeland said. "She was pretty vague about what she was looking for."

"OK, leave her be. I'll organise some response officers to locate Ludlow."

Freeland left Girton's office and headed over to Obigwe's desk. He found her staring at some video footage. He recognised it as the last time Marcus Harrington had been seen.

"Something has always bothered me about this," she said in answer to Freeland's query.

"What?" Freeland asked.

"I don't know," she said in frustration. "But when Katie Stafford and I visited Dominic Monaghan's house earlier, it started nagging at me again."

Freeland pulled up a chair. "Two heads are better than one," he said.

On the screen, Marcus was clambering out of his car on Dominic Monaghan's driveway. The camera was fixed to the eaves of the house, and angled so it covered the driveway, the main entrance to the house, and the double garage. He opened his umbrella against the pounding rain. Obigwe noted the clothes he was wearing; dark jeans, black trainers, a long, brown leather jacket and a red T-shirt emblazoned with 'Bazinga!' the catchphrase of Sheldon Cooper from the TV show *The Big Bang Theory*.

Stepping onto the open porch, Marcus pressed the doorbell, then folded his umbrella. His face was clearly visible as he turned briefly towards the wide-angled camera on the front of the house. Obigwe froze the shot and compared it to a photograph supplied by Andrea.

"He doesn't have a brother and has no male cousins, so unless his father suddenly lost thirty-years, there's no doubt that's him," Freeland agreed.

There was a pause of almost a minute, and Marcus pressed the doorbell a second time. Eventually, the door opened. The figure that let him in didn't look at the camera, but both detectives were satisfied it was Dominic.

Freeland checked the time stamp. "It matches the location history for Marcus' phone," he said.

Obigwe increased the playback speed.

Forty-five minutes passed. The rain continued, and aside from the occasional swaying of trees in the wind, there was no movement on the cameras. Eventually the door opened again, and Marcus appeared. Same leather jacket, same dark jeans, same black trainers. His back was to the camera, so they couldn't see his red T-shirt, but in the second or so before his umbrella obscured him, there was a flash of the same-coloured hair.

Marcus briskly crossed the drive to his car, pulling the front door closed behind him. He rounded the bonnet to the driver's side and opened the door. It was still raining hard, and so he turned and entered the car backside first, closing the umbrella behind him.

Obigwe ground her teeth. What was she not seeing?

Her subconscious brain had spotted something. But she wasn't sure what.

Eventually the headlights and rear lamps came on, then the car performed a three-point turn, and headed out of the drive, and beyond the camera's range.

"Times still match his mobile phone location," Freeland offered.

Obigwe paused the video and rewound the last minute.

The feeling she was missing something was even stronger.

She played the video again.

There was something there, she was certain.

She played it again in slow motion. What was it? What was making the hairs stand up on the back of her neck?

She ran it again, this time zooming in on the car. The picture quality was good, but the angle of the camera, the rain drops and reflections on the passenger side window meant she couldn't make out more than shapes inside the vehicle.

And then she saw it.

Chapter Forty-Three

Andrea had no idea what to do. She knew that if she told Obigwe and Stafford that Marcus had contacted her, then he'd be arrested and she'd never get the chance to speak to him. She'd never get the chance to hear him put across his side of the story. Or have the chance to look into his eyes or listen to his voice to gauge the truth of what he was telling her. For her own peace of mind, she had to know if the man she'd once loved – still loved in some ways – had really done those appalling things.

But despite his protestations, he could be lying. She could be his next target. He'd supposedly already murdered once, and attempted to kill again. Could he harm her also? And it wasn't just her she had to think about. What right did she have to place her babies in danger like that?

And then there were the potential problems from assisting an offender or perverting the course of justice. 'He asked me not to tell anyone, your Honour,' was unlikely to be a sound legal defence.

But it was the last line of the text that chilled her. The line before he signed off with *Mxx*, the way he'd always done, since the day they'd met.

I'm coming over.

What did that mean? Was he going to their old home? The home she shared with Seamus? Or did he mean here? Did he know she was staying with Dominic?

Suddenly, the feeling of insecurity came crashing back, and with it a clarity of thought, and eventually, a compromise.

She knew she needed to be somewhere safe, and the games room-cum-store room was the best option she had. She'd get Dominic to send her the code and then jam it closed from the inside. Then she would video call Marcus and record it. If he wished to speak to her, he could do it from a safe distance. If he said anything incriminating, it would be on file. She had no idea if it was admissible as evidence, and now was hardly the time to google it, but at least she could give the police something.

Then she would text DS Obigwe and let her know that they were talking, and his phone was active. She'd watched enough TV to know they could track his handset.

With that in mind, she texted Dominic.

"Urgent. I need the code to the games room. Marcus back in town. Might not be safe. Andy x"

A few seconds later, another text arrived, again from Marcus.

"We need to speak. Please. Mxx"

She purposefully ignored it. She needed to get everything in place before she agreed to speak to him. But how long did she have? Was he already heading to Dominic's? Was he walking up the drive this very minute?

There was still no response from Dominic. Perhaps he was in a meeting? Should she call him?

The phone rang and rang, until voicemail cut in.

"Damn it!" she swore. She knew she was panicking. Perhaps even over-reacting. But she couldn't help it. All she could focus on was getting into that little room and locking the door behind her.

She tried the door code again. Perhaps the system was just being glitchy? It flashed red.

She tried reversing the digits. It flashed red.

Think, she ordered herself.

Dominic probably opened it using a fingerprint, but she knew that such systems always had a back-up code in case the fingerprint scanner failed.

Maybe she could guess it?

It was six digits, so it could be a date.

If he had taken that route, then perhaps it was something meaningful to him? The code she shared with Seamus was the date that the brothers' parents were married, reversed.

She quickly entered the two brothers' dates of birth, both forward and backwards. As expected, it wasn't that simple. She entered hers and Carole's for good measure. Still nothing.

Time to get morbid. The date Carole supposedly died. Nothing. The date Seamus and Dominic's parents died. Nothing.

She thumped the wall in frustration. Dominic ran a security company; it looked like he followed his own advice and didn't use a code that could be easily guessed.

She checked her phone again. Still no text from Dominic. The final message was the one from Marcus. How far away was he?

She paced back and forth. She was just about to admit defeat and phone DS Obigwe, when the blinking clock on the oven caught her attention. Dominic still hadn't got around to resetting the damn thing after the storm had knocked out the electricity.

Of course, why hadn't she thought of that before?

For safety reasons, the internal household electronic doors sold by MSS defaulted to the 'unlock' position if there was a power cut. That way you couldn't be trapped inside if there was a fire. The external doors that they used had a key back-up to release the door mechanically if the power went off and the bolt locked. Dominic had been on at them to fit electronic locks on their own house but, like the solar panels and the electric vehicle, it was still on their list of 'things to do when the twins are older'.

The night of the storm, Dominic had complained the power had failed because of cheap circuit breakers and dodgy wiring.

It took Andrea almost a minute to find the fuse box. It was located high on the wall in the utility room. Grumbling about being so short – not to mention heavily pregnant – she dragged a chair in from the dining table and kicked off her shoes.

There were two rows of circuit breakers. Unfortunately, the labels meant nothing to her. After a moment of indecision, she decided to turn off all the electricity. If that worked, she'd prop open the door to the games room and restore the power. Hopefully, everything would reset. She was sure Dominic would understand. She flicked a big red switch. Nothing happened. Perhaps the battery back-up kept the power going? How could she switch that off?

The freezer beside her rumbled and then went quiet. She gave a sigh of relief; it had just taken a few seconds for the appliance's capacitor to discharge.

Clambering back off the chair, she went back into the living area. Now it was gone, she noticed the lack of background hum. The lock on the front door had a flashing red light. Walking over to the games room, she saw its keypad was also dark, with just a blinking LED.

Grabbing the handle, she turned and pushed.

Chapter Forty-Four

The technician from the Video Analysis Unit had made it to CID in double-quick time. He was now sitting in front of Obigwe's computer, scanning the CCTV footage from Dominic's house.

"Something always bothered me about the video of Marcus leaving Dominic's that night," Obigwe explained. Girton, Freeland and Stafford were crowded around her workstation.

"Before he pulled out of the driveway, he paused for almost a minute. I zoomed in and I could see he was alone in the car, so he wasn't speaking to someone. And we know from his phone records he hadn't called anyone. I couldn't see his face through the glass, but I could clearly see a shadow of what he was doing."

"Adjusting the seat and mirrors," Freeland said, admiringly.

"Exactly. It was Marcus' car; he'd driven it for years. Why would he need to change the driving position?" Obigwe asked.

"Shit. Good spot, Mercy," Girton said.

"There's more," the analyst interrupted. They were now working on the footage from the night of the fire. The video started in the early evening. "This is when Dominic claimed to have returned home from work that evening," he said. "His phone arrived at his house just after six."

On cue, the Range Rover Dominic had owned back then, swung into view and paused in front of the garage door closest to the front entrance; it was already opening. Dominic's car moved into the garage. A few moments later, he re-emerged, dressed in a suit and jacket, with an open-necked shirt. The motorised door closed behind him, and he let himself into the house.

"There's nothing of any note for several hours," the technician said. "It gets darker until the camera switches to night vision. Then it jumps." He pointed at the screen. Now they'd seen it, it was impossible to miss. The trees, swaying in the autumnal wind, flickered slightly.

"Could it just be a glitch?" Girton asked. "The time stamp doesn't flicker."

The analyst shook his head. "I don't think so. This type of system takes a direct feed from the cameras into the digital recording unit. The video recorder adds the time stamp; it doesn't care what the source of the video feed is. I'll bet he's installed a signal switcher with two inputs: one from the camera, and another from a video source playing a recording from a previous night. All he had to do was switch between them. The cut would be almost seamless, unless you are looking for it."

He hit fast forward, until the video showed Dominic race out of his front door half-dressed and enter the garage.

"That's when he received the call about the fire," Freeland said.

The analyst played the video backwards. This time the cut, fifteen minutes after Dominic returned from work, practically jumped out at them.

"There was no need for him to come outside to enter the garage," Obigwe said. "He has a connecting door from the house."

"He just wanted to be on video to set up his alibi," Girton said.

She turned to Stafford. "I want a team to MSS and another team to Dominic's house to arrest him. I want to know what he was doing the night of the fire. And what the hell happened to Marcus Harrington three days later. And find Pete Ludlow. Any reply from Andrea's mobile, yet?"

"No, it's ringing out, then going to voicemail."

"Shit."

The Night Of The Storm

Chapter Forty-Five

Carole ran, stumbling and sliding in the wet mud. The biting wind and driving rain had soaked her to the skin and the thin plimsoles she wore were sodden. She was already exhausted, but fear and adrenaline drove her on. Branches whipped at her face, the full moon behind the rain clouds just enough to turn the blackened night into shades of dark grey.

Her legs ached; almost no exercise in three years had left her weakened, but she refused to be beaten. This was the chance she'd been waiting for.

Clambering over the wooden fence that ran alongside the embankment, she could just make out road below, the tarmac an even deeper shade of black.

It wasn't her first attempt at an escape. A few weeks after she'd first been imprisoned, Dominic had briefly turned his back after delivering her dinner. She'd hit him with the edge of the plate, the scalding hot lasagne spattering across his bare neck. He'd stumbled to the floor, and she'd jumped over his prone body, heading for the front door. To this day, she wasn't sure if he'd been stunned, or he just decided to let her realise how trapped she was. Regardless, she'd reached the door, to find it locked; the code she frantically entered not recognised.

And then he'd taken her by the arm, firmly but not roughly, and led her back to the games room.

She'd screamed and shouted for almost an hour, pounding the padded walls and kicking the reinforced door, aiming every invective she knew at the unblinking camera in the corner of the room. She'd overturned the bed, smashed the TV – her only companion for these past weeks – and even tried to break the toilet. She'd sprayed water from the shower in an attempt to flood the little room, until Dominic had cut the supply off.

Eventually, she'd collapsed in the corner, sobbing.

Twenty minutes later, the door had opened again, and a freshly-heated plate of lasagne had been slid inside. The handwritten note had simply said, *'I forgive you'*.

But tonight, three years later, had been different. Even inside her sound-proofed prison – now kitted out with a new TV, a mini fridge-freezer and a microwave so she could fend for herself during Dominic's infrequent absences – Carole could hear the storm raging outside. She was watching a boxset on Netflix. That, and a carefully disabled Kindle, were her only sources of entertainment.

Suddenly, the room was plunged into darkness. A pitch black that was as complete as anything she'd ever experienced. Her breath caught in her throat. The claustrophobia she'd experienced during the first weeks and months of her confinement had largely abated, but now it returned with a vengeance.

She knew every square millimetre of her cell, but still she barked her shin against the camp bed, as she stood up. As her eyes tried to adjust to the unexpected darkness, she became aware of a faint, flashing red light somewhere within the room. Turning, she realised it was from the electronic door lock.

Could it ...

Not daring to hope, she'd made her way to the door, and taking a deep breath tried the handle.

It swung open on well-oiled hinges.

Suddenly, her mind went blank. She'd dreamed of this for so long; fantasising about what she'd do. After a few seconds of indecision, she ran straight for the front door. She had no idea how long it would be before Dominic returned from wherever he had gone. She knew he could watch the house's security cameras on his phone. Would he realise the power had failed and he needed to come home?

A flash of lightning, followed almost instantly by a rumble of thunder, lit up the room. Carole was not especially religious – and over the past three years had more reason than most to feel that God had abandoned her. But if that wasn't a sign from Him, then what the hell was?

She tried the front door.

It was still locked.

Of course it was. It was one thing to have the locks on internal doors release during an emergency, but the external doors would do the opposite. Otherwise, all a burglar would need to do is cut the power to the house.

The door to the garage was similarly secure.

She screamed in frustration.

So, what if there was a fire? Dominic was meticulous, and aside from the craziness of the past three years, generally risk averse. There must be a key somewhere. And it would have to be accessible in the event of an emergency.

She cast her eyes around the house, then forced herself to think back to the day she and Seamus had first visited Dominic in his new home. He'd been like a child, excitedly showing them the features of this unique building, and outlining his future plans.

He'd just installed the security system, and he and Seamus had entered into a boring conversation about which of MSS' products he was using. It had been her that asked how they'd get out in an emergency, and Seamus had explained how the locks worked.

"If you ever need to get out and it's locked, there's a mechanical key on the hook on the wall between the door and the connecting door to the garage," Dominic had casually thrown in, before calling their attention to his state-of-the-art cooker.

And there it was. An entirely different shape to every other key on the hook. She almost wept with frustration. If she'd remembered this conversation the first time she'd attempted to escape, maybe the past three years of her life would have been completely different?

Pushing the thought aside, she snatched the key off the hook and fumbled it into the tiny slot below the handle.

There was a loud click, and for the first time in three years, Carole Monaghan was a free woman.

***

The rain and wind were relentless, and Carole's teeth were chattering as she picked her way along the embankment. From what she remembered, there were houses a mile or so along the road, but she was beginning to worry she might not make it that far. Perhaps she'd have to risk flagging down a passing car? She knew that Dominic now drove a Tesla, one of those silent electric vehicles. If she listened for the sound of a combustion engine over the sound of the storm, then she could be sure it wasn't him.

As she continued, her mind drifted back over the past three years.

Dominic was deluded. Pathologically so. How had neither she, nor anyone else ever realised that?

She'd known he was attracted to her. Despite what men think, these things rarely go unnoticed. When she and Seamus got married, he made a big show of finally having a sister, although the way she caught him gazing at her sometimes wasn't always brotherly. But that was OK. He was always the perfect gentleman.

And when things became difficult between her and Seamus after they lost Amelie, she valued his advice and the kindness he showed her. It was he who she had finally confessed to about the road accident, when anonymously unburdening herself online had done nothing to lessen her guilt. He had helped her come to terms with what she had done, counselling her against telling Seamus what really happened that night.

And so, life continued. Dominic had girlfriends – too many to count – but he never seemed to find 'the one'. She even had a go at setting him up with a couple of the single women at her exercise classes, but to no avail. It didn't take long for her to notice he had a 'type'. And when she realised one day that his type bore more than a passing resemblance to herself, she brushed it off. He was Seamus' brother; they were alike in so many ways, it stood to reason they'd have similar tastes in women. If she was honest with herself, she was a little flattered; he was a very attractive man.

And then there came that fateful encounter in the garden. She had no idea what was so different about that night; it wasn't the first time she'd been alone with him in such a state. Her memory was still hazy. Had he taken advantage of her vulnerability? Or had she been so angry at Seamus that she'd let him take advantage?

Either way, she'd woken up feeling sick and guilty. She'd barely been able to look Seamus in the eye, and vowed to keep Dominic at arm's length, avoiding being alone with him.

She'd managed it until the night that Seamus went to Manchester. Dominic had called her sporadically over the previous few weeks, but she'd brushed him off. Eventually, he'd turned up unannounced. He'd been edgy and nervous, pleading for an opportunity to clear the air between them.

It was their last chance, he said, before Seamus came back from Manchester. Already a little tipsy, and chilled out from the weed she'd smoked earlier that evening, she'd finally agreed. He was right, they needed to talk about what had happened in the garden. Hopefully she'd also gain some more answers.

She'd been expecting an apology, but instead, what she got was Dominic pleading with her to give him a chance. She'd tried to let him down gently; she cared deeply about her brother-in-law and didn't want to hurt his feelings. But as the conversation wore on, it turned more desperate.

"You know he's going to leave you, right?" he'd eventually stated. "You must have seen the way he is with Andy."

She'd recoiled as if slapped. It wasn't so much that it was a surprise to her, rather a surprise that she wasn't the only one who'd suspected it.

"I love my brother dearly, but the way he's treated you is shocking," Dominic had continued. "You deserve better. You deserve someone who loves you for who you are."

She'd been too stunned to say anything, and this seemed to spur him on. "Leave him," he urged. "Come and be with me."

"But what about Seamus?" she'd asked, her brain urging her to say something. He seemed to take this as evidence she was at least considering what he had to say.

"He'll be fine," he said dismissively. "He has Andy. We both know Marcus is a dick; that relationship has been on life support for ages. If you leave Seamus, it'll give him and Andy the push they need to finally get together. When the dust settles, everyone will be happier."

She could see in his eyes that to his engineer's brain, it all seemed so logical.

Appalled that he saw relationships in such binary terms, she'd been firm in her rejection of him.

"But we're so right together," he'd pleaded. "Surely you felt it that night?"

Standing up, she'd escorted him to the door.

For the next two days, she'd walked around in a daze, unsure what the future held.

Leaving Seamus for Dominic was unthinkable. But how could she stay with Seamus if what Dominic had said about Andrea was true? Three times she got as far as the front door, car keys in hand, ready to drive down to Andrea's house to beg her to tell her it was all lies. Three times she changed her mind at the last moment, scared of what she might find. With Marcus in Glasgow, and Seamus in Manchester, if Andrea wasn't home, she could think of only one explanation for her absence.

The next time she saw Dominic was the night that Seamus was due back from Manchester. This time, he was even more edgy, but there was also something else in his eyes. A determination she didn't like the look of.

And this time, when she told him that she didn't want to see him, he didn't take no for an answer.

***

Carole continued picking her way along the fence line, her feet slipping and sliding on the sodden grass above the main road. Another flash of lightning lit up the sky.

Those first few days after her kidnap were a blur. Try as she might, so much of what had taken place had been blocked from her memory. A survival mechanism, she guessed. She remembered being bundled into the back of Dominic's car, her wrists bound and her mouth stuffed with something. The Range Rover he'd owned back then had more than enough space for her. Fear and the alcohol and weed she'd consumed that night had robbed her of any sense of time, but by the time Dominic finally returned, she was bursting for a pee. Eventually, she felt the car lurch into gear. The last thing she remembered was the smell of burning.

Her next memories were in the crude cell that Dominic had fashioned out of his games room. Back then, the sound-proofing wasn't as good as it needed to be, and so Dominic would gag her and tie her wrists every time someone came around.

There had been a brief surge of hope a few days after she had been taken (there was no clock, but the food that appeared at regular intervals marked the passage of time). Dominic suddenly burst into the room unannounced. He'd been rougher than usual as he bound her and stuffed a rag in her mouth, before shackling her to the bed frame, and she'd feared the worst was finally about to happen.

But moments after he raced back out of the room, she'd recognised the sound of Marcus's voice.

She'd bucked and kicked, screaming ineffectually through the gag, but it soon became apparent he wasn't there to rescue her.

Finally giving up, she lay back and strained her ears, listening to Marcus as he shouted and ranted at Dominic.

She felt a flash of shame, as her best friend's husband revealed how he'd witnessed her and Dominic having sex in the garden that night. The shame then turned to sadness and betrayal as he went on to explain how he'd followed Seamus to Manchester and captured evidence of his and Andrea's affair. There was no comfort from the fact she hadn't simply been paranoid.

For his part, Dominic had remained icy cold, his low tones barely penetrating into her prison. She'd heard his harsh laugh of derision when Marcus made his demands: a hefty pay rise, equal status to Seamus, and more share options. And if Dominic decided to fire him, because he and Seamus working together was no longer viable, he wanted a generous redundancy package, even more share options, and a glowing reference. Otherwise, future clients might just find out why Seamus had suddenly found himself in need of a new job three years previously. A senior executive with a problem gambling habit and a CEO who protected his brother whilst screwing his sister-in-law, would hardly look good for MSS as it sought to go public.

Dominic's response had been a strident, "fuck off".

And then Marcus had played his trump card.

"Do the police know you visited Carole the night she died?"

His revelation hit Carole like a truck. *The night she died?*

What did that mean? Surely she was just a missing person? Why would they think she was dead? Wouldn't they need a body?

And then she remembered the sound of Dominic grunting and swearing as she lay in the boot of his Range Rover, the car rocking on its shock absorbers as he manhandled something heavy out of the backseat.

Surely he hadn't ...?

"Bull shit," Dominic had loudly said, his voice snapping her back to her predicament, although he had sounded less certain than before.

"Really? I have footage of you turning up that night," Marcus said, his voice triumphant.

Carole's mind went into overdrive. She'd watched enough TV to know that if the police suspected Dominic had been the last person to see her alive, then there was every chance they would visit him to question him. Would they search his house?

Back in the US they'd need probable cause to get a search warrant. Was the procedure in the UK as strict? She had no idea.

Regardless, she had to find a way to turn that to her advantage. To somehow alert the police to her presence, or failing that, find some way of leaving a sign that she had been held captive here.

"Have you shown anyone else that?" Dominic was speaking again.

"Not yet." Marcus' voice was calculating. "This is the only copy."

There came a sudden crash and a surprised shout – from Marcus if she was to guess.

For the next few seconds she strained to picture what was going on from the sounds of grunts and smashes.

Eventually everything went quiet.

For what seemed like forever, the house was silent, before she eventually heard the beeping as the house alarm was set.

And then Carole was left alone, in the dark, weeping.

At the end of the road, a pair of headlights appeared. Instinctively, Carole shrank back, using a tree as cover. Was it Dominic, returning from wherever he'd been that night?

She strained her senses. The lights were dim, not the bright LED lamps of a modern car.

Above the pounding rain, she heard the rattle of an engine. Definitely not the electric whine of the Tesla that Dominic now owned.

Hope surged through her and she let go of the tree, picking her way down the grassy verge. The car approached rapidly and she started to panic. What if she didn't get down there in time to flag it down? She was exhausted. Did she have the strength to continue her journey.

Her foot snagged on an exposed root and suddenly she was tumbling towards the road.

The last thing she remembered was the dazzling glow of the car's headlights, and then an impact, and everything went black.

Now

Six Days After The Storm

Chapter Forty-Six

TEARS POURED DOWN ANDREA's face as she navigated Valley View Road faster than was wise. She pressed the call button on the car's hands-free kit. She had to tell Obigwe how they had got it wrong.

The car's display flashed and emitted a discordant beep.

She risked taking her eyes of the road, and her heart sank.

'No device connected.'

"Shit!" she shouted, the car swerving as she thumped the steering wheel.

Her phone was sitting on the counter in Dominic's kitchen, where she'd left it after she raced out of the house.

All she'd wanted to do was escape. To flee to a place of safety. She pressed the accelerator even harder, and stole a glance in the rear-view mirror, praying she didn't see the red of Dominic's Tesla. The vehicle was a high-performance supercar, there was no way she could outrun it.

She had to let Obigwe know what she'd found in the games room, but there was no way to call. And even if she did have her phone, Obigwe's card was in her purse; she hadn't entered the number into her handset.

She could call 999. Obigwe said that the force control room would give her call priority. They could locate Obigwe and patch her through. At this speed, she was less than two minutes from home. She could use the landline.

An angry blast of horn from an oncoming car as she swung around a bend, forced her back into her own lane, and she made herself ease off the accelerator.

Eventually she saw the familiar trees and hedges marking the start of the cluster of houses where she and Seamus lived. Slamming on the brakes, she ground to a halt in front of the motorised gates at the end of their driveway. Fumbling the remote control, she waited impatiently for them to swing open. Wheels spinning, she powered up the drive, and parked in a shower of gravel next to Seamus' Toyota.

Climbing out of the car, she felt a sharp stab of pain that stole her breath from her.

"Not now, guys, please not now," she gasped. The cramps felt different to those she'd experienced earlier in the week, and she gave a low groan.

Forcing herself to the door as fast as she could, she fumbled for her keys, but dropped them on the floor. Steadying herself against the door frame, she bent as low as she was able, and managed to snag them with a fingernail.

Standing up again brought stars to her eyes and she found herself wheezing.

Finally, she managed to unlock the door and switch the alarm off. Another contraction passed through her. They're just Braxton Hicks, she told herself as she locked the door. The adrenaline and stress were making the twins nervous. It was nothing to worry about.

Another wave of pain, and her knuckles turned white on the door frame.

Dominic had his own set of keys she remembered once the pain had passed. How could she stop him coming in?

After a few seconds, she had an idea. She and Marcus had used to leave the keys in the lock when they went to bed, so they could escape easily in the event of a fire. When she'd moved in with Seamus, she'd continued doing that, not realising his house had a different type of lock. Her reward was a drunken Seamus ringing the doorbell at three a.m., unable to insert his own key to let himself in after a night on the town with his brother.

She couldn't remember if they'd given Dominic a key to the backdoor as well, so she went into the kitchen, took the spare from the key hook, and pushed it into the lock on the French doors.

As she returned to the hallway, she spotted their tablet on the kitchen table. Waking it, she selected the app controlling the CCTV cameras. Breathing a sigh of relief, she saw that only her and Seamus' cars were on the driveway; there was no sign of Dominic's Tesla.

With the house secure, she climbed the stairs, panting as she did so. There was a telephone socket in the office which the broadband router was plugged into.

Pushing open the door, she stopped in her tracks. The router was exactly where it had always been, but only a single lead led from the socket to the rear of the device.

There was no phone handset.

But then, why would there be? Thinking back, she couldn't remember the last time she'd used the landline. They had good mobile phone signal around here, and the only calls they received were in broken English asking if they had been involved in an accident at work. Seamus must have finally disconnected it.

Did they even have the handset anymore?

They must have. Seamus was a typical man; he never threw away a cable or piece of electrical equipment in case he might need it one day.

Lowering herself onto her knees, she crawled under his desk and grabbed the black folding crate pushed against the wall. The plastic creaked and bent, until eventually it overcame the friction with the carpet and slid towards her. By the time it was free, Andrea was sitting on the floor, gasping as she waited for another contraction to subside.

"You aren't helping, you two," she muttered, as she wiped the sweat from her forehead.

The box was a tangle of random USB leads, coaxial cables and even a SCART lead that probably hadn't seen action since Seamus' university days. Finally, buried at the bottom, she found what she was looking for. The base unit for a cordless phone and its accompanying handset.

Too exhausted to get up again, she crawled on all fours to the telephone socket next to the bookcase and plugged it in. Then she crawled backwards to the nearest three-pin plug socket. The base unit lit up like a Christmas tree, and Andrea almost burst into tears.

Picking up the handset, she shakily dialled 999.

Nothing happened.

She shook it as if that would help. It remained stubbornly dead.

"No!" she shouted, in frustration. How many years had it sat in that crate, its battery losing charge?

She placed it in the base unit and after a few seconds an LED started blinking. It was charging, but how long would it take until she had enough juice to make a brief phone call?

Perhaps she could use the tablet instead?

The unit was a very basic model, it really only needed an internet connection. It was never going to leave the house, so they'd seen no reason to pay more for one with a 4G SIM card. But couldn't you make calls over the internet? What was it called? Voice Over IP? There must be an app she could download.

Reaching for it, she snatched her hand back as if she'd been burned. Watching in horror, she saw the cameras displayed on the screen shutting off, one by one.

He was here.

Chapter Forty-Seven

"There's no sign of Dominic Monaghan," Obigwe said. She was standing next to Girton in the centre of the CID office, an Airwave radio clutched in her hand. "His PA says he left work a few minutes ago. His mobile phone is on his desk."

"Where's Andrea?" Girton snapped.

"No answer on her mobile; the signal shows the handset is at Dominic Monaghan's house," one of the civilian support staff answered.

"There's a team on the way there now," a detective interjected. "With blues and twos, they estimate five minutes."

"That's too long," Girton hissed.

"Where's Marcus' phone?" Obigwe asked. They'd received an alert that his phone was back on the network, after a three-year absence. It had sent two text messages to Andrea's phone just a few minutes ago. "Andrea changed her mobile number after she and Seamus kept receiving harassing calls after Carole's apparent death. I don't see how Marcus could have got her new number."

"Meaning someone else was sending those texts," Stafford finished.

"They've located Pete Ludlow," called out another detective, holding a different radio. "He's at his girlfriend's house. There's a bucket of puke by his bed and he looks like death-warmed-over."

"Unless he's one hell of an actor, he's not involved then," Freeland said.

She and Obigwe grabbed their jackets.

"Send me the location of Marcus' phone," Obigwe said as she headed to the door, although she could already guess where it would be heading.

"Don't go in there until uniform backup arrive," Girton shouted after the two women, Obigwe raised a hand in acknowledgement as they disappeared.

"They're going in there aren't they?" Girton said to Freeland.

"If I know Mercy ..."

***

Andrea cast her eyes about in panic. The doors were locked, but that wasn't much of an impediment to a determined man. Why hadn't she driven straight to the police station? She cursed her foolishness.

The night of the fire, the cameras had been turned off by an app registered to Seamus. But by now she knew that was a ruse. The police had originally assumed Marcus had used his own access codes to hack into Seamus' account to shut the cameras down the night of the fire. But it was obvious now that Dominic had been the one to ensure there was no evidence of his presence at the house that night.

She overrode the settings and the camera feeds returned. Dominic's bright red Tesla sat at the end of the driveway. He was grim-faced as he walked towards the house. She squinted at the screen. The long, leather jacket he was wearing appeared familiar, yet she couldn't recall him ever wearing it. After a few seconds, it came back to her, along with a wave of sadness, followed by fear. The coat belonged to Marcus.

Any hope she may have had that Marcus was still alive and had sent her those text messages faded away. He was dead; he'd likely been killed the night he confronted Dominic three days after the fire. The text messages she'd just received were probably an attempt by Dominic to shift the blame for his attempts to kill Carole in the hospital onto her missing husband. And now it looked as though he was trying to set him up for whatever he was planning on doing to her. She had no doubt that by the time the police found her, Marcus' electronic footprint would have been triangulated to her location, and fibres consistent with his clothing would be all over the house. As for Dominic, he'd spent so much time in his brother's home, his DNA and fingerprints would be everywhere anyway.

Her only hope was to evade Dominic until she could get a message to the police.

But where could she hide? Or more accurately, where could she defend herself from? There were only a few rooms in the house, and once he breached the front door, he'd have free rein. The cheap bolt on the bathroom door may as well be made of tissue paper.

She needed a weapon. That meant she needed to head to the kitchen.

Creeping down the stairs, she could see a shadow through the window at the top of the front door.

She paused halfway down. The scratch of a key in the lock sounded deafening. Looking at the tablet's screen she could make out the shape of Dominic as he fought to unlock it. It seemed that for now at least, inserting a key into her side of the door had worked.

Giving up, he took a few steps back, before slamming his shoulder against the door. It rattled in its frame but held.

But for how long?

Another wave of contractions told her that even if she made it to the kitchen, she was in no condition for a knife fight. She'd have to get creative. She'd have to seek the higher ground.

Returning to the landing, she retrieved the sliding loft ladder from the airing cupboard, extended it, and manoeuvred it against the lip of the hatch.

The crashing against the front door had now ceased, and she stole a look at the tablet. He was unlocking the garage, which was odd; there was no connecting door with the house. Her blood ran cold as she remembered the tools that they stored in there. How long would the uPVC door last against them?

Heaving herself up the ladder, she pushed the hatch open, and climbed into the darkened attic. She fumbled with the light cord.

"You two really aren't helping," she muttered again, as she tried to position her bump so she could reach back through the hatch.

It took three attempts for her to finally pull the ladder up behind her, fumbling with its locking mechanism so that she could collapse it to fit into the roof space.

The clatter as she laid it down coincided with the sound of plastic splintering from the front door.

Dropping the hatch lid, she resisted the urge to take a breather and looked around for some way to keep the cover closed. There were plastic crates that she could use to weigh it down, but none of them felt heavy enough to stop him if he pushed hard enough, and there was no way to wedge it shut with the ladder. There came another splintering noise, followed by a bang as the front door thumped against the door stop.

He was in.

She was the heaviest object in the loft.

Gingerly she tested the hatch; it creaked but seemed sturdy. Supporting her weight on her hands, she carefully sat on it. The creaking grew louder, but it held.

Downstairs, she could hear Dominic moving around.

"Andy? We need to talk," he called out. "It's not what it looks like."

It bloody well is, thought Andrea, but said nothing. *You're a fucking nut job who's kept his sister-in-law locked in a room for three years and killed some poor woman to cover it up.*

She reached over for the tablet.

Shit! The video feed from the cameras had frozen, a blue spinning circle indicating poor signal.

She waved the tablet around, until eventually it came back, before freezing again. The Wi-Fi signal in the house was generally pretty good, but they'd never tried it in the insulated loft before.

Squinting at the screen, which she was now holding at arm's length, she could see there was just one bar of signal; not enough bandwidth to stream live video.

"Andy, please. Let me explain."

His voice was directly below her.

Another wave of contractions passed through her, and she felt a warm dampness spreading through her knickers.

Her waters had broken.

Chapter Forty-Eight

There was no way Obigwe and Stafford would get to Dominic's house before their uniformed colleagues, but neither of them could remain at the station and listen to everything relayed over the radio.

Stafford raced along Valley View Road dangerously fast, considering they had no lights or sirens. Obigwe clutched the Airwave in her right hand, and the door handle in her left.

The radio crackled into life.

"We're at Dominic Monaghan's house. Front door is open, but there are no cars, and nobody is answering our calls. Do we enter or wait for backup?"

There was a brief flurry of chatter, before Girton's voice replied. "Yes, enter with caution. Potential risk to life."

Stafford slammed on the brakes and slid into a lay-by before Obigwe could open her mouth.

"No vehicles, and the door is open?" she said, spinning the steering wheel to its full lock, and depressing the accelerator again. "They've been and gone."

The car's tyres spat mud and gravel before it fishtailed back onto the road, heading back from where they'd come.

***

Biting hard, Andrea stifled her whimper as she rode out the pain.

Closing down the CCTV on the tablet to free-up bandwidth, she clicked on the app store. Below her there was a brief silence before she heard metal-on-metal then a thump.

Shit! She'd forgotten the folding decorator's ladder Seamus had borrowed for the nursery.

The app finally opened, asking her if she wished to install an update. She tapped no, fighting the urge to swear.

"I know you're up there," he called out. "I just want to talk."

Tapping the search box, she typed in 'Voice Over IP'.

The spinning icon reappeared, and she held the tablet at arm's length again.

Come on, come on, she silently urged the device.

Below, she heard the creak of his weight on the ladder.

A list of apps appeared.

Choosing the first in the list, she selected install, again holding the tablet at arm's length.

There was a clanking noise as he ascended the ladder.

"Come on Andy, it's not safe up there for you. What if you fall?"

The hatch pushed up, and she heard him grunt.

How big was this bloody app? The download bar crawled across the screen, the percentage increasing slowly.

Beneath her, the hatch pushed up further, before crashing back down. She'd forgotten how strong he was; he and Seamus made full use of the complementary gym in the office space rented by MSS. Pre-pregnancy, she'd weighed barely nine stone. Could he lift her?

Finally, the download reached one hundred per cent.

'Configuring device.'

She fought the urge to scream.

"Andy, you know I'd never hurt you. I just need to speak to you."

"You tried to kill Carole in the hospital," she shouted at him, unable to keep quiet any longer.

"That wasn't me, that was Marcus," he called out. "He's back and you're in danger. Let me get you somewhere safe."

"Bullshit. And what about that poor woman who burned to death in the shed?"

"Again, that was Marcus. I just figured it all out."

His voice was low and reassuring, but she could hear a desperate edge to it.

Finally, the app finished installing and offered her the option to open it. She jabbed the button.

"So why do you have a prison in your games room?" she demanded.

"It's not a prison, it's another downstairs bathroom. The room wasn't being used for anything else."

"I'm not a fucking idiot, Dominic. There's a bed in there, and the walls are sound-proofed. And who installs a video camera in a bathroom?"

He said nothing.

"I've called the police," she said. "They're on their way. Leave now, and maybe they won't Taser your fucking arse."

Now his voice was low and dangerous. "You don't know what you're talking about. And besides, you left your phone at mine, remember?"

The tablet was blinking at her. 'Enter your account details or sign up for a free thirty-day trial.'

She started to type, when there was an almighty heave from below, and she fell off the hatch.

***

Andrea scrambled back to her knees, but a sudden stab of pain ripped through her.

"Oh, fuck," she groaned. The hatch had crashed back down into place, but she knew she only had seconds before he made it up the ladder. The light dangling from its cable swung from the vibrations.

She looked around the loft in panic. What could she use as a weapon?

The pain subsided and she scrambled back towards the hatch. All she could think to do was climb on it again, and hope he got tired trying to lift it repeatedly. She could stand on it and use one of the horizontal roof supports to keep her balance, and perhaps push down on it.

Reaching up she placed her hands on the wooden beam, either side of the swinging light, feeling the heat from its sixty-watt bulb radiating down. She kept her face turned away to avoid being dazzled.

She tentatively reached out a foot, praying the hatch wouldn't cave in if she stood on it.

But she was too late. The hatch burst open with a loud crash. Dominic's angry face stared up at her through the gap.

Pulling his teeth back in a grimace, he started climbing the ladder. Andrea kicked out at him, but he ducked and tried to catch her foot. She scampered back out of range.

She had nothing left.

Even the Christmas decorations were securely boxed away, and the plastic crates were filled with old college notes and crap that should have been taken to the tip years ago.

Dominic's head came through the hatch.

She didn't even have a shoe she could throw at him.

And then she had a light bulb moment. Literally.

She grabbed the dangling lamp by its cable and yanked as hard as she could. The loft was instantly plunged into darkness. A moment later, Dominic let out a piercing scream as she thrust the scalding hot incandescent bulb into his face.

With a crash, he toppled backwards off the ladder.

Jumping over the open hatch, Andrea grabbed a dusty crate filled with Seamus' university course assignments and heaved it through the opening in the floor. There was a satisfying thump, followed by an even more satisfying yelp from Dominic.

Without pausing, Andrea started throwing everything she could lay her hands on through the hatch, finishing with the ladder that she'd hauled up with her.

Eventually she ran out of missiles. She paused for breath, and only then became aware of a familiar voice calling to her.

"It's OK, Andrea, you can stop now. We've got him. It's Mercy. He's under arrest."

One Month Later

Epilogue

A CHILL WIND WHISTLED across the cemetery. Mercy Obigwe and Patrick Freeland stood at a respectful distance. They had been invited by the family to the internment, but they didn't want to intrude.

A light-haired man in his late-thirties was shaking hands with mourners; the turnout was modest, but it seemed Angelica Carshalton had been loved by some. Finally, he made his way over.

"Thank you so much for coming," he said. His voice caught. "Thank you for finally bringing my little sister home."

"We're very sorry for your loss," Freeland said, shaking his hand. Obigwe repeated her own condolences.

"I suppose I always knew this day would come," Fergus Carshalton said. "Despite everything, Angel and I were close. She'd call me once a week and would try and pop by to see her nieces as often as she could." He inclined his head towards two young girls standing with their mother. "I knew she had stopped working the streets, and was trying to get clean, but I guess she wasn't quite there yet." He sniffed. "When she stopped calling, I knew something was wrong. But I didn't know what to do. I wasn't even sure what town she was living in. Anyway, thank you for finally giving us answers."

"I wish we could have told you something different," Obigwe said.

The urn containing the ashes of Angelica Carshalton that Seamus had mourned as his wife, had been reunited with the urn that Carole's parents had tended back in Wyoming. If any of the contents had been scattered elsewhere, nobody felt it necessary to tell Carshalton's family.

"Oh, they're gorgeous," Obigwe said as Andrea Harrington manoeuvred the double pushchair over, after Angelica's last remaining close relative took his leave of them.

"I'm so glad they're healthy, and you look really well," Freeland said.

"Three hours sleep a day suits me," Andrea said, forcing a weary smile. "Who'd have thought?"

Dominic Monaghan had been lying stunned at the bottom of the loft ladder when Obigwe and Stafford had made it into the house. He'd made no attempt to resist arrest, and Stafford had cuffed him whilst they waited for backup to arrive. Obigwe had climbed into the darkened loft to find Andrea well into labour. For a time, it looked as though Obigwe might be adding midwife to the list of skills on her CV, but fortunately, the paramedics had arrived in time, and they'd managed to help Andrea down the ladder and into the back of an ambulance.

A frantic Seamus, already panicked after neither his wife nor brother had answered their phones as he caught the train back from Scotland, had been given a high-speed police escort from the station to University Hospital. He'd made it with just minutes to spare and welcomed his two daughters into the world.

Obigwe then had the unenviable task of sitting him down and telling him what had happened in his absence. She'd never forget how the new father's euphoria had turned to disbelief that his late wife had come back from the dead, then horror when she told him what his brother had done.

"How's Seamus holding up?" Obigwe asked.

Andrea sighed. "He's hanging in there," she said. "Fortunately, these two are keeping us plenty busy, so he's not spending too time much dwelling on things." A look of worry crossed her face. "When things have settled down a bit, there's a lot that needs to be dealt with. He couldn't face coming today."

"I can imagine," Obigwe said.

"Dominic's pleading not guilty to murder," Andrea said, changing the subject. "He's going for manslaughter on the grounds of diminished responsibility for Angelica Carshalton, and self-defence for Marcus."

"I heard," Obigwe said cautiously. The Crown Prosecution Service weren't having any of it. As far as they were concerned, the degree of planning that had gone into Carole's kidnap and imprisonment, and the kidnap and murder of Carshalton, were evidence Dominic was of sound mind. No matter what the experts Oldroyd and Parker had engaged might claim.

Marcus' body had been found buried under Dominic's beautifully landscaped garden. After three years, all the post-mortem could show was that he had died from blunt-force trauma to the head and had cocaine and alcohol in his system. The injuries were consistent with Dominic's claim that Marcus had appeared at his house in a drug and alcohol-fuelled rage and attacked him. He'd defended himself and Marcus had fallen and hit his head on the kitchen counter. Unfortunately, Dominic had replaced the counter, so there was no evidence either way to support his story.

Dominic had then disguised himself as Marcus and driven his car to Birkenhead, then used Marcus' phone to transfer money out of his and Andrea's joint accounts to strengthen the narrative that he'd gone on the run. Detailed analysis of Dominic's financial records had revealed him paying hundreds of pounds for a series of taxis that hopped between major train stations, bringing him back from Birkenhead. There had been no reason to look at Dominic's finances at the time of the original investigation to uncover his ruse. They'd never know if he had pulled the same trick with the CCTV feed when Marcus visited that he had used to hide his movements on the night of the fire. Video from the day after Marcus visited him was never collected and would have long since been written over.

Dominic refused to say how he'd got Marcus to unlock his banking apps, and the prosecution would imply that he may have tortured him into doing so. When Dominic had visited Andrea, the morning after her husband went missing, he'd stolen Marcus' passport and planted the photos of Carole he'd obsessively collected over the years on his laptop. Again, he'd have needed Marcus' passwords.

Because of that, the CPS were going to push for a second murder conviction.

Andrea sighed. "Part of me wants to see him locked up for life for killing two people, not to mention kidnap. But another part ... well he's Seamus' brother and in his own way, I believe he really did love Carole. I think he's ill, and I don't think prison is the right place for him. He needs proper help."

"How is Carole?" Freeland asked. He'd agreed to give evidence at the trial but had stayed largely uninvolved as Obigwe prepared her case.

"Slow progress," Andrea said. "She's fully conscious now, and has started to say a few words, but there's years of work to be done. Her parents want to fly her back to the States to a private rehabilitation clinic, but there's a court order preventing her leaving the UK until the CPS has decided what to do about the fatal road accident. It's a complete mess." Tears started to form in her eyes, and she quickly bent over to fuss with the twins' blankets.

"We think she understands what happened to her, at least in general terms," she said once she'd regained her composure. "The video from Dominic's house cameras revealed no evidence he sexually or physically abused her, and that he even used to let her join him in the evenings, or go out in the garden for exercise ... But there's only footage from the last six weeks. He held her for almost three years. Who knows what happened in that time? It looks as if she had learned to go along with things to a degree. To give him what he wanted."

She shook her head. "That's why I think he probably was insane. Surely any rational person would have realised that even if she did eventually fall in love with him, the rest of the world thought she was dead? What was he planning on doing? Moving abroad, or was he going to keep her in that sound-proofed room forever?"

Obigwe watched her with concern but bit her tongue. She couldn't express an opinion either way about Dominic's mental state, given that it would likely be a linchpin of his defence.

Andrea wiped at her face. "What gets me the most – and I know it keeps Seamus awake at night – is that for three years, we ate around his house, watched TV in his living room, even had parties just metres away from her. Did she even know we were there? For three years, he never went away for more than a long weekend, and as soon as any girlfriends got serious, he'd end the relationship." Her voice turned bitter. "To think we were worried about him. Seamus even asked him if he was gay. Now of course, it all makes sense ... And then there are those WhatsApp messages. For weeks he must have been hidden at the end of our driveway, late at night, fabricating conversations between his phone and that burner phone he wanted us to believe was Carole's."

Obigwe said nothing, pushing down a flash of shame. They'd had the evidence all along, but as usual neither the time nor the resources to examine it fully. The location histories for Dominic's mobile phone, and the burner phone they'd believed was Carole's, showed that when the messages were sent, both phones had been connected to the same cell tower; the one closest to Carole and Seamus' house. They were also confident that Dominic had used Seamus' password to cause intermittent CCTV outages at their home over the preceding months, to make the lack of footage from the night of the fire less suspicious. More reasons the CPS weren't accepting diminished responsibility.

Andrea sniffed. "Part of me hopes that if things were really bad in the beginning, she doesn't remember it. What would be the point? We haven't told her about me and Seamus yet. But I guess we'll have to eventually. We're waiting for the courts to figure out whether she and Seamus are still married first." She smiled bleakly. "Our solicitor is rather more excited about our situation than we are. I imagine he'll be dining out on this for a while. In the meantime, the insurance company want the money back that they paid out for Carole's death – which is fair enough, I suppose, given that she isn't dead anymore. But Seamus used it to pay off the mortgage and a rather impressive gambling debt the stupid bastard had accumulated shortly before Carole died, and which he'd neglected to tell me about. So, we'll need to sell the house."

Her voice was bitter. Before she could say anything else, one of the babies started to fuss.

"I think that's my cue to leave," Andrea said. "As soon as one starts, the other joins in. I need to find somewhere to feed them."

She shook hands with Freeland, then offered her hand to Obigwe. It turned into a spontaneous hug.

"I really hope everything turns out right for you," Obigwe whispered in her ear. "You've both been through enough. And I hope that you and Carole find peace."

"Thank you," Andrea whispered back. "For everything."

As she pushed the buggy out of earshot, Freeland muttered quietly to Obigwe. "I wouldn't want to bet her and Seamus are still together in twelve months."

Obigwe sighed sadly. "I'll be praying for them. They deserve some happiness after all they've been through."

"Amen to that."

Acknowledgments

Thank you for reading this book. *The Aftermath* is something of a departure for me. After ten years of writing my DCI Warren Jones police procedurals, I had a growing desire to try something a bit different. As a huge fan of domestic thrillers – books where nice people, with nice lives, in nice houses have horrible things happen to them – I really wanted to write my own.

As always, I couldn't have done this without the help and support of friends and family. My first readers are always my beta readers, my wife and parents. Their feedback on my initial draft was invaluable. A massive shout-out must also go to Justin Nash, whose advice and wisdom helped me change the focus of the novel, hugely improving it. Thanks for everything, Justin.

The book that you hold in your hands wouldn't be nearly as polished without the advice and editorial support of Heather Fitt. Thank you so much for your hard work.

Then there is the cover. Isn't it great? That's all down to Peter from Bespoke Book Covers. He took my rambling ideas and turned them into reality – note to self, next time, get Peter to design my cover before I finish my final draft. His initial design included a couple of fantastic elements that sadly didn't appear in the story, so couldn't be used – but he has really good instincts! He should write his own novel one day!

One of the best things I did as a fledgling crime writer was join The Crime Writers' Association. Over the years, I have enjoyed the friendship of many other members and whenever I need advice, there's always someone I can ask.

A big thank you to the hard-working librarians who have helped champion my books (and provided a quiet place for me to write when I really need to get out of the house). For anyone unsure of the essential role libraries play in our society, I urge you to visit one in the middle of a random weekday. Not only will you enter a place filled with books and those that love them, you will also see a safe and welcoming space for those who struggle to fit in sometimes.

Finally, thank you to the many readers who have supported me over the past decade, buying, borrowing and talking about my books. I know this is a bit different to what you are used to, but I hope you enjoy reading it as much as I enjoyed writing it.

Best wishes,
Paul

Have you enjoyed this book?

Why not let me know or leave a review?
Email me at **dcijones@outlook.com**
Visit my website and sign up to my newsletter
www.paulgitsham.com

or follow me on Social Media
Twitter/X: **@DCIJonesWriter**
Instagram: **@paulgitsham**
Facebook: **facebook.com/dcijones**

Or why not check out some more of my writing?

DCI Warren Jones: The Last Straw

When Professor Alan Tunbridge is discovered in his office with his throat slashed, the suspects start queuing up. The brilliant but unpleasant microbiologist had a genius for making enemies. For Warren Jones, newly appointed Detective Chief Inspector to the Middlesbury force, a high-profile murder is the ideal opportunity. He's determined to run a thorough and professional investigation but political pressure to resolve the case quickly and tensions in the office and at home make life anything but easy.

Everything seems to point to one vengeful man but the financial potential of the professor's pioneering research takes the inquiry in an intriguing and, for Jones and his team, dangerous direction.

"Crime Writing at its very best."
Kate Rhodes, author of *Cross Bones Yard* and the *Alice Quentin* series.

DCI Warren Jones: No Smoke Without Fire

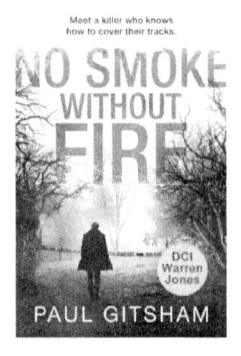

Meet a killer who knows how to cover their tracks ...

DCI Warren Jones has a bad feeling when the body of a young woman turns up in Beaconsfield Woods. She's been raped and strangled but the murderer has been careful to leave no DNA evidence. There are, of course, suspects - boyfriend, father - to check out but, worryingly, it looks more and more like a stranger murder.

Warren's worst fears are confirmed when another young woman is killed in the same way.

The MO fits that of Richard Cameron who served twelve years for rape. But Cameron never killed his victims and he has a cast-iron alibi.

Then personal tragedy intervenes and Warren is off the case. But the pressure is mounting and another woman goes missing. Warren is back but will the break he desperately needs come before there's another victim?

"Excellent! Best read in years and I have read A LOT of crime fiction!"
Amazon Reviewer

DCI Warren Jones: Silent As The Grave

It's DCI Warren Jones' coldest case yet ...

The body of Reginald Williamson had been well concealed under a bush in Middlesbury Common and the murder efficiently carried out – a single stab wound to the chest. Reggie's dog had been killed just as efficiently. With no clues or obvious motive, the case is going nowhere. Then Warren gets a break.

Warren's instincts tell him that the informant is dodgy – a former police officer under investigation. But when Warren hears the incredible story he has to tell, he's glad to have given him a chance to speak. Suddenly, a wide criminal conspiracy, involving high-level police corruption, a gangster and a trained killer, is blown wide open...and Warren finds that this time, it's not just his career under threat, but his family – and his life.

"I completely devoured this book."
NetGalley Reviewer

DCI Warren Jones: The Common Enemy

How do you catch a man's killer when everyone wanted him dead?

In Middlesbury, a rally is being held by the British Allegiance Party – a far-right group protesting against the opening of a new Mosque.

When the crowd disperses, a body is found in an alleyway. Tommy Meegan, the loud-mouthed leader of the group, has been stabbed through the heart.

Across town, a Muslim community centre catches fire in a clear act of arson, leaving a small child in a critical condition. And the tension which has been building in the town for years boils over.

DCI Warren Jones knows he can't afford to take sides – and must solve both cases before further acts of violent revenge take place. But, in a town at war with itself, and investigating the brutal killing of one of the country's most-hated men, where does he begin?

"Highly recommend... a book that you will struggle to put down."

Reader Review

DCI Warren Jones: Forgive Me Father

Who could kill a man of God?

A fire breaks out in a chapel, and DCI Warren Jones is alarmed by what is discovered at the scene. Curled up in the ash and debris is a body – and it's soon clear that the chapel doors were locked from the inside.

The disappearance of a local priest, Father Nolan, and a cryptic note left in his room, point to an unusually violent suicide. But when further evidence confuses the picture, Warren begins to suspect foul play – and murder. Clearly, someone wanted this seemingly innocent man to suffer.

And when a discovery on a quiet riverbank sends the investigation reeling, Warren knows he must act quickly to discover who is behind this spate of grisly deaths – before another man of God is found dead.

"Highly Recommended! This was an amazing discovery, one of those that makes you go and buy quite a number of the previous books in the series."
Amazon Reviewer

DCI Warren Jones: A Price To Pay

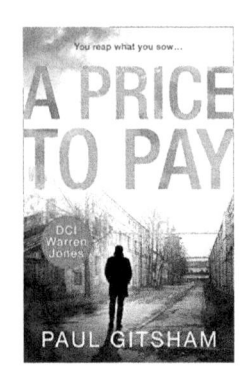

If you play with fire, you're going to get burned ...

It should be an easy solve: a murder in broad daylight with two eyewitnesses. But the victim is the son of a notorious local crime family who has a habit of hitting on other men's wives; the witnesses are Serbian nationals who speak limited English.

For DCI Warren Jones, this is his most challenging case yet. As the suspects pile up, the victim's family work to protect their son's memory by destroying any evidence that could betray his criminal past – or might have led to his killer.

Somehow Warren must uncover the truth about the murder – but there are secrets at the heart of the case more dangerous than anyone could have imagined, and the fallout could tear Warren's team apart...

"Rollercoaster of a read where the action never stops... An excellent addition to the series... Definitely recommended."
NetGalley Reviewer

DCI Warren Jones: Out Of Sight

His biggest mistake was trusting someone he shouldn't have ...

When a body is found abandoned under a bridge, teeth and fingerprints removed, DCI Warren Jones and his team have little to go on. And once they finally identify the victim, the case doesn't get any easier.

Estranged from his family but desperate to reconnect, the victim led a solitary life – apart from secretive liaisons with a series of partners he met online. Could one of them be guilty of his murder? Or does the truth lie closer to home?

The more Warren digs, the murkier the picture becomes – re-written family wills, sabotaged CCTV footage and black-market deals are just the beginning. Only one thing is for sure: whoever was behind the brutal murder, they carefully won the trust of their victim before ending his life...

'A cracker of a page-turner... Highly recommended'
Neil Lancaster, bestselling author of *Dead Man's Grave*

DCI Warren Jones: Time To Kill

Seven days until the killer strikes again – but who is next?

DCI Warren Jones is deep into the investigation into an apparent murder-suicide when another case is thrust onto his desk. Winnie Palmer, missing for two months, has been found dead, her body stripped and propped against a tree in the woods.

Two cases are more than enough to handle – but things get even harder for the team when they realise the cases might be linked. And when a third suspicious death is added to the pile, it raises a horrible question. Is there a serial killer on the loose?

With all the murders taking place on Sundays, it's a race against time to find the killer before they strike again. As the days tick by Warren desperately searches for a link between the victims – but the only thing he knows for sure is that absolutely anyone could be next...

"A smart and exciting crime thriller that'll keep you second guessing from start to finish... Full of cleverly plotted misdirections and a riveting chase that barrels towards a shocking conclusion."'

Karin Nordin, author of *Where Ravens Roost*

DCI Warren Jones: Web Of Lies

The Truth Will Come Out ...

When mother-of-two Louisa doesn't return home from work one night, her husband raises the alarm. Investigating the workshop where she ran her mail-order business reveals signs she was taken by force – and DCI Warren Jones is put on the case.

As Warren and his team begin to dig into the missing woman's life, a complex network of relationships emerges. Who is Louisa's husband talking to on his second, secret phone? What's the truth about her relationship with the convicted criminal who works next door? And what happened to Louisa's university housemate a decade ago?

Can the team break through the lies and get to the truth?

"A complex and tangled web of deceit, secrets and lies... Tense and compelling... I read into the wee hours."
Liz Mistry, author of the Detective Nikki Parekh series

Printed in Great Britain
by Amazon